THE MARINARA MURDERS

Also by Joanne Pence

Ancient Secrets Series

ANCIENT ECHOES - ANCIENT SHADOWS

ANCIENT ILLUSIONS - ANCIENT DECEPTIONS

The Donnelly Cabin Inn

IF I LOVED YOU - THIS CAN'T BE LOVE

SENTIMENTAL JOURNEY - A CERTAIN SMILE

TIME AFTER TIME

The Rebecca Mayfield Mysteries

ONE O'CLOCK HUSTLE - TWO O'CLOCK HEIST

THREE O'CLOCK SÉANCE - FOUR O'CLOCK SIZZLE

FIVE O'CLOCK TWIST - SIX O'CLOCK SILENCE

SEVEN O'CLOCK TARGET - EIGHT O'CLOCK SPLIT

NINE O'CLOCK RETREAT - THE 13th SANTA (Novella)

The Cook and Inspector Mysteries

DEATH ON A SILVER PLATTER - A QUICHE BEFORE DYING -
THE MARINARA MURDERS -

CLOSE ENCOUNTERS OF THE DEADLY KIND

Others

SEEMS LIKE OLD TIMES - DANGEROUS JOURNEY

DANCE WITH A GUNFIGHTER - THE DRAGON'S LADY

THE GHOST OF SQUIRE HOUSE

THE MARINARA MURDERS

THE COOK AND INSPECTOR MYSTERIES
BOOK THREE

JOANNE PENCE

QUAIL HILL PUBLISHING

Quail Hill Publishing

Eagle, ID 83616

Visit our website at www.quailhillpublishing.net

First Quail Hill Publishing E-book: March 2024

First Quail Hill Print Book: March 2024

1

___

He sat in the cold, cramped lime-green Honda, his legs and spine stiff and aching.

Earlier, he had watched the fog advance from the Pacific to immerse the neighborhood and its bundled together houses under a suffocating shroud. Shapes had become blurred and obscure in the frigid dampness, the streets slick and treacherous.

Now it was night. The thick fog had faded into a fine mist that powdered his windshield.

No one seemed to notice him sitting there. No one had paid any attention to him last evening either, or the evening before that. Alone, he kept his vigil over the homicide inspector's brown-shingled cottage. If tonight didn't work out, he'd return tomorrow. What did one day, or five, or even ten, matter? His patience would be rewarded.

Everything had been meticulously planned. Even the unexpected had been anticipated, reasoned. He had learned that when people rushed, they grew careless, made mistakes. But, even taking his time, it should be over by Easter. He chuckled at the symbolism.

The low, throaty rumble of a Ferrari Portofino engine reverberated in the pit of his stomach as it turned the corner onto the quiet street. Once, he'd have given his eyeteeth for wheels like that, but he'd cleansed his flesh of such material desires. His desires in this lifetime were far more pure, more simple. More... what was a nice way to put it? Physical. Yes, that was it.

The Ferrari stopped in front of the cottage he'd been watching. Its headlights switched off and the door of the low riding car swung open. He adjusted his glasses higher on his nose and leaned forward to watch, as if the few inches would matter with his near-sightedness.

A foot in a high-heeled shoe emerged, a narrow ankle, a shapely calf, then another. As the woman eased her way from the car, her black skirt rode up, exposing the curves of her legs. She was petite, beautiful, and dressed to match the expensive elegance of the sports car.

Starting the Honda's engine, he waited until he was sure she was headed toward the cop's house, then made his way slowly toward her.

Angelina Amalfi turned around at the rackety pings of the approaching car and watched as it pulled up alongside hers. The driver leaned toward the passenger door and rolled down the window. The nearby street lamp illuminated a long, narrow face with thick, black-framed glasses and a San Francisco Giants baseball cap pulled low over his brow.

"Complimentary copy of the *Chronicle* for you." He side-armed a rolled-up newspaper over the hood of the Ferrari. It skidded to a stop at her feet.

She picked it up and read the date. "This morning's news. How exciting." It was nine o'clock at night! She was tempted to fling it right back, but she'd never been any good with Frisbees.

"Wait," he called as she tucked the paper under her arm and walked toward the house. "Are you the lady of the house? Two months for the price of one."

"Sorry, not interested." She kept going.

"Maybe your husband is?"

She glanced back over her shoulder. "He's not my husband, but I'm sure he's not interested either."

"Maybe someday, real soon."

"What?" His puzzling words caused her to stop and face him, but he'd already lurched the car forward, the tires squealing on the wet pavement. He stopped at the next house and tossed a paper onto the front steps and then went on to the house after that.

She'd have to tell one of her friends down at the *Chronicle* that they needed to hire a better class of salesman. There was something vaguely troubling about this late working one.

"I thought I heard your car."

The voice startled her from her thoughts. Homicide Inspector Paavo Smith stood in his doorway, one hand against the frame, the other on the doorknob. Her heart felt like it was doing handsprings.

"What are you doing out there?" he asked. He had a just-awakened, slightly disoriented look, his blue eyes soft instead of sharp and controlled, and his wavy, dark brown hair falling onto his brow instead of neatly combed to the side. His gray sweatshirt was rumpled, and bare feet showed beneath his jeans. To her, he looked darling.

"Did I wake you?" She hurried up the front steps to him, put her hands on his shoulders and gave him a quick "hello" kiss.

"It's all right," he said, looking baffled at her being there.

It had been two weeks since he'd helped her return to her apartment in San Francisco after she had packed up her clothes and computer and went to her parents' home in Hillsborough to "find herself" and to figure out if she wanted to have a serious relationship with him.

But then, the way he'd found her, waited for her, held her, and kissed her, had convinced her that his feelings for her were as real as hers were for him. She wanted to be with him, and she believed he felt the same.

She returned to her apartment in San Francisco. But once back in the city, the cautious inspector returned. She knew why. According to his co-workers as well as her father, they would *both* be better off without the other in their lives. As a result, Paavo said, and she agreed, they needed to "move slowly."

Frankly, she'd hoped he would tell his friends to go stuff themselves, just as she'd told her father—in much nicer terms. But Paavo was much more diplomatic than she had ever been.

He led her into the house and shut the door. "I had to pull an all-nighter, so when I finally made it home this evening, I fell asleep on the couch. I was having this great dream..." he smiled, still looking a bit sleepy, "and here you are."

She put the newspaper down on the coffee table, placed her handbag on top of it, then took off her jacket and dropped it over an easy chair. The living room, with its mismatched, over-stuffed furniture and array of well-read books and magazines, was comforting to her, and had been a haven during some harrowing times. "I thought you only dreamed about murder cases, Inspector."

"Not always," he murmured, following her. He studied her a moment, then shook his head and admitted, "Just because my job gets in the way, it doesn't mean I don't miss you."

"Do you? Sometime I wonder," she said, as she sat on the sofa.

Pale blue eyes captured hers, and as he sat beside her, touching her arm, she could see the desire in them, as well as the sadness. "Don't," he said. "Don't ever doubt how I feel about you."

"I know, and I also know how much we enjoy being together. So, instead of 'moving slowly' by not seeing each other as often as we'd liked, I think we should feel free to see each other all the time the way best friends do."

His eyebrows rose. "Friends, Angie? Really?"

"Why not? I don't see why we can't talk and help each other, especially at times when we're troubled. Like I am now."

His brow knitted. "You're troubled?" His hand covered hers.

She nodded and dropped her gaze to the floor. "Yes." Then she quickly looked at him again.

"Tell me what's wrong."

She took a deep breath. "Now that I'm here, it seems so silly. I shouldn't be bothering you."

"You aren't."

"I mean, it's not a homicide or anything like you deal with. It's just about my job, my career."

He looked puzzled. "That sounds serious enough to me."

She bit her bottom lip. Now that she was here and facing him, her plight really did feel silly. But she had little choice except to continue. "Well, since I'm going to keep away from TV *and* radio cooking shows from now on, I was thrilled when the editor of *Haute Cuisine* magazine suggested I write an article with a review of an interesting new restaurant in the city." Her excitement was obvious with each word she said. "It should be a great opportunity for me. If the article is good, and interesting, it could be the start of a serious career as a restaurant critic!"

"That sounds great," he said, putting an arm around her as he took in every nuance of her expression.

She let herself lean against him, enjoying the comfort he offered. Here goes nothing, she thought, praying he wouldn't laugh. "It would be, except that I've searched everywhere trying to find an interesting restaurant to write about. There's nothing out there. I'm so discouraged!"

"Angie," her name was a sigh of relief that the situation was hardly dire.

She felt foolish and went over to Paavo's big yellow tabby, Hercules, and using her long, raspberry-colored nails, she scratched the top of his head and around his ears. He purred and then contentedly shut his eyes. "I know it's not very important," she said finally, "but I don't know what to do."

He folded his hands on his stomach. "Okay, *friend.* Explain the problem to me. We both know this city is lousy with restaurants. I don't get it."

"The problem is that nobody wants to read another magazine article about Chef La-di-dah's latest epicurean adventure," she said, still looking at the cat. Finally, she faced him. "That's old hat. I want to write about something unique. Something that will make people sit up and take notice—of *me,* if not the restaurant. Plus, I'm tired of not having a decent job to call my own."

"Something will turn up for you, Angie. Give it time." His voice held comfort and assurance. "Believe me."

"I hope you're right," she said softly, returning to the sofa once more.

"Are you mostly driving around, looking at places as you drive by?" he asked.

She nodded.

"Try what they teach new beat cops. If you want to get to know your people, walk the streets with them. You might find a neighborhood that interests you, then park and walk to the restaurants, big and little. You once mentioned to me that you can tell a lot just by sniffing the air as you pass a restaurant's open door, or when you first walk in. If you like the aroma, check it out."

She cocked her head, amazed he'd remembered. "I did say that, didn't I?"

"Maybe you should listen to yourself more often," he suggested with a grin.

I do, she was tempted to say. *And that's exactly why I'm here.* But she didn't say any of that. Instead, she said, "Thank you, friend. And I'll be on my way so you can get back to sleep. I know you often don't get nearly enough."

With a quick peck on his lips, she put on her jacket and sauntered from his house. Step one of mission accomplished.

2

As the green Honda climbed California Street, its wheels spun on cable car tracks wet from the drizzling mist. Damn! If he'd been able to find a parking place, he wouldn't be having this problem. But finding parking at midnight on Nob Hill was impossible except for ridiculously expensive parking garages. He wasn't about to pay the money.

Earlier, he'd waited at the cop's cottage some twenty minutes for the broad to come out, but she didn't. He guessed she might be spending the night there. If a woman that good-looking came knocking on his door, he'd keep her with him all night. No doubt about it.

But he had better things to do than sit and think about the cop and the woman and what they were doing. He had a different friend to check on.

A special friend.

Just past Taylor Street, a silver, boat-sized Mercedes sat in valet parking a few steps from the Coventry Hotel. He knew who it belonged to. It was there when he'd arrived here at ten-thirty, and it was still there now that it was nearly midnight.

The Coventry seemed like pretty plush digs to be used for a by-the-hour trysting place. But that's what it was.

For that same hour and a half, since he'd found no parking, he'd driven up and down the city streets, waiting, compelled by the need to be sure. A lesser man would have discovered the existence of a more direct target and would have stopped there. But not him. He had to double-check everything. Everything had to be exact.

Two days ago, he'd visited his special friend's Twin Peaks apartment and gave her a complimentary copy of the *Chronicle*. Women were suckers for freebies like that.

She was blonde and attractive, with a body that was ripe, fleshy and well-rounded; the kind that would fall to fat hips and sagging breasts in a few years, but in the meantime, was made for pleasure. A man's pleasure. She was also a bit dense. He'd had to explain what he meant by a two-for-one offer.

Just then, two figures emerged from the hotel. It was them! He needed to stop his car to watch them. The only open space he could find was a garage driveway. He pulled in there and cut the Honda's headlights.

It was eleven fifty-three.

As they passed under yellow street-lights, the features of the tall, silver-haired man and the young woman walking with him were illuminated. She was indeed the dull-witted blonde he'd met at the Twin Peaks apartment. But his real interest was directed at the man.

The man escorted her to her white Chevy Malibu also in the parking lot, and then with a smug, self-confident expression, watched her drive off before hurrying to his Mercedes. He glanced once, dismissively, at the bespectacled man in the illegally parked Honda, then got into his car.

The next morning, the green Honda cruised by the brown-shingled cottage once again. The Ferrari and the cop's car, an old Mustang, were both gone.

It didn't matter. They'd be back. No need to hurry. He'd planned too carefully to blow it now.

Ten years was a long time to plan. A long time to make up for.

He deserved something for those ten years. And for Heather.

This was all about Heather.

He sped through the winding, wooded paths of the Presidio to emerge at the east gate. On Baker Street, he parked directly across from the Palace of Fine Arts, the orange-hued Grecian landmark of the elegant Marina district. A half hour later, the front door of a large stucco home opened. An elderly, shrunken man, nattily dressed in a gray slacks, a gray-plaid sports coat and bowler hat, stepped out. He watched the old man slowly walk down the long flight of stairs to the sidewalk and turn toward what everyone called the Marina Green, the popular, lawn-covered play area that ran along the north coast of the city from the Presidio to Fort Mason.

After waiting a couple of minutes, he stepped from his car and ran up the stairs to the front door, dropped a *Chronicle* in front of it, rang the bell, and raced back down to the sidewalk.

Soon, an elderly woman appeared in a pink floral house-coat, her white hair in tight little ringlets.

He waved at her, pointed to the rolled newspapers in his arms and then to her door stoop. When she saw the paper lying at her feet, she smiled and nodded, waved back to him, then took the newspaper indoors with her.

It was going to be almost too easy, he thought.

3

"You better button it up, Vinnie," Butch Pagozzi shouted, running half-way down the basement stairs. Over sixty years old, he was small, light-weight and felt every bit as spry as forty years ago when he fought Tiny Alvarez for the bantamweight title. Butch lost. "We got a customer. For dinner. A dame!"

"You gotta be kiddin'. What kinda dame would wanna eat in a joint like this?" Vinnie Freiman stood his pick ax against the cement wall right beside the sledge hammer, picked up his cigar and chewed the end as smoke billowed around his balding head. A Coleman lantern lit the area beside him. When he looked up at Butch, the light caused shadows on the layers of bags under his eyes, giving him even more of a basset hound look than usual.

"I don't know," Butch muttered. "What am I gonna do?"

"Get ridda her."

"I cooked somethin' up just in case somebody wanted to eat. But what if she don't like it?"

Vinnie, a short, stocky man, pulled a huge, rumpled handkerchief out of the back pocket of his baggy brown trousers and mopped his brow and the back of his neck. "Who the hell cares? We don't want her here anyway, remember?"

"You're right. Who cares? But you never know. She might like it." Butch wrung his hands. "I mean, nobody ever complained about my cookin' before."

Vinnie took the cigar out of his mouth. "That's 'cause they was too busy barfin'."

"Jesus! What am I doin' here?" Butch grumbled. He sat down on the steps. "How'd I get into this mess?"

"Get up there and get ridda the dame," Vinnie ordered. "I got work to do. Or maybe you think doin' this is better than standin' over a stove? You want we should change places?"

"But you don't cook," Butch said.

"Not a lick."

"I'll take care of the customer."

"I thought so."

Butch ran back up to the kitchen of what had once been a small but thriving restaurant. The kitchen was fully equipped and clean. After some of the places he'd cooked, Butch still marveled every time he stepped into his new quarters.

Still, the thought of a paying customer in the dining room made his right eye twitch so badly he could barely keep it open. He checked the seasoning in his spaghetti sauce. He guessed it was okay. It seemed okay. Sort of.

"'Ey Butch," Earl White yelled, pushing through the swinging doors from the dining room. Earl, the third member of the trio, had the assignment of working the dining room since he was the only one with experience of dealing with customers. He once worked as a bouncer in Vegas. The job didn't last too long, though. Tough as he was, he found that five-foot-five bouncers sometimes got bounced themselves. "Da dame ain't leavin'. What am I s'posed to do?"

"Give her a menu."

"A menu? But you only cook spaghetti an' meatballs."

"So?"

"But I t'ought I was s'posed to get ridda her," Earl said quietly, not wanting to press the obvious. He didn't want Butch to get mad at him.

Butch eyed the door to the basement. Vinnie's cracks about his cooking still smarted. "Well, maybe she wants to eat somethin' first. This is a restaurant, you know."

Heaving a sigh, Earl searched for a menu.

Angie glanced over her shoulder at the sign in the window. It definitely said "Open." Too bad no one connected with the restaurant knew it. When she walked in, the waiter had stared at her without a word and then ran into the kitchen.

As she waited at the entrance, she looked over the empty dining area, a small, cozy room with wood-stained walls and big, round, white light fixtures. It might have had some charm except that the tables were topped with gray formica, had aluminum legs, and were surrounded by aluminum chairs with padded gray vinyl seats. Glass salt and pepper shakers completed the decor. This was hardly the accouterment she expected in a restaurant with the ethereal, whimsical name of The Wings Of An Angel.

Then it struck her. This had to be one of those fifties nostalgia places. That was why it looked so tacky. It was supposed to. She felt a little slow, but then, she was a twenty-first century kind of gal.

The chubby little man who'd run away earlier peered at her from the kitchen and then stepped through the swinging doors into the dining room. He wore a yellow shirt and brown polyester slacks—the sartorial equivalent of gray formica and vinyl, she guessed.

"You wanna eat?" he asked. His thick, curly-brown toupee

looked almost shellacked, reminding her of those 1950s dolls she'd seen in so-called antique shops with plugs of shiny vinyl hair stuck into their scalps. She was impressed. This place really went all out for authenticity.

"The restaurant is open, isn't it?" she asked, still staring at his hair.

"I guess." He didn't move. When she didn't move either, he waved an arm toward the empty tables and said, "Have a seat."

"Thanks." She was growing more dubious about staying. But maybe the waiter had a weird sense of humor. He certainly had a weird accent. He had to be from either San Francisco's North Beach or Mission districts—or Brooklyn. Their accents were amazingly similar.

She chose a spot by the window overlooking Columbus Avenue. This part of the avenue, a few blocks from the popular cafe and bistro area of North Beach, was fairly quiet. A drugstore, card shop, jewelers, locksmith and small corner grocery served the people who lived and worked nearby. But she loved this part of the city and so, taking Paavo's advice, she'd walked it, and ended up finding this place. The waiter dropped an old, greasy menu on the table in front of her. The name across the top, Columbus Avenue Cafe, had been lined through with a ball-point pen. The new name hadn't been written in.

"I understand this restaurant just opened," she said.

"Couple days ago."

"How's business?"

He shrugged. "Okay."

Why didn't she believe him?

"Good," she said, eying the menu again. She'd always thought preparing a menu and seeing the restaurant's name printed on it would be one of the biggest thrills a new owner could have. For the owner to still be using the former cafe's menu made no sense to her at all.

As the waiter walked away, she turned her attention to the dinner entrees. Pasta Primavera. Ravioli. Veal Parmigiana. All the regulars. It was a surprisingly complete menu, and the smells coming from the kitchen were inviting.

This place had been closed for months, ever since The Columbus Avenue Cafe, a well-respected but unprofitable establishment, went under. The building's owners had been desperate, she'd heard, and willing to rent out the restaurant space for a song. The problem was the location. A little too far north of fashionable North Beach restaurants to pick up the trendy crowd, yet too far south of Fisherman's Wharf to get its tourist trade. The location ended up serving only people who unknowingly wandered away from the other restaurants and grew desperate. A tough way to make a living.

She beckoned the waiter to come to her again, which wasn't a problem, given the complete emptiness of the place.

"I'll try your manicotti. With it, I'd like a small salad, Italian dressing on the side, served with the main course, not before, and the house red."

He squinted as if in pain. She noticed that his face was heavily lined under the toupee. "Uh, we don't have no manicotti today."

"Oh. That's too bad. How's the lasagna?"

"Same as da manicotti."

She wasn't sure she'd heard right. "Veal Parmigiana?"

He shook his head.

She shut the menu. "What *do* you have?"

"Spaghetti an' meatballs."

She handed him back the menu. "Fine."

He half-waddled, half-ran back to the kitchen. Maybe she'd be smart to just leave without waiting for dinner. But she was hungry, and this was a new restaurant in town. Wearily, she leaned back in the chair and rubbed her fingers across her scalp, lifting her shiny, dark hair and brushing it back off her face, not even caring that the added blonde high-lights were all askew. Being a free-lance restaurant reviewer meant she had to be adventurous, despite the occasional disastrous meal. On the other hand, if the food here was espe-cially good, this could be regarded as her personal find. A feather in her cap.

Right now, though, she had the sinking feeling her cap would soon resemble a plucked turkey.

Somehow, she was going to have to come up with a job that paid a decent salary. She lived in a beautiful apartment in a building owned by her parents, and her Ferrari had been a gift from them. But it was time to become independent, self-suffi-cient—especially if she planned to settle down and get serious about her life, her career, and her feelings about a certain homicide inspector.

Somehow, through some of the scariest, strangest situations she'd ever encountered in a hitherto safe and rather boring lie, she'd managed to fall in love with him. At least, she guessed this must be love, having never felt anything like it before with the fellows she'd dated.

She couldn't imagine feeling this way about anyone else, and she wanted to be with him forever. Did that mean she could finally be growing up? Finally be thinking in terms of marriage?

Okay, she knew marriage wasn't high on a lot of her girl-friends' list of things to do, especially since so many marriages ended in divorce these days. But she was raised as an Italian Catholic girl, close to her family, and getting married was what was expected of her, not only by her parents but also by her four, older, married sisters. It was a burden, but that's who she was.

Still, she found it bad enough not being sure what "love" meant, but "marriage" was another level of bewilderment alto-gether. Sure, she saw it with her family, but she'd never really considered what it would mean to her, to the way she lived her life.

Yet, as her feelings for Paavo deepened, she found herself doing just that.

The thought of marrying someone was simultaneously exciting and scary. She needed to learn more about it, and since she was teaching an adult ed history class and was working on a book on San Francisco history, she knew all about research. Why not research marriage?

The sight of Curly-locks heading her way, juggling a heaping plate of spaghetti and meatballs, plus a basket of French bread and butter, broke her out of her reverie. As he placed it on the table, he stared at her forehead.

"Thank you," she said, trying unsuccessfully to make eye contact. "It looks wonderful."

"Yeah." He continued to stare.

"This restaurant has a beautiful name," she said uneasily. Was there such a thing as a forehead fetish? "The Wings Of An Angel. I was expecting gossamer curtains on the windows and warm wooden furnishings."

"Yeah? Well, dis ain't so classy. Maybe you wanna leave now?"

"Leave? I haven't eaten yet."

"You got some doit."

"Doit?"

"On your forehead. Doit."

She tugged at her bangs, pulling a few strands of hair back onto her forehead. "Not dirt, it's ash. Today's Ash Wednesday. I went to evening mass at St. Peter and Paul's Church up the street, and then wandered around a bit and found you."

"We was wonderin' how you found us."

"I guess that makes me God's gift to you," she said, and then grinned. "Not only that, your restaurant has the word Angel in its name, and my name's Angelina. Sounds like fate to me."

The waiter blanched and started to back away. He couldn't possibly think she was being serious, could he? "Just leave da money on da table," he said.

"I'm joking," she called, but he didn't stop. "How much is it?"

Over his shoulder he shouted, "Five bucks."

Five bucks? Impossible. Twenty would be a moderate price in this city. Nothing cost five dollars anymore, except maybe a plain cup of coffee. This restaurant was too strange. She twisted some spaghetti around her fork and took a bite. Hmm....

She took another bite, shut her eyes and chewed. The sauce was delicious. Different, she had to admit. A little odd. But still, delicious. She tasted the meatballs. They'd been cooked in the red sauce, and the combination of flavors had merged in a mysteriously heavenly way. There were all the regular meatball and spaghetti sauce flavors—ground beef, tomato paste, garlic, onion, basil, oregano, fennel, a touch of ground pork... and something else as well. What? It was a trifle salty, whatever it was, but quite good.

She kept eating, trying to figure out the mix of ingredients, but couldn't. "Waiter!" she called. "Waiter!"

He stuck his head out between the swinging doors. "You ain't chokin', are you?" he asked.

"No. I was wondering if I could have a word with your cook."

"He don't talk to nobody." His head disappeared.

She listened to the sound of hammering coming from the kitchen. Maybe they were still doing some construction, and that's why things were so out of kilter here. She took another bite. Delicious.

That did it. She was going to find out what was in those meatballs if it killed her.

4

Paavo sat at his gray-metal desk in the tightly crammed room of the homicide bureau and reached for his phone. Around him, stacks of books and papers balanced precariously, the only clear space being a small area in front of his computer. For the sixth time in the past three hours, he called Angie's number. For as many times, he'd listened as his call went to voicemail, "...can't answer your call right now, but please leave your name and number and I'll—"

He hung up in disgust. Last night, when she'd shown up looking so beautiful and desirable, and then announced they should be friends, he didn't know what to do. The temptation to tell her, or better yet, to show her, how he felt about her was overwhelming. And it definitely wasn't mere "friendship."

But instead of saying or doing anything, he'd let her leave.

She told him she'd be home this evening. So he made plans to surprise her by taking her out to dinner. Too often, his evenings would be interrupted by a case. But Homicide had been mercifully quiet this week. The deaths they'd gotten were clear cases of suicide, overdoses, or gang killings that were turned over to the special Gang Task Force.

He'd waited to call her until he was as sure as possible without a working crystal ball that they could spend the evening together, and now she wasn't answering.

Homicide was empty, except for him. Benson and Calderon were out in the field doing an investigation, and the others had gone home. Paavo soon finished his report on a suicide out on Castro Street—the third this month.

This city was known for its high suicide rate, but despite all the psychological rot about why they happened here—two centuries of "go west, young man," the end of the trail, and so forth—three suicides within thirty days was too much. Homicide had to check out each one to be sure it wasn't a cleverly disguised murder. But in this case, he'd learned the victim had a painful, fatal illness. His gut reaction was that the dying man simply wanted to end his misery.

Paavo leaned back in his chair and glared at his phone. Where had Angie gone? Why hadn't she told him last night she'd be out?

Maybe something came up with her family. With four older sisters, all married and with kids, plus doting parents, not to mention enough cousins to fill the bleachers at the city's baseball stadium, she could spend hours and hours with just family, not even counting her friends.

He phoned her neighbor, Stanfield Bonnette. He could barely stomach Bonnette, but Angie seemed to like the guy, and sometimes she dropped in over there. Bonnette lived in a small one-bedroom place across the hall from Angie's big apartment.

"Hello! Stan the man, here."

Paavo nearly hung up the phone right then. "This is Paavo Smith. I'm trying to locate Angie. Have you seen her?"

"Ah, Inspector! Well, well, what a surprise." Paavo hated the smug sound of Bonnette's voice. "I'm sorry to admit I haven't seen Angie today. She usually tells me where she's going, too.

I'm surprised she didn't this time. I guess she doesn't tell you her whereabouts anymore either, does she?"

Paavo didn't like what Bonnette was implying by that "anymore" crack. "Thanks for your help," he said, then hung up.

Just what had Bonnette meant? Had Angie told him of her plan for them to be just friends now?

Hell, Bonnette was just trying to get his goat, and—dammit—he'd succeeded.

Paavo considered calling Angie's mother and asking if Angie was there, but immediately dismissed that thought. Once Serafina got him on the phone, she'd grill him on how he and Angie were getting along, and what their plans were for the future. As if he should know. They couldn't even make plans for this evening!

The truth of the matter was that they hadn't known each other all that long. Most couples he knew dated for months, sometimes years, before "getting serious." And even then, they'd often end up splitting up, or if they got married, they'd get divorced. Especially if one of them was a cop.

He knew the statistics all too well.

On the other hand, although the time he and Angie were together wasn't long by a calendar, it was beyond intense with people trying to kill her or her co-workers. And the whole time they were both trying to deny any serious attraction existed between them.

Until, finally, they couldn't deny it any longer.

"No luck, Paav?" his partner, Toshiro Yoshiwara, asked. He'd stopped to drop off evidence and was now on his way home. He knew Paavo had hoped to spend that evening with Angie.

Yosh had transferred to the San Francisco Police Department a couple of months earlier from Seattle where he had been highly regarded. He was a big man, tall as Paavo, broad-shouldered, with huge, strong hands and a head that bore only a stubble of black hair from his buzz cut. He had been teamed with Paavo after Paavo's long-time partner was killed by gun smugglers. Yosh was as boisterous and out-going as Paavo was quiet and reserved.

"She's been out all evening. For some reason, she's not answering her phone."

"Tell you what," Yosh said, "let's go down to The Court House and have a beer. You can try phoning her from there. She might turn up. No sense going all the way home when you're much closer to her place right here."

"If she goes home."

"It's worth a try." As he spoke, he swung around in his swivel chair. "Hey, look who's here. It's Mr. Jolly!"

Luis Calderon had just entered the room. Frowning, without a word to anyone, he walked straight to his desk.

"Hey there, Luis," Yosh called out. "How ya doing?"

Calderon's expression grew more dyspeptic. "Lousy."

"Lousy?" Yosh repeated, acting shocked. "What's wrong?"

"I hate this time of year. It's the worst. When I was a kid I was supposed to give up something for Lent. But we were so poor I didn't have anything to give up."

Paavo gave a quick shake of his head, hoping to stop Yosh. Everyone who'd ever worked with Calderon had heard this before. Every year, every season, a litany of Calderon complaints. Even before his wife, Carlota, left him, the guy viewed life through misery-colored glasses.

Instead of stopping, though, Yosh winked. "And soon," he said, in a mock soothing tone, "all that changes with the beauty of Easter."

"Sure. All that candy making kids sick. Who wants to see all that puking? Or Easter bunnies? You know what my family used to do with Easter bunnies? Eat them. I grew up scarfing down Peter Rabbit."

Yosh got up from his chair and plunked his bulky, well-muscled body on the edge of his desk. "I thought you said Christmas was the worst time of year?"

"Yeah." Calderon sighed. "It stinks too. Holidays stink. I hate 'em. So, you two supposed to stick around and cheer me up tonight, or what?"

"I'm heading for the Court House," Yosh said, then turned to Paavo. "You coming?"

"Paavo doesn't go for that stuff," Calderon said. "Anyway, I got a jumper. Have to wait for the ME's to call with the autopsy results so I can finish my write-up. Anyone want to help?"

"Off the Golden Gate?" Paavo asked.

"Where else?"

"Calderon can handle it on his own, Paavo," Yosh said. "Might cheer him up."

Paavo wasn't one to stop at the neighborhood watering hole and everyone in Homicide knew it. Usually he'd just go home when work quieted down. Tonight, though, he felt antsy, and the thought of staying with Calderon had less than zero appeal.

He grabbed his jacket. "Okay, Yosh," he said. "Lead the way."

Homicide was located in the Hall of Justice, an ugly, block-sized monstrosity that housed the police administration offices, coroner, office of the District Attorney, courtrooms, judges' chambers, and a variety of other city government offices.

One block away stood The Court House, a decent bar in a neighborhood of dives. Hall of Justice employees from bailiffs to the Chief of Inspectors lifted glasses in there. Lawyers for the defense rubbed shoulders with district attorneys. It was said that more pleas had been bargained in that bar than in all the offices in the Hall put together.

The smoke-filled lounge was packed when Paavo and Yosh entered, despite indoor smoking being illegal in the city.

"Hey, Paavo," called one of the assistant DA's, Hanover Judd. "Long time no see."

The DA's offices were on the third floor of the Hall, and Homicide directly above them on the fourth. Paavo would, at times, work with Judd on a homicide prosecutions.

Now, Judd stood at the bar, a scotch and soda in his hand. In his early thirties, he managed to maintain an exuberance and idealism about his job that Paavo found refreshing after the politics and power-mongering that usually went along with much of the work at the Hall of Justice.

Paavo went over to him and shook hands. "How's it going, H.J.?" He introduced Yosh.

"I got a call today from someone you might know," Judd said. "A retired judge, name of Lucas St. Clair. Called to report that he's being harassed by someone, wondered what we could do about it."

Paavo ordered a Dos Equis amber and Yosh an IPA. "I remember St. Clair," Paavo said. "What's going on?"

"The guy he's complaining about hasn't done anything except loiter around the neighborhood. But today, he gave the judge's wife a copy of the *Chronicle*."

"Considering that paper," Yosh said, "I'd say that's definitely a criminal offense—for misinformation if nothing else."

"Does the judge have any idea who he might be?" Paavo asked.

"St. Clair can't give us a good description. The guy's always wearing dark glasses and a baseball cap. Thing is, the judge lives right across from the Palace of Fine Arts. He said the guy often parks next to the duck pond. It's a weird town, Paavo. The fellow might just have a duck fetish."

Paavo doubted it. "Did the judge go through the newspaper? See if there were any stories that meant anything to him?"

"I didn't ask. He said he'd already read the paper that morning."

"It might be worth looking into—a message of some kind." The *Chronicle*—Angie had left a copy of her newspaper at his place the other night. Seemed a lot of people were giving away *Chronicles* for some reason.

Yosh had been listening to this conversation with interest. "You know this judge, Paavo?"

"He was one of the toughest," Paavo said.

Judd chuckled. "The DA's thanked their own saints when they got St. Clair, but the defense lawyers called him The Judge from Hell."

"Uh, oh," Yosh said under his breath. "Speaking of DA's, I think I'd better get out of here."

"Why's that?"

"I see Lloyd Fletcher over there. He's still pissed off by the way I answered the judge at the Marlowe arraignment. But I wasn't about to perjure myself just because he had a lousy case."

"He knows that."

"He might know it, but he won't forgive it."

Paavo glanced at a silver-haired man in a corner booth, so aloof and polished in a charcoal Brooks Brothers suit that he seemed out of place here. "He used to be a reasonable guy."

"That was before he started thinking he'd like to be mayor," Judd said.

"Fletcher? He's never held any office."

"You got it. That's why he thinks he's got a chance. No one knows for sure if he'd be a good mayor or a bad one. He can run as an open-minded liberal who's also against crime and win big in this town. No one will know whether or not he's telling the truth."

As Fletcher and the man he'd been talking to, Maxim Wainwright, a member of the Board of Supervisors, stood up to leave, he noticed Paavo and Yosh. He made his way to them.

"Well, well," Fletcher said. "What brings Homicide's finest to these shores? Hello there, H.J.," he added, then immediately turned back to the inspectors. "I thought you two never touched anything stronger than Snapple."

"We're down here seeing how the other half lives, Lloyd," Yosh said. "Buy you a drink?"

The tall man cocked an eyebrow as if unsure how to take Yosh's remark. "No, better not. I'm on my way home. By the way, Smith, you did a great job on the Barker case."

"The guy confessed. That makes it easy," Paavo said, remembering why he hated coming to places like this. He hadn't been here long, and he was already wanting to leave.

"Yes, well..." Fletcher glanced at Yoshiwara. "You know, Yosh, I heard you were thinking about going back to Seattle. People have been saying you might be happier there. That true?"

"What a laugh," Yosh said with a big, friendly grin. "I'm having the time of my life here. You must have heard somebody's wishful thinking."

Paavo wondered if Fletcher knew Yosh was being sarcastic as all hell, or saw him as Mr. Congeniality in action.

"Good, good," Fletcher said. "Hate to lose a good man in Homicide. See you boys around." With that, holding his hand aloft like the politician he hoped to become, and waving goodbye to friend and foe alike, Lloyd Fletcher left the bar.

He sat in his green Honda and watched the procession come and go from The Court House. A couple of beat cops strolled out, then a sheriff's deputy. Three women went in, dressed to kill. They were probably receptionists or secretaries for some bigwigs. They didn't look old, tired, or ugly enough to be any of the professional women who seemed to be taking over the running of this city.

Lloyd Fletcher had stood outside the door for a long while, waving and smiling at everyone who came out or went in. And, like the sycophants they were, they bowed, scraped and fawned over the powerful D.A.

It made him want to throw up. No one had ever fawned over him. Quite the opposite, in fact. Ten years ago they kept saying he had to have been crazy to do what he'd done. He wouldn't tell them the real reason. He wouldn't tell them that he did it for Heather.

Everything was for Heather.

He leaned forward to watch as the cop soon followed Lloyd Fletcher out the door. He was glad he hadn't needed to wait very long before Smith left. Now, if only he'd go to his girlfriend's house...

He hadn't been able to track down where she lived yet.

But he would.

The cop went into the Hall of Justice parking lot and in a while reappeared in his old blue Mustang. He let him go ahead, then pulled into traffic two cars behind him. Once he found out where the girlfriend lived, he'd have all the information he needed. Then, life would be perfect.

5

"Is she still eatin'?" Butch asked, stirring the spaghetti sauce so that chunks of the canned tomato he used wouldn't stick to the bottom of the old aluminum kettle.

"Looks like she likes it," Earl said.

"You think so?" Butch's eyes lit up. "Maybe I oughta cook up a couple more things?" He walked to the kitchen door and took a peek at their only customer. Wearing a self-satisfied grin he turned to Earl. "Tell Vinnie to pipe down in the cellar. What kinda joint will she think this is?"

"You tell him." Earl was no fool.

"Nobody's gotta tell me," Vinnie announced, just emerging from the cellar steps. He stomped to the middle of the kitchen floor and glared from Butch to Earl and back again. Despite the slump age had put in his back, his black eyes were still piercing under thick eyebrows.

"What the hell you two bozos doin' feedin' people dinner?" he asked. "What do you think this is? A goddamn restaurant? We got work to do. We gotta be fast. In and out, before anyone asks questions. Or maybe you think everybody's as dumb as you are?"

"Look, Vinnie, we can't go throwin' out customers," Butch said, going back to stir his sauce. "What if she complains to somebody? We gotta look legitimate."

Vinnie's face turned fiery red. "You ain't looked legitimate since the day you was born."

"Hey! You don't talk like that about my mother, hear?"

"What mother? You was hatched."

Butch crossed the room and stuck his face close to Vinnie's. "Just remember, I was a contender for boxing Champion of the World."

Vinnie didn't look impressed. "Yeah, yeah."

"Besides," Butch folded his arms and lifted his chin, "if I quit, you wouldn't have nobody to cook. Then what would you do?"

"Ever hear of TV dinners? They probably taste better than your slop, anyway."

"Okay, I *will* quit!"

"You can't." Vinnie turned his back on Butch. "Earl, hurry her up. Get her out. Give her the bill or somethin'."

"She ain't done eatin' yet," Earl said meekly.

"So? What do you think this is, the Ritz? Give her the bill and make sure she takes the hint."

Earl swallowed hard. "I don't t'ink she takes no hints, Vinnie."

"Oh, waiter," Angie called out gaily. She waited a second. No answer. "Waiter?" Nothing but muffled voices from the kitchen. What dreadful service.

Finally the waiter stuck his head through the swinging kitchen doors. "Whaddya want dis time?"

"This spaghetti sauce and these meatballs are absolutely wonderful," she said, ignoring his bad manners. "I really would like to talk to your cook. I'm sort of in the business myself, you see."

"He don't wanna see you," Earl shouted.

"Why not?" The restaurant was still empty. "It can't be because he's too busy. I'm not asking that he come out here. In fact," she said as she stood, "I'll go into the kitchen to talk to him. Believe me, if he uses this sauce on just two or three more dishes, this restaurant will do wonderfully."

Earl hurried toward her, holding his arms spread wide the way he'd learned to do in Vegas when someone lunged for a Blackjack dealer. "There ain't no way you can talk to him."

She folded her arms. "Won't you ask him?"

"He's shy," Earl said.

"Shy?"

"Look, it's gettin' late. You want some dessert?"

Somehow, she couldn't imagine a restaurant with only one entrée offering anything decent in desserts. "I've given up desserts for Lent."

"Yeah? I t'ink dis place has, too."

The waiter spoke with such a deadpan style, Angie had to laugh. She sat back down, unsure if he was serious or not. Even if she couldn't see the cook this time, she would eventually. She wasn't about to give up finding out what made the meatballs and sauce so special. If only the restaurant had a bit more to offer, it might have been a find for her—an interesting place to write about for her magazine article. Right now, though, it wasn't even one dot in a three-dot journalism column.

The lack of a presentable menu was irritating. After all, any fool could stumble across a good high-priced restaurant in this city. It took someone clever to discover a cheap place worth going to. Someone like her, in fact.

She glanced at her wristwatch. It was eight-thirty, not late at all. If she went home now, she'd probably sit around watching TV or trying to figure out her relationship with Paavo. He was most likely busy as ever with his cases and would see her when he could. He was pretty good at dropping by unexpectedly for a visit, but she didn't want to get into a rut of going home to wait for him. It wasn't as if their relationship had progressed beyond kisses. Not even an "I love you." Although, she felt he felt that way, and she was pretty sure he felt she felt that way, too. But neither of them felt confident enough to say so. Frankly, all this "feeling" with no action was the pits.

She was a modern woman with freedom, choice, and opportunity. She just had to figure out what to do with them.

"I'll have a caffè latte," she said suddenly.

"A caffè latte?" Earl repeated.

"That's right."

"Okay."

Earl ran into the kitchen. "Now she wants a caffè latte. What's dat?"

Butch glanced toward heaven. "Didn't you learn nothin' before you went to the big house? It's half strong coffee and half milk."

"So why don't you just make da coffee weaker?"

Butch shook his head. "There's a pot of coffee all made. It's Chase and Sanborn, but I made it around noon, so it's probably strong enough to take the wax off the floor. Plug in that espresso machine, and the gizmo on the end there will make the milk all foamy, then you pour it into the coffee. It's easy. You understand?"

Earl looked at the machine. He never saw anything like it before. "'Course I understand. It's easy."

"Okay. So do it. Oh, one more thing. You got to serve it in a tall glass." Butch went back down into the cellar to help Vinnie.

"Yeah. I can do dat."

Earl turned on the machine before he took a half gallon of milk from the refrigerator. He poured it into a wide-mouthed pitcher and held the pitcher below the espresso machine's steam arm. He twisted the valve and a jet of steam shot some of the milk out of the pitcher onto his shirt. But it didn't look any more foamy than when he started.

He cursed and tried again. This time the milk sprayed his slacks. He gave it another try. Milk rained onto his hair.

He twisted the knob faster this time. A jet of milk shot straight into his eye, nearly blinding him as more foul language erupted.

He shoved the pitcher as high as it would go onto the steam arm and turned the valve with all his might. Milk hit the ceiling. Still no foam.

The milk that had landed on his toupee earlier seeped through it and began to trickle down onto his forehead. He wiped it away.

Rage turned to cold determination.

He moved the milk into a bowl, put it under the beaters of a big, industrial size mixer and turned it on.

The milk spun around in the bowl at a fantastic speed, but it still didn't get foamy. He added an egg.

That helped a little.

A bottle of blue Dawn sat on the counter by the sink. Just a splash. Who'd ever know? Like magic, bubbles appeared.

Now we're in business, he thought. Leaving the machine running, he began to search for the type of glass Butch had described. There were short, fat glasses, and tall, thin glasses, but nothing tall, yet thick enough to hold hot coffee. He didn't want the customer to burn her fingers.

Pulling up a chair, he stood on it so that he could reach into the back of the upper shelves of the cabinet where restaurant owners past had left behind mismatched cups, plates and glasses that they didn't want to cart away with them. After several minutes searching, he found a tall, thick glass with a handle.

Perfect. He grabbed the glass, got off the chair, turned

around and to his horror saw that the milk had foamed up and out of the bowl, across the counter and down onto the floor. It was heading for the dining room.

He carefully tiptoed through the slippery foam to turn off the mixer, then continued on to the pot of coffee. He poured the coffee into the glass. Despite the handle, it still felt hot, so he found a small, flat plate to put it on. Nice.

He then plopped several spoonfuls of sudsy milk on top. Although he'd only used a small amount of detergent, a slightly soapy chemical scent wafted out of the cup, mixed with the smell of bitter coffee. Maybe she'd think they used really clean glasses.

He was headed toward the dining room when Butch came up from the basement where he'd been helping Vinnie. "What the hell! What'd you do to my kitchen?" He lunged toward Earl.

Earl tried to run but the soles of his shoes were slick from the detergent on the floor. His feet scrambled wildly. He held the plate tight, watching the glass as it slid from one side of the plate to the other. With each slip of the glass, he angled the plate in the opposite direction, so that, like a juggler, he managed to keep the glass upright and filled with coffee while his feet, legs and body gyrated.

But then, as Butch hit the slippery floor, he hydroplaned across it and smacked right into Earl's back.

Earl's legs flew out from under him. He went down on his backside into the frothy muck. The push he'd gotten from Butch caused him to slide right through the swinging doors into the dining room.

Angie turned around to see man, foam and caffè latte shooting toward her.

He came to a halt and somehow, miraculously, still held the coffee upright in its tall glass on its flat plate.

Angie stood as the waiter picked himself up and carried her the coffee.

"Are you all right?" she asked.

"Yeah. It's nothin'." With a deep sigh he placed the coffee on the table, but right on top of her fork. The plate made a little rocking motion then tilted. The glass slid off the plate, hit the table top, tipped over and the caffè latte rushed out of the glass across the table and dripped right onto Earl's shoes.

"Oh, that's too bad," Angie said. "Well, I wasn't really in the mood for coffee, anyway. I think I'll take in a movie."

She opened her purse, took out a five-dollar bill, plus two singles for the tip, and placed them on the table. "Ciao," she said, and sauntered out of the restaurant.

6

"Angie, you should be talking with Paavo about your relationship, not me." Bianca, the oldest of Angie's four sisters, emptied the morning's first load of wash from the dryer into a basket. She quickly refilled the dryer with another load, then picked up the basket and came back into the family room to join Angie.

"I'm not ready to yet. First, I need to understand what a serious relationship would mean to me. To us. After all, what if he says he doesn't feel like he's ready to be serious about anybody, and looks at me as if I'm pathetic for asking? The problem is, though, I think about it day and night." Angie sat on the sofa, her chin in her hands. "I can't eat. I can't sleep. I can't even think about my article for *Haute Cuisine*. You've got to help me!"

"Have you talked to mamma or papà?" Bianca was fourteen years older than Angie and at least fourteen pounds heavier, with straight dark brown, chin-length hair. She began to sort out underwear between husband, older and younger sons—a chore Angie couldn't imagine herself emulating any time soon.

"Are you kidding?" Angie said miserably.

"You're right. Mamma would have you walking down the aisle before you're ready, and papà would have you shipped off to a nunnery."

"That's why I've come to you. I've got to know if I'm being pushy. You know I have the patience of a gnat. I want to know where I stand with him! If he doesn't care that much, I need to stay available to others. To tie myself down to a man who doesn't want me would be stupid. I need you, Bianca. To tell me everything."

"The real picture?" Bianca looked dubious.

Angie nodded. "The hard truth."

"The cold facts?"

"The ugly details."

"Of marriage."

"Well... since that's where my thoughts might lead," Angie murmured, her stomach fluttering even hearing the word, "Go for it. I want the better and worse. Actually, the worse. I can handle the better."

Bianca held up a pair of jockey shorts and studied them. "Hmm, the tag with their size fell off." With a shrug, she tossed them in with her older son's clothes. "It's a tall order, Angie. Marriage, more than anything else I can think of, is in the eye of the beholder. I can give you one person's opinion, but I think you need to talk to a few other people as well."

"I will!" Angie started folding bath towels. "I mean, this is my life we're talking about. 'Look before you leap,' that's my motto. God, you've got a lot of towels here. What are you doing? Starting a bath house?"

"Teenage boys. When they discover girls, they discover soap and water. And since when is that your motto? I thought it was 'No time like the present.'" Bianca gave Angie a pointed, big-sisterly look.

"That aside, I need your help."

"What's marriage like..." Bianca said thoughtfully, matching pairs of white socks and folding them together. "Well, let's look at music and going out to hear it live. Peter loves classical."

"You know I love opera."

"And you can give me Michael Bublé any day," Bianca added.

Angie nodded. "Paavo loves blues and soul."

"Anyway, a good marriage is when you compromise."

"What did you go see?"

"A fine performance of wannabe Irish dancers."

Angie's eyes widened.

Bianca shrugged. "It wasn't terrible."

7

R ed and blue lights atop three police cars spiraled and flashed. Business men and women, shoppers, tourists, and the city's usual wide and motley crowd of street people stood eerily silent in the wake of senseless, brutal death. Beyond them, all the noise and traffic of downtown city life on a weekday morning continued as usual, oblivious to the tragedy that had struck here.

Sans Souci was a small, exclusive jewelry shop tucked between a women's boutique and a large stationer's on Post Street. At ten o'clock that morning, someone had walked into the jeweler's, shot and killed the clerk, and escaped. The motive, most likely, was robbery.

Paavo stopped his Mustang behind a black-and-white. He and Yosh trained their eyes on the crime scene, already cordoned off by the patrolmen who'd first answered the call. The paramedics leaned against their ambulance, waiting patiently for the homicide team to arrive. They were in shirt sleeves, enjoying the warm, sunny spring morning, and Paavo couldn't help but notice the irony of it.

As he and Yosh walked toward the shop, a patrolman filled

them in on the few details he'd learned. Pulling out their note-books, the two inspectors began scribbling raw data. By unspoken prior agreement, Paavo would take the inside, Yosh the outside.

Yosh glanced inside the shop to get a feel for the situation, to see the victim and where he'd fallen. Then he began questioning the people who hovered around on the sidewalk—taking down their names, addresses and initial reactions before they drifted away or said too much to each other, causing their own views and sightings to become confused or distorted by what others' saw.

Inside the shop, Paavo didn't head directly toward the body, but edged along the perimeter of the store, jotting down and rough-sketching each detail noted, including the way the victim lay and the spatter from his body.

The victim, Nathan Ellis, was a white male, about age 30, six feet tall, 180 pounds, with short blond hair, and a pale complexion. He was tastefully dressed in a brown and gray tweed blazer, gray slacks, white shirt, and brown tie, and with a watch and wedding band. He lay on his side, almost in a fetal position, in a pool of blood stemming from a gunshot wound to the chest.

None of the merchandise in the store seemed disturbed, yet the store owner, discovering Ellis' body, had called this in as a robbery. Why?

Minutes after Paavo and Yosh arrived, the medical examiner showed up with her team, and soon after, the photographer and crime scene investigations unit arrived. As Paavo wrote, questioned and studied, the photographer took videos and stills of the inside and outside of the store, while the CSI unit began the collection of trace evidence and fingerprinting. The ME soon completed her exam and her team waited for Paavo's okay to remove the body.

He was in no hurry. Until he was sure he'd learned everything the dead man could tell him about the way he died and by whom, he'd keep the body right where it was.

The removal team rolled their eyes at each other at the delay. Paavo saw their gesture and dismissed it. Same for the jewelry store owner who was pacing back and forth in front of the store anxious to get in and figure out how much was left of his money and jewels. From what Paavo could see, he didn't have anything to worry about.

"Let me go!"

Paavo whirled around at the sound of a woman's cry. A young African-American woman, nicely dressed in a business suit and high heels, struggled with the uniformed officer guarding the crime scene. As Paavo approached her, she stopped struggling. Fear at what she might learn filled her dark eyes.

"I'm Inspector Smith," he said.

Her tear-stained face would have been beautiful were it not etched with worry. "I heard it on the radio," she said, her voice trembling. "On the traffic report. A shooting at a jeweler's on Post Street. I called, but it wasn't Nathan who answered the phone. It was a police officer." Her icy fingers grasped Paavo's hands. "He's going to be all right, isn't he? Tell me he'll be all right."

"Are you his wife?" Paavo asked.

She nodded.

"I'm sorry," he said gently with a slight shake of his head.

"No! You're wrong!" she screamed, her grip tightening. "Let me see him."

"Mrs. Ellis—"

"He's all right!" she cried. "Please, God."

Paavo gestured at the patrolman beside her. "This is Officer Crossen. He'll take care of you, Mrs. Ellis."

"Nathan!" She sobbed hysterically as Paavo gave her hands a gentle squeeze and then backed away. The young patrolman, taking charge, led her slowly toward his police car. He'd take her home and find someone to stay with her.

Paavo shut his eyes a moment, running his fingers through his hair as her desperate cries echoed in his mind. He faced the dead man, checking, double-checking, and all the while pondering the man who had been Nathan Ellis and all he'd lost this day.

Finally, he took a deep breath and scanned the crowd until he found the anxious, white-haired man he'd spotted earlier. "I understand you're the owner," he said.

"Yes." The man's voice quavered.

Paavo drew him away from the crowd and gave the ME the okay to remove the body.

"Your full name?" he asked.

"Philip Justin Pierpont."

"You're the one who discovered that Mr. Ellis had been shot?"

"Yes. I was coming back from the bank and I heard a loud noise. I thought a car had back-fired, but then I saw people running away from the shop, screaming. I hid in a doorway, I'm sorry to say. When it was quiet again, I came here and found Nathan."

"You called the police and reported a robbery."

"Yes."

In the jewelry shop, diamond rings and necklaces on black velvet had sparkled under the lights. Paavo had seen nothing broken into, nothing disturbed. The cash register was still filled with cash. "What made you think it was a robbery?"

The man's cheeks turned red, his hands moved spasmodically as if out of control. "What reason other than robbery could anyone have been here? Why else would anyone shoot Nathan Ellis?"

At five o'clock, Paavo finally arrived at his desk to enter into his computer the lengthy notes he'd taken at the jewelry store that morning and throughout the day as he'd spoken with friends, relatives and co-workers of the victim, as well as potential witnesses up and down the block where the jeweler was located. It had been a frustrating day. So far, he and Yosh had found no witnesses to the crime, and no one had seen anyone go into or come out of the jeweler's that morning. The robber had to have gone out the back door into an alley, which meant he had cased the place before robbing it.

It was, in fact, a robbery. Not five minutes after Paavo and Yosh left the store, Philip Pierpont had phoned to tell him that three inexpensive reproductions of Russia's priceless Fabergé eggs were missing—blown crystal eggs, encrusted with gold, worth no more than a few hundred dollars each. The priceless originals were in museums, but here, someone had killed a man over a set of copies. It didn't make sense.

Paavo stared grimly at the words he'd placed on his computer screen. The downtown area around Post and Grant Streets was one of San Francisco's busiest. That no one saw anything was hard to believe. He couldn't help but suspect he was dealing with the big city problem of people not wanting to get involved in any problems that didn't affect them personally. The fact that a thirty-year-old man was gunned down sense-lessly seemed to mean little to anyone except his family and friends.

Sometimes Paavo wondered why it meant anything to him.

His phone rang. It was Visa's security division, giving him the home telephone numbers that matched the cards of two customers who were in Carole Anne's Dress Shoppe, next door to Sans Souci Jewelers, just minutes before the shooting occurred. There was a slight chance one or both of the women had been on the street in front of the jewelers when the gunman entered. If so, he had to get to them fast.

Generally, eyewitnesses to murders didn't provide much help. Their memories were too easily influenced. The bigger the case, the more they tended to "remember" what was shown on TV news. But he wanted to find out why they'd left so quickly. Why they weren't among the people Yosh had interviewed.

He dialed the first number. No one answered. He called the second number. No answer there either. Where were they?

The unanswered telephone calls brought an eerie déjà vu from last night. Up until eleven o'clock he'd kept trying to reach Angie. He'd even checked to see if there'd been any auto accidents involving a Ferrari Portofino. There hadn't been.

After eleven, he gave up. He hadn't left a message. She'd probably gone to visit one of her sisters. Maybe a girlfriend. It wasn't as if the words Stan had spoken about her no longer telling him where she was going or what she was doing had bothered him. He had scarcely thought about them at all except for one or two or ten times.

When he arrived at work that morning he'd skimmed the accident reports again and felt like a jerk doing it. If he didn't watch himself, he'd start calling hospital emergency rooms next.

He had no reason to expect her to tell him every time she went out in the evening. She could go where she pleased, with whomever. After all, they'd never spoken of an exclusive commitment.

He'd made some assumptions, though. Some big assumptions. Maybe even some foolish ones.

He forced himself to shove aside thoughts of where she might have gone. It was her business, not his. What he needed to do was to type up his notes while his scribbles still made sense. Later, he'd call. Tonight, though, with a fresh murder case to investigate, he probably wasn't going anywhere.

Before long, he became lost in speculation about the case

and in deciphering the day's findings. Looking up from his computer, he glanced at the clock on the wall. Seven-forty. Then at his desk calendar.

His desk calendar had somehow gotten stuck on Friday. But today was Tuesday... Tuesday night. That seemed to mean something. He'd been too busy the last couple of days to flip the pages. Now he did.

And discovered he was in big trouble.

Angie had bought ballet tickets for the two of them for tonight. He rubbed his forehead. He'd never been to the ballet before. Had never wanted to go. Still didn't.

But she had been looking forward to it and he'd promised to join her. He'd even told her that if he didn't call her beforehand, he'd meet her in front of the Opera House in time for the eight o'clock performance. She was probably already there waiting.

He glanced down at his clothes. Dark gray jacket and pants, white shirt, navy tie. A day of rooting around a crime scene and hunting down witnesses hadn't done wonders for them, not to mention his way-past-five o'clock shadow, or the fact that he'd forgotten about lunch and hadn't had time for dinner.

Yosh walked into the squad room. "Here's that encyclopedia article you wanted."

Paavo took the photocopied pages.

Peter Carl Fabergé, b. May 30, 1846, d. Sept. 24, 1920, was a Russian goldsmith whose studios achieved fame for the skill exemplified in the objets d'art created by its artisans who worked in gold, silver, enamel, and precious stones, set in ingenious designs.... Some of the most imaginative pieces were for the Russian courts of Alexander III and Nicholas II, including the famous series of decorated enamel Easter eggs given as presents by the tsars.

"So, what do you think, Paav? The killer have a hen fetish or something?" Yosh asked, then chuckled.

Although black humor was a big part of the way homicide

inspectors dealt with the ugliness they saw every day, there were times Paavo couldn't join in. Some cases wheedled their way under even the thickest skins. Usually, they were the ones that involved kids. But today, Debbie Ellis' grief-chilled hands had made him see Nathan Ellis as a person, not just another statistic added to the city's murder rate.

"I got it!" called Inspector Bo Benson from the other side of the quiet room. Calderon's partner, he was spending most of his time lately trying to crack a gang-related teen party shooting. He walked toward them, a big smile on his face. "The guy was trying to figure out which came first, the chicken or the egg, and the clerk must have—"

Yosh grabbed Benson's arm and swung him around. "Coffee time, Bo," Yosh said, leading Benson away from Paavo's glare.

Paavo threw down the encyclopedia pages in disgust. Three modern Fabergé eggs. Why were they taken? Anyone would be lucky to get a fence to give a sawbuck for the lot of them. The kind of people who would be interested in that kind of decoration weren't the kind who frequented pawn shops or ran with fences.

And most puzzling, why steal eggs when there were diamonds to grab? Even a junkie desperate for a fix doesn't grab playthings when face-to-face with diamonds.

Did Nathan Ellis spook the gunman? Maybe the killer fired in a sudden panic, snatched the nearest thing at hand, and fled.

Then again, could the gunman have come to kill Ellis and lifted the eggs to confuse everyone? But if so, wouldn't lifting diamonds have been a better ploy?

Too many possibilities, too many questions only the gunman could answer—when he was caught.

Paavo glanced at the clock again: seven fifty-three. The ballet would last a couple of hours, he'd see Angie home and hopefully be back here by eleven. He grabbed his jacket and prayed a taxi would be near. It would be faster than trying to find parking around the Opera House.

Angie stood in front of the Opera House. She should have known Paavo would be late. If she'd been thinking, she'd have left his ticket at the box office. That way she, at least, could have seen the beginning of *Romeo and Juliet*. She had so looked forward to having him see it with her, though—the beautiful dancing, Prokofiev's luscious music, and most of all the tragic love story—the beauty of love and commitment more important than life itself. And she couldn't even get her man to the theater on time. Where had she gone wrong?

With startling clarity, her conversation with Bianca came back to her. Was she right to blame for Paavo not being here? Had she been unwilling to compromise?

He was probably busy—and had been too busy all day to call. She'd heard on the news about a killing at a downtown jeweler's. But he'd expressly told her that if he didn't call he'd be here. He'd canceled out on her before, but he'd never stood her up. He'd told her not to call—apparently the guys he worked with joked about how often she phoned or texted him. So, she didn't. He said he'd be here, and she'd believed him.

She'd have known if he phoned. But her cell phone had been quiet all day, despite the many "missed calls" she'd had from Paavo the night before as she'd gone to church, dinner, and a movie—alone. She'd silenced her phone for church, and decided to leave it that way during dinner and the movie. When she finally checked her phone back home, she saw that he apparently couldn't be bothered to leave a message. She, in turn, had no reason to call him back. Today, she hadn't even taken the phone out of her purse.

She took it out now and discovered her battery was dead. How had that happened? Now what was she supposed to do?

Paavo most likely was working the jewelry store murder. She hated it that there was another death in this city that had seen more than its share of violence. Right across Van Ness Avenue from her stood City Hall, its high, round dome lighting up the night sky, majestic and noble. That was only for appearance, however. Beneath the dome, battles for control of the city were legion, and everyone in the city knew the story of how, years back, a member of the Board of Supervisors had murdered the mayor and a fellow supervisor.

A shiver ran down her back. Maybe it was just some paperwork that was keeping Paavo, and he didn't have to deal with this latest murder.

She glanced up and down the street. Now that the ballet had started, the sidewalk was empty except for two street people who'd wandered over from Civic Center Plaza to ask the supposedly wealthy ballet-goers for handouts.

She raised the collar of her evening coat against her neck and backed up toward the tall glass doors, wanting to be inside, enjoying the warmth of the building instead of out here.

A taxi pulled ahead of a line of cars stopped at a red light, cut across two lanes, and screeched to a halt in front of the Opera House. Paavo jumped out and thrust some money at the cab driver. Angie folded her arms, lifted her nose in the air, and gazed past him. A small green car stopped behind the taxi. Something about it momentarily caught her attention.

Paavo raced up the stairs to her side. "Sorry," he said.

"It's already started," she replied matter-of-factly.

"I was afraid of that," he said guiltily. "Do you want to go in, anyway? Or just forget it this time?"

Her words came fast and sharp. "I'd like to go in. But I suppose you'll hate it, won't you?"

"Hate it? I've never seen—"

"That's why you weren't here on time."

"No, I—"

"You could have told me. I'm able to compromise."

He looked puzzled. "Compromise? Angie, what are you talking about?"

"I had orchestra seats for us, too. I thought you'd enjoy seeing the ballet."

"I hope to enjoy it," he said very quickly.

She paused. "You do?"

"Yes. I do."

Slowly, her face spread into a smile. "Oh, well, in that case, what are we waiting for? We'll stand in the back so we don't disturb anyone, and during intermission we'll take our seats. I know you're going to love it!" Ignoring his puzzled expression, she took his arm and allowed him to escort her into the Opera House.

8

He eased a double set of surgical gloves onto his hands, the latex like an extra layer of skin. He flexed his fingers. No more planning or preparation: it was payoff time.

After a quick glance over his surroundings—rows of apartment buildings done in post-war stark, box-like architecture, the only thing making them at all attractive being the view of the city this Twin Peaks location provided—he scanned the name tags on the mailboxes.

There it was.

He pushed the buzzer beneath her name. His covered fingertips tingled as his tightly controlled excitement mounted.

No answer.

The silent intercom mocked his expectations. She had to be there. After all, he'd followed her all the way from City Hall earlier that evening. She couldn't have left already. What was the damned bitch doing?

He jabbed at the button.

More silence. He tasted the sweat that had formed on his upper lip.

"Yes?" came a hesitant voice from the intercom.

"Delivery."

"This time of night? I'm not expecting anything."

"It's a gift, ma'am. Roses. Nice, long-stemmed roses." He spoke with steady deliberation, fighting a growing impatience.

"Roses?"

"These are beautiful, ma'am. Best bouquet we have. My boss said the tall, gray-haired guy who bought them insisted on delivery tonight. Said it was special or something. I guess it's all in the card. I'll read it to if you'd like."

"I'll read it myself. I'll buzz you in." Her pleasure was evident.

The door's lock sang with an electric hum as he pushed it open.

Inside he paused, breathing deeply. The heavy glass door swung shut behind him. He cleared his mind of all thoughts other than those of the woman in apartment 320. Then he began his ascent up the stairs, calmly and silently.

When he reached the third floor landing he carefully placed the box of roses on the floor. He didn't want her to recognize him as the *Chronicle* salesman from the other day. With practiced efficiency, he removed his glasses and slipped them into the breast pocket of his shirt, attached a fake brown mustache to his upper lip, and put on the John Deere baseball cap he carried under his jacket. Satisfied with his transformation, he picked up the flowers, walked to Tiffany Rogers' apartment door, and knocked.

She opened the door, clutching her thin, clinging robe to her chin. With her other hand, she touched the damp hair curling around her oval face. The closeness of her barely concealed body, full, soft, and reeking of pure, raw sex, both excited and troubled him.

"I was in the shower when you rang," she said, taking a half-step backward.

"Ma'am." He crossed the threshold and touched the brim of his cap.

"Oh... uh, come in." Her voice was hesitant. "It is drafty out there, isn't it?"

"Yes, ma'am."

She was walking toward the purse on her living room table when he shut the door behind him. At the sound of the click she stopped, half-turned and looked at him.

"I want to tip you," she said. "I'll only be a moment."

His reply was a thin, awkward smile.

She rummaged in her purse, then turned around with the three dollars she'd taken from her wallet.

She gasped in surprise. He had silently followed her into the living room and stood close, too close. "Here," she said, and thrust the dollar bills in his direction.

He wanted to put his glasses on, to see her better. Ignoring the extended hand with the money, his eyes explored her. The robe clung and accentuated her soft curves, its vee neck all but exposed her pendulous breasts to his gaze. His breath caught and he could feel beads of perspiration at his temples.

"Here... the money," she said, her voice rising. "Give me the flowers."

He pushed the flower box toward her with one hand as he snatched the dollar bills with the other. The woman, clutching the box to her body with both arms, moved back, away from him. A puzzled look crossed her face. She stared at him. He could see the distaste in her gaze as she took in his sweat-streaked face, his weak, myopic eyes.

"I just wanted my flowers," she stammered with a false, fearful smile.

"And this, too," he said. In his hand, a six-inch carbon steel combat knife gleamed.

She hadn't even screamed. It figured. She was the type who took whatever a man gave her. He smiled with contempt at the bloody, semi-nude heap on the crimson rug. With a quick slash of the knife, he opened the box of roses and tossed them around her, then picked up the largest, fullest one. He walked to her bedroom and placed it on her bed.

Back in the living room, standing over her, he pulled a rag from his pocket and wiped off the knife with a slow, up and down motion. Then he slid it back into the sheath under his jacket.

This one was for Heather.

9

"Actually, Angie, Charles and I never go to concerts anymore. Not rock or opera. Not even supper clubs," said Caterina, Angie's second sister. Cat, who had been called Trina and had dark brown hair when she was growing up, had somehow metamorphosed into a platinum blonde Supermom with her own interior design business. Franz Kafka had nothing on her.

Angie sat in the family room of Cat's Tiburon home and watched her sister make a shadow box of the Pilgrim's landing.

"So coming up with dumb compromises isn't a problem for you anymore?" Angie asked hopefully.

"Not at all. Movies are our most common entertainment now when we can find the time. I'm always so busy!"

"Reminds me of Paavo. He's always too busy for me, it seems," Angie murmured. "Say, isn't Kenny supposed to make that shadow box himself?"

"Really, Angie! Have you ever seen an eight-year-old's shadow box? One of his classmate's father is in the Army Corps of Engineers. Kenny needs a fighting chance at a good grade."

Angie didn't think that was the idea of the lesson, but she held her tongue. "So now you and Charles go to the movies."

"Not *go* to the movies. We stream them." Cat placed a big rock with PLYMOUTH written on it into the box, then stepped back and eyed it as if she were studying the placement of a Louis XV writing desk. "Married people don't go to the movies much."

"They don't?"

"Heck, when you're newly married, who needs them?" Cat adjusted the rock about a centimeter to the left and contemplated its new position. "Then for a while, after the initial blush —so to speak—of wedded bliss, you do go to shows. But soon, quick as a wink, all that ends."

"It does?"

"That's right." Cat put some glue on the bottom of a cut-out of the Mayflower and stuck it in the box. "Before you know it, you've got kids. Then you know what you do?"

Angie shook her head.

"You buy kids' streaming services and watch age-appropriate movies. By the time the movie ends and the kids are asleep, you are too. And so's your old man."

"Oh, dear..."

The Mayflower was listing badly.

10

Paavo pulled together the last couple of pieces of information from the crime scene unit before going to talk with Nathan Ellis' wife. Robbery might well have been the motive behind Ellis' murder, but he wanted to be sure that he wasn't jumping to an obvious conclusion and overlooking other possibilities. Talking to the grief-stricken Debbie Ellis about something her husband might have been involved in, wasn't on his list of favorite things to do.

As he was ready to leave, his cell phone vibrated. The caller was Angie. He answered.

"Paavo! I'm so glad I reached you!" Angie's voice bubbled through the phone lines. He was relieved she'd called. She seemed more than a little unhappy with him last night when he'd brought her home right after the ballet and left immediately to return to Homicide. But then he realized her call might have been because something bad had happened.

"Are you all right?" he asked.

"I'm fine."

"Your family?"

"Nothing's wrong, Paavo. I can call you about good news, can't I?"

He took a deep breath. "Sure. What is it?"

"I'll give you one guess. But I warn you, it's so unbelievable, so absolutely remarkably stupendous, you'll never guess it."

"Angie, I've got a lot of—"

"Don't be such a fuss-budget. Come on. One guess."

Fuss-budget? "All right. You sold your article to *Haute Cuisine.*"

"That would scarcely be stupendous. Besides, I haven't even figured out what to write about yet." She sounded down at that admission.

"Sorry," he said.

"It's okay. Guess again."

"Look, Yosh is waiting. I've got to—"

"All right, all right. Are you sitting?"

"I'm sitting."

"Well, I went to visit my sister, Cat, this morning, and when I got back, I had a message waiting. I didn't recognize the name, so I called back and—you won't believe it—it was a director at KROW-TV!"

"KROW? I've never heard of it."

"You haven't? It's on streaming and even cable. They have the best Farsi shows in the Bay Area."

Paavo did sit now. "How could I have missed it?"

"Don't be sarcastic! Anyway, they're expanding their repertoire and they've decided to add a cooking show."

"In Farsi?"

"No! In English. And guess who they'd like to star in it?"

"Gordon Ramsay?"

"Paavo! Not him! Me!"

He laughed. "Angie, that's great news. But didn't you just say you were giving up on TV and radio cooking shows?"

"I was upset. Temporary insanity. They can't *all* be deadly. I had a run of bad luck, that's all."

"In that case, I'm glad for you."

"Thank you! But there's just one problem. It'll be about Italian cooking and they've come up with a terrible name —*Angelina in the Cucina*. That's Italian for kitchen."

"You're right. That *is* a terrible name."

"Maybe I can talk them out of it. But anyway, this is it, Paavo. My big break. My big start on the way to fame. Hollywood—or is it Burbank?—here I come!"

Her words gave him pause. She was right. His fingers tightened on the phone. "I guess so," he said softly, "Congratulations."

"I have to do an audition, of course. I've never done one before, but how much of a problem can it be, right? They said I just have to go down to the studio and cook something in front of a camera. Sounds easy to me."

His voice was flat. "I'm sure you'll have no problem at all."

She paused. "Aren't you happy for me, Paavo?"

Why did he feel as if someone had just kicked him in the gut? But then, he'd always suspected she'd be a big achiever. "Of course, I am. It's fantastic, Angie. Really. Good news."

"Let's go out and celebrate, okay?"

"I've got this investigation."

"I mean tonight."

"I'm not sure."

There was a long silence. "Right. I should have known. You're busy."

He heard the hurt in her voice. "Soon, Angie. Okay?"

"Sure, Paavo. Soon."

The phone went dead. She hadn't even said goodbye.

Paavo put word out to all the pawn shops that if a replica of a Fabergé egg came in, he was to be contacted immediately. He silently congratulated himself on his good humor at the deluge of Easter egg and Easter bunny jokes he was hit with. It made him wonder if he was mellowing.

He went to the crime lab to see what they had learned about a couple of round, black stains the crime scene investigators had found on the jewelry store's light gray carpet. Since the cleaning crew vacuumed and sponged off any dirt marks the night before, it was suspected the thief might have it on something on his shoe.

"I was just getting ready to call you, Paavo," Inspector Howard said. "We've got a match, but it's not much."

"What is it?"

"Bubblegum."

"Bubblegum?"

"Looks like the thief stepped onto a big wad of bubblegum and it stuck to the bottom of his shoe. That's it, Paav."

"You're right, Al. It's not much."

***

The clock on the computer screen read 3:30 p.m. After visiting her sister, Angie had spent the rest of the day trying to concentrate on her historical study of San Francisco. She figured that anyone with degrees in English and history, who'd attended some of the best universities in the world, should write at least one book. But the book was taking a long time to write, and she wasn't even half-way through yet. Maybe she wasn't cut out to be a historian. Especially since she was spending more time researching marriage than looking up factoids about the city's history.

After her phone call with Paavo, she was struck once again

at how incompatible they were. How could he not have jumped at the chance to celebrate with her?

She leaned back in the new white leather, ergonomic chair in her den and stretched, trying to get the kinks out of her back, neck and shoulders. She'd never ached this way in her old, high-backed chair. It had been generously padded with soft, down cushions.

Not so this one. The seat, foot rests, elbow and wrist supports moved every which way but comfortable. The chair looked like something from the Starship Enterprise. She got up and tried adjusting it for the umpteenth time.

A shave-and-a-haircut beat rapped on her apartment door. She knew that knock. *Why me, Lord?*

As she crossed her living room, she gazed with renewed affection at the non-ergonomic antiques collected over the past few years. If chairs like that were good enough for Hepplewhite...

Before opening the door, she looked through the peephole —a precaution Paavo had convinced her she needed to take. As expected, her neighbor, Stanfield Bonnette, stood in the hall, a dopey smile spread across his otherwise pleasant face.

She opened the door a crack. "I'm busy, Stan."

He straight-armed the door, preventing her from closing it. "I haven't seen you for a while, Angie!" he said with a quiver to his lower lip. "I came by to make sure you were all right."

He was playing her for a sucker. She knew it. But how could she shut the door on someone who could make his lower lip tremble on cue? "All right, come in. But I've only got a minute."

"Thanks!" He walked into the living room then turned to face her with an expectant smile. "Do I smell coffee?"

She guessed Stan could seem disarmingly charming if she didn't know him so well. He was twenty-nine, tall, thin, with silky light brown hair and brown eyes, and considered himself an up-and-coming bank executive. No one else seemed to think of him as such, however. Especially not his bosses, which included his own father.

"I don't think you can smell coffee when I haven't made any since morning."

"It must be the sweet aroma of anticipation." He walked into the kitchen and went straight to the refrigerator. "Let's see what we can find here."

There was no stopping Stan in pursuit of food. "There's not much of interest except in the freezer," Angie said.

He opened the freezer door. "Oh! Looky there. Whatever it is, it looks great."

"It's called *tortoni*." As she'd suspected all along, hunger, not sympathy, was the true cause of his angst in the doorway.

"Should we split it?" he asked, lifting out the custard cup filled with Italian-style ice cream. "Though it is awfully small."

"I've given up desserts for Lent," she said. "I made that last night for Paavo, but things didn't work out, I'm afraid."

Stan fished a teaspoon out of the drawer and shoved a heaping spoonful of *tortoni* into his mouth. "Delicious. That Smith is more of a fool than I thought he was."

"Sometimes I have to agree," she murmured.

"Pardon?"

"Nothing." She made him an Americano with her espresso machine and carried it into the living room. Quickly finishing off the *tortoni,* Stan grabbed a couple of biscotti from the cookie jar and followed her.

"So tell me what's up," he said as he took a seat in the center of the sofa.

Suddenly she smiled and with barely contained excitement said, "I'm going to audition for my own TV show."

His face brightened. "Angie, that's wonderful news! What kind of show?"

Laughing, Angie sat on the Hepplewhite chair next to the sofa. "Cooking. What else?"

"Wow!" Stan jumped to his feet, pulled her from the chair and waltzed her around in circles. "Let's go celebrate."

"What?"

"Me and you."

The thought of going out with Stan was appalling. He was a friend—and a rather annoying one at that.

"We should go dancing." He grinned roguishly as, holding her hand, he lifted his arm and had her spin under it. "Hot salsa, Western line, slam. Name your poison."

Letting go and stepping away from him, she sat again. "Are you joking?"

"Not at all." He also sat. "When was the last time you went to the Sound Works?"

"God... the Sound Works." Thoughts of the huge, raucous dance club brought a smile to her lips. "Let's see. It was before I met Paavo, that's for sure. Ah, I remember. I went with Dmitri, so it had to have been sometime last summer."

"Dmitri?"

"You met him. He was the Russian violinist. Absolutely mad. Fun, though."

"Oh, him." Stan grimaced. "Sometimes I wonder about your taste in men, Angie. Anyway, Doctor Bonnette says you need to go dancing tonight. With him."

She stared at him. The man was actually serious. "Thanks, Stan, but I don't think so."

"What are you going to do instead? Mope around here and hope the detective gets tired of looking at corpses and decides to give you the time of day?"

"He'll come by when he can."

"Stop kidding yourself, Angie. He's not right for you. Ditch him!"

"Stan!"

"All right, don't ditch him, then. But how often does someone get asked to audition for a TV show? You deserve a celebration. And the best part is, you don't even have to dance with me if you don't want to."

She smiled, but shook her head.

"Don't say no. If he doesn't call or show up by nine tonight, that means he'll be working late, right? Then you and I can go celebrate your good fortune. Okay?"

"Well..." It might be interesting to take her marriage survey to the Sound Works. She'd never bothered to notice how many —if any—of the couples there were married. And, if they weren't, what did that say about married life? She gazed at Stan. What did *he* think of marriage? She did want a man's opinion, and he was a friend.

He jumped to his feet. "Angie, come back! You were *way* out there. I'll see you at nine-oh-five."

"Just one thing, Stan. I want to drive by Paavo's house on the way. I don't want to call. I just want to see if he's there or not."

"Sure, Angie, whatever you say."

11

The six inspectors who made up the Homicide Bureau of the City and County of San Francisco were divided into three two-man teams. From 9 a.m. Monday morning until 9 a.m. Friday, one team was on-call and responsible for every homicide that took place in the city, around the clock; another team was on call for weekend homicides—9 a.m. Friday through Monday morning. When not on-call, the inspectors were expected to do all the paperwork, work with assistant DA's on cases being prepared for trial, and appear in court—grand jury, preliminary hearings and actual trials. And yes, find the murderers.

They rotated duties every week.

Paavo looked at the clock on the wall in Homicide. It read 8:30 p.m. Since it was Thursday night, he and Yosh only had another twelve and a half hours to go as the on-call team. During that time, they'd had two murders—Nathan Ellis' and one that resulted from a bar fight. The suspect, who had ten eye-witnesses to his pulling out a gun and blasting the victim outside the bar, was in custody.

Ellis' murder was another matter. Early that morning Paavo had finally been successful reaching the two women who'd bought dresses the day before at Carole Anne's Shoppe, next door to Sans Souci Jewelers. Both assured him they'd seen nothing unusual. Nonetheless, he'd asked them to come to Homicide to talk to him in person, and found that each could remember a couple of men and women loitering near the jewelers. One in particular, a small, bearded old man, caught both their attention. It wasn't much, but better than nothing.

Since the store owner had his cleaning service wash the glass cases each evening, the only prints found on the glass belonged to the victim, Nathan Ellis.

"You must be exhausted, Paavo." Inspector Rebecca Mayfield stopped beside his desk and smiled at him. She was Homicide's newest member. Tall, perfectly proportioned, with long blond hair often pulled back in a ponytail, she could almost guarantee an entire squad of patrol officers volunteering to help with any investigation she was involved with.

"You're here pretty late yourself," Paavo replied.

"I'm helping Calderon with his jumper. No note, and from all appearances, the guy had everything to live for. Anyway, my own cases seem to be running me around in circles." She pulled a chair alongside his desk and sat down. "Maybe a little breather will give me a fresh eye. Could be I'll pick up on something I'm missing now."

"Good idea."

She put her elbows on his desk and leaned closer. "It's a good idea for you, too, Paav. How about some dinner?"

"I want to finish typing up my notes." He flipped back and forth through his notebook. He and Yosh had split up the list of people whose offices overlooked the alley behind the jewelry shop. No one remembered anything strange. But putting all their statements together just might turn up something.

"Come on," she said softly. "You won't forget what you need to write down. You have time for one fast-food hamburger, don't you?"

Nothing about Nathan Ellis had made him a likely target for a killer. He'd been married three years. His wife worked as a legal secretary at a law firm five blocks away from the jeweler's, which explained how she was able to get there so quickly after the robbery. Paavo frowned. What was he missing?

"Yoo-hoo, Paavo?" Rebecca called. "Dinner."

"Oh, sorry, Rebecca. I'm not hungry. Thanks anyway."

She cocked her head. "The building's on fire."

Paavo stared at some scribbles in his notebook, trying to decipher them. The robbery was the most troublesome aspect of this case. Why would anyone pass up diamonds to take replicas of some museum pieces? He glanced at Rebecca. "If it was, the alarms would be going off."

"I give up," she murmured, pushing herself away from him, her back against the chair and her arms folded.

Calderon marched into Homicide. "You still here, Mayfield?"

"Just a couple minutes more, then I'm leaving."

"Any luck?"

Rebecca gazed at Paavo. "None at all." Then she faced Calderon. "Oh, your reports. Yes, they're on your desk."

Calderon grunted, the nearest he ever came to thanking anyone. Rebecca stood up. "You want to go to dinner, Luis?"

"I already ate."

"Well, then, I guess I'll go home. So long," she said, and then called, "See you tomorrow, Paavo."

"See you," he replied, never looking up from his computer screen.

A short while later he shut the jewelry robbery folder and put it in his desk drawer. Yosh had left for home long ago.

Apparently the last couple of nights, staying late to work on the Ellis case, his wife was feeling neglected. Tonight was fence-mending time.

One more example, Paavo realized, of how marriage and homicide don't mix. This caused him to think of Angie, and the reason why it did was so obvious it made him shudder. Every rational pore told him to not let things get serious with her, that he wasn't marriage material, and it was unfair to try to be a part of her life.

But another part, a more selfish part, wouldn't let her go. That part told him he didn't want to lose her—every petite, saucy, ambitious, warm-hearted, generous, maddening inch of her. They were as unlikely a pair as he'd ever come across, but when he was with her, he felt as if the whole world smiled. God, where had *that* come from?

He thought about her phone call earlier that day, about her excitement at auditioning for the TV program, and her disappointment that he couldn't celebrate with her.

He pushed his chair back from his desk, not wanting to be here anymore. Suddenly, he knew exactly where he wanted to be.

He got up, lifted his jacket from the back of his chair and left.

The minute Angie saw Paavo's house, she knew he wasn't home. The lights were off, and his car wasn't in the driveway. Stan was in the Ferrari with her. They should continue on to the Sound Works. Why bother to stop? But then, given the off-chance Yosh had given Paavo a ride home, she parked and ran up to the front door. She didn't like him being alone and so she asked for a key to his house so she could get to him in case of emergency. He thought she was overreacting, so she gave him a key to her apartment for the same reason. He took it and then gave her his. It was, to her, a commitment of sorts.

But now, it didn't seem right to go barging in for no good reason. Instead, she knocked on the door and rang the bell, hoping against hope that he was there.

He wasn't.

The frustration she felt told her more than anything how much she had wanted to see him that night. She'd put on a dynamite new black Dolce and Gabbana dress. Short, slinky and shiny, with a flattering halter top, it fit like a layer of skin. Black leather sandals with towering heels gave her the leggy look of models far taller than she. Big, bold gold earrings and a spritz of Coco Chanel's Mademoiselle completed the ensemble.

The whole time she was dressing, she'd imagined Paavo opening his door, looking surprised, pleased, and unable to bear not taking her in his arms right then and there. Of course, she'd insist they go dancing first, but soon—maybe very soon— she'd consent to going home with him and then *really* celebrate her audition request.

Now, the only man she had to show off for was Stan.

Disappointed, she turned back to her car.

A green Honda Civic pulled out of the parking space and sped to the corner. Even on city streets, the driver was probably going to have to floor the accelerator to keep up with the Ferrari he was following.

At almost the same moment, Paavo turned onto his street from the opposite end of the block. By the time he reached his house, the green Honda was no more than a distant set of tail lights. He paid scant attention, though, his thoughts centered on a phone call to Angie and his hope that, after he'd had a quick shower and shave, she'd be willing to have him over. He had a lot to make up to her for.

12

As the last note sounded, Angie turned to the latest in her long line of dance partners, "Thank you," she said, smiling sweetly. "Goodbye, now."

During her pre-Paavo dating days, she'd learned how to deliver a definitive "Get lost, Buster" message without hurting a guy's feelings—or, at least, not too badly.

Tonight she'd doled out 'get lost' messages by the bushel. She was tired, her feet hurt, and she wasn't having any fun. Each man who introduced himself and asked her to dance was measured against Paavo. Each came up lacking. She hadn't met a single one who, if Paavo wasn't in her life, she'd consider dating, let alone anything more. Dancing itself, while fun, didn't hold as much allure for her as it once did. She wondered if it had really been the dancing that she'd found so entertaining, or the flirting that went along with it. So far, she'd spotted only one obviously married couple. A few others were there wearing wedding rings, but they didn't appear to be married to each other.

She was ready to go home.

She tried to spot Stan from where she stood, a nearly

impossible task. Earlier, as Stan got them drinks, discussing marriage with him had been as unrewarding as, in her heart, she knew it would be.

"What do you think of getting married, Stan?" she had blurted. She realized as soon as she said it how the question sounded.

Quick on the uptake, Stan replied, "Angie, this is so unexpected."

"But you know I'm mad about you," she said, then laughed. "Now, tell me what you really think."

"I accept."

"Stan, forget it." She sipped her Whiskey Sour, wondering why she'd even bothered to try to be serious with him.

She danced one dance with Stan and then wandered away. Others asked her to dance, and she went along, for a while at least. She saw Stan a couple of times wrapped in the arms of a large redhead. To find him now, to tell him she wanted to leave, she'd have to plow through the crowd, and even then, she'd need a considerable amount of luck. The heat and stuffiness of this room was getting to her, as was the loud, blaring music. She lifted her hair from the back of her neck and wandered toward an open window far back in the club, away from the dancers and the tables that circled them.

The area was fairly dark—the only real lights were those on the dance floor. The area surrounding it was darkened giving it a moody, intimate feel. Angie reached the window and bent forward, her hands on the window sill, enjoying the feel of the cool breeze against her face and shoulders; enjoying being alone for the first time that evening.

"Warm, isn't it?" said a silky smooth male voice.

She glanced up. A tall, muscular man with heavily tinted glasses and a neatly-trimmed beard and mustache stood beside her, a little too close. He smiled at her. "Yes, very," she said, polite but cool, and again faced the window.

"This is my first time here," he said.

She didn't reply.

"It's rather intimidating," he continued. "All these people. You never know if any of them will talk to you or not. My friends told me to give it a try, though. They said... they said most people were pretty nice."

What was this guy doing, trying to pick her up or hold a group therapy session? "And some want to be left alone," she said pointedly.

"That's very true. Do you come here often?" he asked.

He was dense or persistent or both. She folded her arms, staring out at an alley with its garbage cans and backs of buildings. "No."

"Oh? Why not?" he asked. He leaned his shoulder against the window frame and cocked his head, a casual pose, as if they were having a friendly chat. It was presumptuous. She wished he'd go away from *her* window.

She stiffened. "I haven't wanted to."

"Ah. Well, you're lucky. Yours is a much better reason than mine."

She'd had it. This boor struck her as a walking cliché. "I know, you were too busy working, right? Something involving high finance, making lots of money, I suppose? Pardon me if I'm not impressed." She'd delivered the words with a sneering tone that should make any self-respecting male leave in a huff. It didn't.

"No, that's not it at all. But still, I don't blame you for not being impressed. There's nothing impressive about me, I'm afraid." She glanced his way. These were the first words he'd spoken that had any ring of truth. He shook his head, then bowed it. "I've been alone too much," he added.

This guy had quite a line going. He'd almost taken her in, too. He was pretty good at this. "Well, I'm sure there are plenty of women out there on the dance floor who'll solve that problem."

He chuckled. "I can see you don't believe me. I don't blame you. My... my reason isn't very believable, I'm afraid."

"Now that I *do* believe," she said, not sure why she was still being civil. Well, sort of civil.

He adjusted his glasses. "Actually, it was pretty terrible."

That did it. "Excuse me," she said, and turned to leave.

"Wait. I'm sorry. I'm making quite a mess of explaining." He quickly stepped in front of her. "You see, my wife died some months ago."

"Sure." She tried to get around him.

"Here I thought you were a decent human being!" His lip curled in disgust and he stepped back as if fearful of being tainted by her.

She stared at him in shock.

"I don't know the kind of people you normally associate with, lady," he said, "but I assure you, I wouldn't lie about my wife's death. You may be lovely, but no one is *that* beautiful." His voice broke, and he faced the window.

She felt guilty and very, very small over the way she'd spoken. When had she become so jaded? "Wait! I'm sorry." She touched his arm. "It was just after being hit on all evening, I was feeling, well... it was a callous thing to say."

He nodded, saying nothing, his back rigid as he stared through those strange, heavily tinted glasses.

Uneasily she said, "It'll take time." She began backing away. "But you'll be all right, I'm sure."

"It's hard." He took a step toward her, then stopped. "Very hard." His voice was hushed, almost a whisper.

She forced herself to stop backing up even though he made her feel uncomfortable. She had to remember that he was a new widower. He was facing the down-side of marriage—from the ultimate togetherness, to being alone.

Suddenly, her mind filled with the memory of watching Paavo get shot, of seeing him fall to the ground, not moving, and her fear he had been killed. Her heart ached for what this stranger must have gone through. "I'm sorry," she said.

"What's your name?" he asked.

"Angelina."

"Angelina what?"

"Just Angelina."

He gave a tentative smile. "Well, Just Angelina, my name's Reese."

"Saying Just Angelina that way is an old joke, you know."

He held his arms out at his sides. "I'm no spring chicken," he said, and laughed. She did her best to join him.

"I must confess," he continued, "I noticed you when you came in with that handsome blond fellow. Is he your steady?"

Perhaps their meeting by the open window hadn't been as much by chance as she'd assumed. This stranger, Reese, was far too inquisitive. "He's my fiancé," she said, remembering her earlier conversation with Stan. Also, being betrothed was a way to keep men such as Reese at arm's length.

"Ah. A lucky man," he said.

"Thank you."

One of the band's few slow dances began. "Since you're engaged," Reese said, "and the last thing I want is a woman who's available, would you do me the honor of this dance?"

"I'm afraid not. Thank you anyway."

"Oh. Well, I can't say that I blame you." An embarrassed blush rose on his cheeks. "I don't think I'd want to dance with me, either. I haven't been on a dance floor since who knows when. My wife was sick for a number of years before she died, you see. I just thought it'd be nice to see what it felt like again, in a safe situation. You're so lovely, though, I shouldn't have presumed... I'm sorry. I didn't mean to offend you."

Again he bent his head and shook it slightly, as if berating himself for being foolish enough to ask her to dance.

"You didn't offend me."

"You mean you will dance with me?" His lips, his voice, smiled. But his eyes? Not being able to really see them was disconcerting. "You're too kind." He held out his hand to her.

She hadn't meant that. She wanted to tell him he could easily find someone else to dance with. But his hand stayed outstretched, waiting. Well, what harm would one dance do?

She placed her hand in his, and his fingers quickly folded around it. They were firm and strong. His thumb lightly stroked her knuckles. "Soft," he said.

"What?"

"Your hand is very soft." He led her onto the dance floor and his arms circled her. "You're soft. I'd forgotten how soft a woman can be."

"Actually, I think I see my fiancé..."

"One dance." His arm tightened. "We'll dance our way over to him. "She held herself back, feeling a sudden urge to run from him. Resting her hand lightly on his shoulder, she could feel his bulky muscles, much like a body-builder's. The strength he must possess scared her. But when he didn't try to draw her any closer, she tried to convince herself she'd been overreacting. Paavo always accused her of doing that.

Still, up close, even in the dimness of the club, she could see that his mustache and beard were strange, and his teeth seemed too big for his mouth, almost as if they were an actor's prop.

She fixed her attention on a nearby couple, her mind clearly playing tricks on her where this man was concerned.

Hot, sweaty bodies packed the center of the dance floor. Elbows jabbed her. Someone stepped on her foot. Another person spun his partner into her back, knocking her flat against

Reese as they danced. His body felt even more muscular than she'd thought. "Excuse me," she murmured.

"It's all right." His lips grazed her ear as he whispered the words. A cold shudder trickled through her.

She broke free. "I must find my fiancé," she said. "Goodbye."

He grabbed her arm and held it tight. Too tight. "Not goodbye, Angelina. Until we meet again."

13

"Who's been telling you these stories, Angie?" Marianne Perrault, a staff writer at *Haute Cuisine,* chased a piece of rubbery squid *sashimi* around her plate with chopsticks. "Hugh and I have been married ten months and we're forever going places and doing things together. Just last night we went out to dinner."

This was music to Angie's ears. Suddenly, her *sushi* lunch tasted much better. "That's so good to hear, Marianne," Angie said. "I remember last week we were talking about that new Afghanistani restaurant and you said how much you wanted to go. Did Hugh take you?"

"No..."

"Or that interesting Malaysian place you mentioned. Was that where you went?"

Marianne took a sip of warm *sake* from a small porcelain cup. "Actually, Hugh's a meat and potatoes kind of guy. He didn't want to try anything that might have ingredients he wasn't familiar with. Come to think of it, we were sort of rushed. I guess our dinner out wasn't such a great example."

"What do you mean? Where did you two end up?"
"Buffalo Wild Wings."

14

Stanfield Bonnette trudged up the Jones Street hill. The bus had he rode after work let him off on Union Street, one block down from his apartment building. No bus tried to climb to the top of Russian Hill. It was too steep.

Someday, he might be able to afford a car, he thought bitterly. But even if he had one, parking was nearly impossible in this city unless you had a garage, which were prohibitively expensive. It was cheaper to bus and Uber everywhere. Especially when most of your money went to paying rent, like his did.

But he enjoyed his top-floor apartment. It always impressed his dates, and he only went out with women he wanted to impress. "It's just as easy to fall in love with a rich woman as a poor one," he told himself all the time. Unfortunately, the only rich woman he'd met so far that aroused more than a passing interest, cared far more about some homicide inspector than she did about him. Last night, she'd given him a start with her question about marriage. He should have known better than to react the way he did, tipping his hand that way. That she laughed made the bitter pill even harder to swallow.

And anyway, just what did that detective have that he didn't?

He stopped walking a moment to catch his breath. This hill was so steep that every so often some steps appeared, built right into the concrete sidewalk.

He'd made it to the top of the hill, the corner of Jones and Green Streets, where his apartment building stood and entered the lobby. A man wearing sunglasses, a San Jose Sharks cap and carrying a bouquet of roses jumped back from the mailboxes. Startled by Stan's appearance, he bent his head downward, the brim of his cap hiding all but his chin from view.

"Sorry," the delivery man mumbled. "There don't seem to be no doorman."

Stan didn't usually talk to strangers, not even ones carrying flowers. He'd lived in the city long enough to be paranoid about everyone and everything. "One is usually here," he said, keeping his distance. "He must have stepped away for a minute."

"I got some flowers for Angelina, the address is this building, but I don't know her apartment number."

"Angelina? You mean Angelina Amalfi?"

"Amalfi. Yeah, that's her."

More flowers for Angie, Stan thought. Probably from her hot-shot detective. The guy probably heard he took her dancing last night and now the cop wants to mend fences. Why didn't she just ditch the guy like he suggested? Well, the heck with him. If he couldn't get her address straight, that was too damn bad.

Then a wicked thought occurred to him. Why not hijack the flowers? Redirect them to his own apartment and never let Angie know Paavo had sent them. All's fair in love and war, he reminded himself, feeling good about how clever he was.

"She lives right here, in apartment 12... 1202," he said, giving his number.

"1202," the man repeated, his head still down-turned as if bowing to Stan. "Thanks. I'll take them up."

"I'm going up there," Stan said. "I live across the hall, so I don't mind saving you a trip. Anyway, she's never home in the afternoon."

"Oh... she's not? Okay, then. Thanks, pal." The man shoved the flowers at Stan and hurried away.

By the time the elevator let Stan off on the twelfth floor, he was feeling a little guilty about what he'd done. Just a little.

Paavo knocked on Angie's door. He had left work early, almost unheard of for him, driven across town to shower and change and made it to Angie's place before their six o'clock date. The last thing he wanted was to be late.

Last night, he'd phoned and phoned, not giving up until he reached her instead of her answering machine. It was midnight. She didn't tell him where she'd been, which wasn't like her at all. It made him feel strange. Suspicious. Where had she gone? With whom? But to show that he trusted her, he didn't ask.

Instead, he made a date with her for this evening, and he planned to keep it. His on-call shift had ended, and the Nathan Ellis murder investigation was going nowhere fast. He should be concentrating more on it, but instead, his thoughts kept turning to Angie.

He felt as if their relationship was on a downward trajectory. The good news was that he didn't need to worry about their compatibility, what the future might bring, and all that madness. Instead, he could enjoy her company while it lasted. The bad news was that it was ending. With her getting her own TV show, it wouldn't be long before she left the city for a place to grow her career—Los Angeles or New York, most likely. He wouldn't be able to compete with the type of men she'd meet once that happened.

For all he knew, she was already growing tired of him and that's why she'd been out so much lately and not saying where. And why she suggested they simply be "friends." He wondered if she hadn't already met someone new or was, at minimum, having second thoughts about their relationship. He didn't blame her. When he heard the doorknob turn, his pulse quickened. She opened the door.

She wore an ivory-colored silk halter top and matching silk slacks. The outfit was soft, expensive, and sexy—just like Angie. She smiled, and he gave her a gentle kiss in greeting, just as she had given him when she came to his home so many days ago.

"I've missed you," he said. But then all his earlier doubts about her feelings for him foolishly came back to him, despite the glow of her smile. He stepped away from her. "I hope I didn't wrinkle your pretty new outfit."

"Wrinkle it," she ordered.

His grin, he suspected, was too wide, too lopsided, and too out-and-out dopey, but that was how she made him feel. How easily she could get him to smile, even laugh, still surprised him. Before meeting her, he'd almost forgotten how. He didn't take her up on her suggestion, but asked, "Where would you like to go to dinner?"

"*Chez* Angelina."

"What?"

"We're eating right here."

"Here? I didn't want you to work. I wanted to take you out."

"You expect me to give up a chance to keep you all to myself? No way!"

Relief poured through him as he took off his sports jacket and loosened his tie. "All right, Miss Amalfi," he said, "if you want me to yourself that much, then you've got me." He dropped his jacket on a chair. "What can I do to help?"

She placed her hands against his shoulders. "What indeed?" she said, not even trying to hide the suggestive quality in her voice.

His eyebrows lifted as he put his hands on her waist. "Really?" he murmured and put his arms around her drawing her close. Their lips met at the same time as something began to ring... and ring... and ring...

"Oh! The timer." She pulled away.

"What timer?" he asked.

Smoothing her outfit, she headed toward the kitchen. "Dinner is almost ready, but now you will need to help."

"Sure."

"You're going to love it," she said.

He followed her into the kitchen and checked pots, pans and bowls as she proudly announced a dinner of filets mignon, lobster tails, asparagus tips, saffron rice, caesar salad, red and white wine, and sourdough bread. For dessert, one Italian rum tart for Paavo. She'd given up dessert for Lent, after all. The only thing left to do was to fire up the heavy skillet and put the two thick filets mignon in the bed of melted garlic butter.

A shave-and-a-haircut beat sounded at the door.

"Watch the filets," she said to Paavo, who was slicing the sour dough. "Medium rare for me. I'll take care of this."

She hurried across the living room and peeked through the peephole before opening the door. "I'm busy."

"And hello to you, too," Stan said cheerfully, slipping past her into the apartment. "Where were you all afternoon?"

"I don't have time to talk, Stan. Go home." She stayed at the door.

"Everything smells so delicious! I even brought some dessert for us." He tossed her a paper bag. "Also, I wanted to tell you about my day today. A strange delivery man was at the door when I got home." He walked into the living room.

"That sounds fascinating," she said drily. Leaving the door open she looked inside the bag. "One cookie?"

"But it's a Mrs. Fields. Very rich. We can split it. I can tell you about the delivery while we eat."

"Angie, you'd better check these steaks," Paavo said, stepping into the dining area from the kitchen. He stopped short, his eyes narrowing as he gave Angie's neighbor a quick once over. "Well, well, look who's here."

Stan jumped at the sight of Paavo. "Oh, I didn't know you had company, Angie. And here I thought you'd want some intellectual conversation. Oh, well, some other time." He snatched back the paper bag with the cookie. "By the way," he said, lowering his voice seductively, "thanks *a lot* for last night." He lifted an eyebrow at Paavo as he sauntered from the room. Angie shut the door behind him.

"You went out with Bonnette last night?" Paavo asked, his eyes glacial.

"It was nothing." Angie tried to push him back into the kitchen.

"Bonnette seemed to find it special."

"Pay no attention to him."

"You haven't said where you two went."

"No..." How could she tell him she'd gone with Stan to take a cold, calculated look at the singles scene? And that she'd found it wanting. Badly. "We went to the Sound Works."

"A dance club?"

She nodded.

His face tightened. "I see."

"No, I don't think you do. Stan said we should go out to celebrate my up-coming audition. I agreed."

His gaze was hard. "That's right. I was busy last night, wasn't I?"

"I waited, but—"

"It's okay, Angie," he said quietly. "I understand."

"Stop saying you understand! Stan's just a friend."

"Right. And the Sound Works is the kind of place to go to with a friend. Lots of single people go there—to dance, meet other singles. Why shouldn't you go as well?"

Could all that sarcasm be masking a twinge of jealousy? "Exactly. I knew you'd understand," she said her voice as calm as she could make it. "Let's go eat."

The man looked positively baffled as he followed her to the table. Once the food was on the table, they quickly put aside Stan and his cheap innuendo.

"You're a genius," he said, dipping his last bite of lobster into the warm, clarified butter.

"I know. And I've got one last piece for you." She took the piece of her lobster with her fingers, slathered it in butter, and lifted it to his lips.

He ate, then caught her hand and licked the butter from her fingertips one by one. Sparks of desire curled and coiled throughout her body. She could scarcely breathe as she reveled in the slow, lazy sensuousness of his tongue against her fingertips. When he finished with her pinky, she was speechless, never expecting anything like that from him.

"I know what's even better," he murmured, taking her hand, he stood and drew her from her chair to stand before him. "You," he whispered as his arms circled her, and he kissed her, a real kiss, not a friendly peck in greeting. A kiss of passion. His hands slid down her waist to her hips, drawing her tight against him. Where he touched, she sizzled.

She felt she would burst with feelings for him as she lifted her head, wanting to see his eyes, his expression. "I miss you so much when we're not together," she whispered. "The days seem so empty."

"And the nights," he murmured, carefully pulling her top free from the waistband of her slacks. It was clear he had thoughts about where this evening together would end up. It was time to move their relationship to the next step... or was it?

Her heart pounded. She wanted him, her body wanted him, but she needed to talk, too.

She drew back, dropping her arms. "I have to talk to you, Paavo," she said seriously, her mouth growing drier with each critical, relationship-changing word she uttered. "I know we agreed that our relationship needed time to grow slowly, to mature, and to see how things might work out between us, but..."

His stared at her, his expression grim. "But?" he whispered.

Suddenly, her nearby cellphone rang. They both nearly jumped out of their skins at the shrill sound.

It rang again. "You'd better answer it, Angie. It might be important."

"I'm sure it's not. Let it go to voice mail."

He stepped away from her, his gaze questioning.

"All right, I'll get it," she said. As she picked up the phone and saw the name of the caller, her heart sank.

"Yes?" she said curtly.

"Hey, there, Angie. How ya doin'?"

She groaned inwardly. She was in no mood for the jubilant voice of Paavo's homicide partner.

"Actually, I'm kind of busy."

"Say, is the Big P.S. there? That's short for Paavo Smith, you know. P.S. Don't you love it? He's not answering his phone."

She winced. P.S.—an after-thought. That's what she would become once Paavo took this phone call. "I guess his phone is in his jacket, in the living room. We were having dinner," she said with a sigh. "Hold on."

She handed Paavo the phone. "It's your partner."

He put the phone to his ear. "Yosh, what's up?"

He listened for a couple of minutes, then frowned. "What was her name?"

Angie caught the "was." God, no, she thought. Another homicide. She prayed she was wrong.

"City Hall? Is that why the Chief's worried?"

Was someone killed at City Hall? Just a couple of nights ago she'd been thinking about the history of the building, the handsome mayor and likable supervisor killed there. This couldn't be anything like that, she hoped. She rubbed the chill from her arms.

"Got it," he said, then ended the call. As he turned, the expression on his face told her Yosh's call was more than just informational.

"You don't have to leave, do you?" she asked.

"It's a special situation, apparently. City Hall is involved. Chief Hollins wants me and Yosh in charge. I'm sorry."

"My God, Paavo!" She spat out the words. "There *are* other homicide inspectors in this city! We were supposed to have some time together."

"I'm sorry, Angie. This isn't the way I wanted our evening to end."

She shut her eyes a moment, drawing in her breath and forcing herself to calm down. "I'm sorry, too. I shouldn't have snapped at you. I know it's not your fault."

He put his hands on her shoulders. "Maybe it's for the best. Maybe that talk you want to have... maybe we need more time before we have it."

Her jaw tightened, and then she nodded. "Okay," she whispered.

He put on his jacket and walked to the door. "See you soon," he murmured.

She didn't answer, didn't follow him to the door, but simply watched him leave, her expression as stoic as she could make it.

15

Paavo and Yosh arrived outside the homicide victim's Twin Peaks apartment building at just about the same time. That this was normally a quiet neighborhood where murder was still a rarity was evident by the number of on-lookers the appearance of a police car had produced. A uniformed police officer waited for them and led them through the spectators, into the building and then upstairs to the third floor where a group of tenants had gathered in the hallway.

Another officer stood outside the door of the deceased's apartment, guarding the crime scene.

"Looks like she's been dead a couple days," Officer McPherson said, his complexion a decided gray as he described going into the apartment with the landlady and finding the woman.

Just then Rebecca Mayfield joined them. "According to the landlady," she said, "the victim's name is Tiffany Rogers. She was about twenty-seven, single, and white. And she worked at City Hall as an administrative aide to Supervisor Wainwright. As soon as I heard that, I reported it. Chief Hollins called, and said, given that, he wanted someone with experience to take over the case. That clearly isn't me, and since Bill Sutter wasn't even here yet, Hollins changed things around. Sorry about this, guys."

"Not your fault, Rebecca," Yosh said. "You'll help us, and you'll learn. We've all had to start somewhere."

"Thanks, Yosh," she said.

A middle-aged woman wearing a floral blouse over turquoise slacks, her short, black hair streaked with gray, approached them. "I'm Harriet Donovan, the owner of this building."

Paavo and Yosh introduced themselves. "Are you the one who found the victim?" Paavo asked.

"Yes, I did." Her voice shook nervously. "I immediately called the police. I didn't touch anything, I don't think."

"How did you get into the apartment?"

"I knocked, but the door was locked." She worried her bottom lip as if unsure about making the next statement. "I have a key. I... I think I'm within my rights to use it, I mean—"

"It's all right, Miss Donovan," Yosh said soothingly. "You certainly had to check on her."

"Yes." She raked her hair behind one ear. "That's what I thought, too."

"What caused you to look for her in there?" Paavo asked.

"I got a call from her sister, Connie. Connie Rogers. Apparently, for a couple of days, Tiffany hadn't shown up at work at City Hall and didn't call in sick. When she didn't show up again today, and didn't answer her telephone, her boss phoned the sister. Connie called me to see if Tiffany was sick and her phone had died or something."

"Does her sister live nearby?"

"Yes, over by West Portal."

"Have you told her about this?"

"No." She put her hand to her throat and took a step backwards. "I'm sorry. I guess I should have, but..."

"That's all right, Miss Donovan," Yosh said. "We'll take care of it. You've been a big help to us already, we want you to know. And I suspect we're going to need your help us a lot more before this is over, so you stay right nearby, okay?"

She nodded quickly, her eyes wide.

"I knew we could count on you," Yosh said.

While Rebecca hung back and watched, Yosh and Paavo stood before the victim's apartment door and put on gloves. Paavo gave a light push, and the door swung open easily. Rogers' body lay on her back in the center of the living room, the once white carpet beneath her nearly black and thick with blood. Her face was colorless, her eyes and mouth open, the eyeballs clouded, and her lips dry and leathery. The odor wasn't unbearable yet.

They stepped closer, easing along the perimeter of the room where it was least likely they might disturb any evidence. A robe covered the victim's arms and shoulders, but the front lay open. The robe had been her only piece of clothing. Long-stemmed red roses, wilted and dead, had been haphazardly tossed around her body, the blood beneath them eerily appearing as if it had flowed from them.

The stab wounds were deep and long. Paavo turned away in disgust. Whoever had done this was sick. The sheer number and placement looked like the work of a sexual psychopath.

San Francisco had been spared one of those for some time. There were the infamous Zodiac murders in the late '60s and early '70s, and later, the Trailside killer. Both had been serial killers, choosing their victims at random. Both had preyed on young, single women.

He could only hope this wasn't another. They were the most difficult to catch, and the ones who, if not caught quickly, were the most likely kill again.

His gaze met Yosh's. Each knew what was uppermost in the other's thoughts.

The photographer arrived, and soon after, the crime scene investigators. Taking one look at the blood, they dressed themselves in clear plastic booties, overalls and gloves, then began the ritual of recording the scene. Paavo and Yosh stood back from the body, careful not to contaminate any evidence. They hadn't approached it, and wouldn't, until after the CSI unit finished their job.

That the victim worked in City Hall was an added complexity to what had the potential to be an ugly case. The City Hall involvement could go nowhere, or go straight to the Mayor himself. Chief Hollins had decided not to take any chances and assigned it to his best detectives.

While the crime scene unit worked, the inspectors went through the apartment building talking to Rogers' neighbors. Most of the tenants were single, living alone or with roommates, worked all day, and had busy evenings. Most hadn't seen Tiffany for days and hadn't expected to since she wasn't a homebody at all. A couple of them heard rumors she had an "important" boyfriend who she'd meet with two or three times a week. She never brought him to her place. They figured he must be married.

The inspectors also asked if anyone had heard any strange sounds or noticed anything out of the ordinary around the apartment building over the last few days. No one had.

"Here's the sister's name and phone number," Miss Donovan said, handing Paavo a slip of paper. "She's waiting to hear from me."

The name "Connie" was written in a tight, precise hand.

Paavo went out to the landing to punch the number into his phone. As gently as possible, he broke the news. He asked her if she felt up to coming to the apartment building, and offered to send a squad car to pick her up. Not only did he and Yosh need to talk to her, but—after the body was removed—she could help them determine if anything had been taken or was drastically out of place in the apartment.

His gut reaction doubted it, though. Looking at Tiffany's mutilated body, robbery wasn't the motive here.

Hours and hours had gone by and still he sat in the green Honda across the street from Angelina's apartment building. His bladder was full, but that was all right. He was thinking, planning. He liked to figure out puzzles and to him, Angelina was a puzzle.

He had followed Smith from his home to the Green Street apartments. The way Smith was dressed, his hair neat, he looked like a man going on a date. But then he left after only a little more than an hour with the woman. Leaving so soon didn't make sense. He should have stayed longer, like all night. *He* would have.

Instead, Smith had left. Alone. He followed him to what he thought might be another rendezvous, only to end up at a crime scene filled with cops.

He hotfooted it out of there fast to come back to the Green Street place. He wondered if Angelina would leave—maybe with the blond fellow? It made no sense. So he watched and waited.

He didn't get it. Was Smith in love with Angelina? Was she really engaged to the blond fellow who took her to the Sound Works? They'd scarcely danced with each other. Maybe she'd lied to him when she told him the blond was her fiancé? Or maybe she was two-timing both men?

Women were such liars. Who could tell what they were up to? They all lied and cheated. Except Heather.

A vague memory tried to take shape, but he pushed it away. Heather was perfection, everything a woman should be.

Not like this Angelina.

Damn! He pounded the dash. Was she the cop's slut or not? He had to find out.

He'd enjoy finding out, in fact. Getting to know her better. A lot better. Angelina was a beautiful woman. Small. Delicate. Like Heather. He had liked the way Angelina felt while they danced. The way she had smelled. Her perfume had the scent of roses. Roses. How perfect.

He remembered the way she'd smiled at him. Flirted, even teased. She laughed at his jokes, his wit. By the time he was through charming her, she was wild for him. He could tell.

And when they danced, he saw her surprise at his body, his strength. She waggled her tail good then, rubbing against him, letting him know how much she wanted him. But her fiancé was there, so she had to hold back. Damn the man.

But later that night, when she and her so-called fiancé were off somewhere screwing, maybe she had shut her eyes and thought of him. Imagined it was *him* that she was touching, *him* deep inside her.

His breathing grew heavier. Thick and raspy. He lowered his hand *there*, even though it wasn't nice to touch himself. Not nice. He pressed hard, enjoying the discomfort. The throbbing.

This Angelina was so much like Heather. His Heather. Heather had been hot for him, too.

It would be like Heather. All over again.

16

As Paavo and Yosh crossed the grand foyer under the dome of City Hall, their shoes made a loud clicking sound on the marble floor. The building was surprisingly quiet and empty in the early morning hour, just minutes after opening to the public.

Tiffany Rogers had been the administrative assistant to one of the most influential members of the Board of Supervisors—longtime member, Maxim Wainwright. Paavo and Yosh had an appointment with him and requested that everyone else who had worked with the murdered woman be available for questions.

"Come right in." A white-haired, navy-blue suited woman, reeking of secretarial efficiency, held the door open for the inspectors. "Supervisor Wainwright is expecting you."

She showed them into a small, but smartly furnished office. The oak desk looked as if it must be worth several grand.

"I'm absolutely shocked by this!" Wainwright, a tall, gray-haired man exclaimed as soon as the introductions were made. "So is everyone who knew her. She was a wonderful young woman. Vivacious and charming."

Paavo took in the wringing of the man's hands, his strained, overly-helpful, concerned manner. At the same time, he gave scant credence to the supervisor's words. All new murder victims were wonderful people—or, at least they were the first time a homicide inspector spoke with their friends and relatives. But that façade often faded after another visit or two.

Paavo pulled his notebook from his breast pocket. As soon as Wainwright stopped enumerating Tiffany's virtues, Paavo and Yosh began their routine series of questions about Miss Roger's job, her relationship with her boss, her co-workers, and if she'd ever complained about co-workers or anyone else stalking her, threatening her, or bothering her in any way. To each question asked, Wainwright replied that he saw no indication that there had ever been a problem. Tiffany had only worked for him for two months. She'd been a clerk in accounting and came highly recommended. Her current position had been as an assistant to Mrs. Brinks, the woman who had greeted them. In fact, Wainwright added, he had scarcely ever spoken with Miss Rogers. All his conversations had been with Mrs. Brinks.

When asked who had so highly recommended Miss Rogers, his reply was "everyone." He couldn't think of any single individual.

Letty Devon, an elderly woman, had been Tiffany's supervisor in Accounting. "She was precious. A lovely girl. She would have gone far as a civil servant," Letty wiped the tears from the corner of her eyes.

"How long did she work for you?" Paavo asked.

"Five months. She'd been in the typing pool before that for three months, I believe."

"You know, Mrs. Devon," Yosh said, "or Letty? May I call you Letty? It's a pretty name. Old-fashioned."

Mrs. Devon smiled and nodded. A red half-dollar sized spot appeared on each withered cheeks.

"I was thinking, Letty," Yosh continued, "didn't Tiffany move up awfully fast? I mean, only three months in the typing pool, then only five here before she was promoted to working for a Supervisor seems pretty remarkable."

"Yes. It was fast." She pursed her lips.

"I bet a lot of people spend their entire career in Accounting. A very good career, too."

"You're quite right." Her shoulders stiffened, and she held her head a little higher.

"Would *you* have moved her that fast?" Yosh asked. "Did you recommend her to Wainwright?"

"Well," she squirmed.

"You can tell me," Yosh nodded encouragingly.

"Actually," she lowered her voice as if afraid someone was eavesdropping, "I recommended against it."

"Oh?"

"She wasn't ready. Not at all."

"Then how'd she get the job?"

"I don't know the specifics, but I know in general."

"Yes?" Yosh leaned closer.

Letty Devon cupped her hand over her mouth as she said one word. "Connections."

Wainwright had mentioned that Tiffany's closest friend at work had been an accounting clerk named Manuela Rodriguez. Paavo told Mrs. Devon he'd like to speak to Rodriguez. Devon offered her office to the inspectors for their interview. "Whatever I can do to help," she announced.

Manuela Rodriguez was in her mid-twenties with raven black hair and enormous, soulful eyes. Her plum suit was tasteful, yet tight enough and short enough to be alluring instead of businesslike. As she entered the office, she tightly gripped a large man-sized white handkerchief.

Her gaze was blank as she studied Yosh, but grew lively when she noticed Paavo. She met his clear blue eyes with frank interest before giving him a slow, suggestive smile.

Usually Yosh was Mr. Congeniality with potential witnesses, and Paavo was the one who sat back, noted reactions, and then asked the most biting questions—the bad cop to Yosh's good. But seeing Manuela's reaction to Paavo, the two inspectors switched roles without saying a word to each other.

At Paavo's first question—how long she'd known Tiffany—Manuela's already red-rimmed eyes began to tear up. "We met when Tiffany was in the typing pool. We used to like to go to parties and all kinds of stuff, you know, when neither one of us was dating anybody special. You know what I'm saying?" Paavo nodded and Manuela crossed her legs, her already short shirt riding even higher. "For the last couple months, though, she didn't go no place with me. She was, like, seeing somebody. But I don't know who. And she wouldn't say."

"Why not?" Paavo asked.

"Top secret, that's all. I figured, like, the guy was somebody here at work."

"Had she dated men from work before?"

"Yeah, sure. Didn't work out, though."

"Miss Rodriguez," Paavo said, "did Miss Rogers tell you about those other affairs?"

"Yeah, sure."

"Why didn't she this time?"

Manuela shrugged. "He was, like, you know, some big shot. Or married. Probably both. She'd never dated a married man before. I didn't think she would now, but she..." She stopped there and folded her hands over one knee.

"Go on," Paavo urged.

"I shouldn't say." Manuela shook her head. "I'm just, like, guessing."

"That's all right, you were her friend," Paavo replied. "Anything you guess interests us."

"Well, she was, like, you know, ambitious. If some big shot took an interest in her, even if he was married, I think she'd go out with him."

"What do you mean by ambitious?" Yosh asked.

Manuela gave him a long look, then shrugged.

"Tell us," Yosh insisted, still playing the bad cop. "Did she want to get ahead here at work? Was she looking for someone to set her up? What?"

"You name it," Manuela shrugged.

"No, Miss Rodriguez," Yosh said. "You name it."

"It would be a big help to us," Paavo added, his tone friendly.

Manuela looked at him with gratitude. "Tiffany liked nice things, you know." She drew in her breath. "She always went out with men who'd give her presents. Expensive presents. But mainly, she wanted to get a job that made enough money that she could tell all men to go to... uh, *where* to go, if she wanted to."

Paavo leaned back in his chair. Manuela's gaze slowly traveled from his shoes along his long, lean body up to his eyes. She gave him a sultry smile.

"Before she got the job in Wainwright's office, had she been seeing anyone?" he asked.

"Not seriously. We went to a ton of parties. Had a real good time. You know what I mean?"

"What about after?"

"After?"

"After she got her job with Wainwright."

Manuela studied her fingernail polish. "We didn't go no place together after. She was already seeing her mystery guy."

"Do you remember the last party the two of you went to together?"

"Sure. We were, like, invited to a party with a crowd from the Hall of Justice, mostly. A few from City Hall."

"Cops?" Yosh asked.

"No. No cops. We didn't hang around with cops. Too much trouble, you know. The dudes there were big shots. Real big."

"Names?"

"I don't remember. But it was at Bimbo's 365 Club. Other people might remember. Not me."

Paavo nodded. "Okay, Miss Rodriguez. If you do remember anything, give me a call." He handed her his card.

She studied the card a minute, then faced him again. "You got really nice eyes, you know," she said, then smiled. "Maybe I got to, like, rethink my thing about cops."

Angie woke up groggy with a horrible headache. She'd tossed and turned until after three a.m. thinking about Paavo. What made her tell him she'd wanted to talk? Talk about crashing their "party" like a lead balloon. But then, the phone call he'd received would have ruined their evening no matter what she'd said or didn't say.

So instead of sleeping, she'd played different scenarios in her head until exhaustion finally overtook her. And sleeping was even worse.

She'd dreamed of talking about their relationship with him, talking about commitment, and each time his reaction was more negative.

The last dream was an out-and-out nightmare. In it, she was

sitting on his lap, kissing him, and then she whispered the word *Marriage.*

He stood up, and she hit the floor. "Got to go to work, Angie. Sorry," he said, stepping over her as he rushed out the door.

The dream backed up and once again, she whispered, *Marriage.*

He stood up. This time, she was in an elevator which began to plummet to the basement. Paavo's head peered over the shaft at her as she dropped. "Got to go to work, Angie. Sorry," he called, his head growing smaller and smaller as she fell.

Marriage.

He stood up. She tumbled backwards over the orange railing of the Golden Gate Bridge. She screamed as she plunged toward the cold waters of San Francisco Bay. Paavo leaned over the railing. "Got to go to work, Angie. Sorry," he shouted, then he turned and left.

She woke up before she hit the water.

No use going back to sleep, she decided and stumbled into the kitchen. Making herself a strong cup of coffee, she had to admit that attempting to discuss their feelings about each other with Paavo was definitely one of her dumber moves. She wasn't ready yet.

And clearly, neither was he.

And thoughts of marriage were even worse, despite her mother and girlfriends all gushing about "wedded bliss" and how it was something she should want for herself.

Did she? What was marriage, anyway? While on the one hand it was cut and dry—you meet a guy, you fall in love, you get married—what could be more natural? More logical? On the other hand, why *that* one guy?

What made a woman decide that on a particular man, when faced with, to paraphrase Carl Sagan, "Billions and billions of men"? Why was there one man who could cause you to believe that if you didn't marry him, your whole life would have a horrible emptiness you could never overcome? It didn't make sense.

She thought about her little survey and her sisters' and friend's reaction to her simple, straightforward questions. She didn't have an answer. Not yet, anyway. She wondered if she ever would.

As she sipped her coffee, the cloudy, grogginess began to clear from her brain, and the world came into focus once more. After last night's big meal, she didn't feel like eating breakfast. She probably shouldn't eat for a week if she didn't want all those calories to go straight to her hips. Her battle against becoming pear-shaped was constant and vigilant. She eyed some little round biscotti her mother had given her—hard, made with very little sugar if one discounted the smidgen of white icing on each. They were made for dunking into hot coffee.

No, she'd given up dessert for Lent. Maybe she should give up thinking about Paavo as well. The more she thought about him, the more confused she became.

She couldn't sit here all day moping. She had important things to do, to plan for, such as how long she'd have to wait before auditioning for the television job, or a more immediate concern, what she'd write about for *Haute Cuisine* magazine.

She wanted the magazine article to be something special, if for no other reason than her arch-rival, Nona Farraday, had recently written her way from free-lancing for the magazine, to a position as a staff writer. To Angie, Nona was like Lex Luther to her Superman, like the Joker to her Batman, like Bevis to her Butthead. No, scratch that.

Like Professor Moriarity to her Sherlock Holmes. Much better.

And just as Holmes and Superman rose above their rivals and defeated them, so must she come up with an article that would turn heads and gain her the attention and respect of the press, the public, and the culinary world.

She had to find something so unique, an experience so exceptional, that people would take note.

The Wings of an Angel. Visions—angelic visions—came floating back to her of the strange little restaurant. Hosanna in the highest.

The flavor of the meatballs and sauce returned as sharply as if she had a plate of food before her. It was unique, wonderful. She'd never tasted that particular flavor before. The chef had a gold mine in that sauce.

But the men running it clearly needed help.

Why not her help?

She knew a fair amount about running a restaurant. She'd reviewed them for over a year, and worked at LaTour's restaurant for a short while before it closed down, along with the *Lunch with Henri* radio program—due to no fault of hers. Plus, she knew a number of restaurateurs in the Bay Area.

Besides that, helping the owners would give her something to do while she waited for her TV audition. Magically, her headache vanished, her grogginess and ill-temper lifted, and the perfect plan popped into her head.

She dressed with care, wanting to look chic but casual, and settled on a Balmain white and black pants outfit. She'd get Wings' chef's attention yet.

She rode the elevator to the basement garage and drove her Ferrari down Union Street to Columbus Avenue. She stopped off at a grocery store—double-parked while she bought some food —and then continued on to the restaurant, only circling the block three times before a parking space opened up. A good sign.

When she arrived, she was pleased to see a young couple sitting in the window eating heaping platters of spaghetti and meatballs. "Hi," she said cheerfully to the same waiter she'd had the last time she was here—a cross between Joe Pesci and Fred Flintstone.

She had slipped the shopping bag with her few groceries onto her arm, holding it like a purse. She didn't want the waiter to pay any special attention to it.

The waiter stopped in his tracks and stared as if he couldn't believe what he saw. "It's you."

"I couldn't stay away. The food's delicious and the service truly memorable."

"Yeah?"

"May I sit?"

"Go ahead."

Since he wasn't about to seat her, Angie found herself a table. "I'm glad to see you're getting more customers."

"Yeah, well, we tol' Vinnie we didn' have no choice."

"No choice? You make it sound as if he didn't want anyone here."

The waiter frowned. "It's a long story."

"I see," Angie said, although she didn't. She took the menu from him. "What's your name, by the way?" she asked.

He pronounced it carefully. "Oil."

"Oil? That's an odd name."

"Yeah. My ma was real fond of royalty, I t'ink."

"Royalty?" What royalty was associated with oil? "Ah, you mean like a sheik?"

"Yeah. Chic. Dat's me. Yeah, well, I gotta help dem udder people." The waiter toddled off to take care of the couple. Angie had the distinct feeling she'd missed something. She opened the menu. It still said "Columbus Avenue Cafe."

"Oh, Oil!" Angie called as the waiter headed toward the kitchen. He stopped and faced her. "Excuse me, but is there any reason for me to look at this menu? I mean, is the cook serving anything besides spaghetti and meatballs today?"

"No."

She handed back the menu. "I'll have spaghetti and meatballs."

"Whadda you wanna drink? And we don't have no caffè latte no more."

"I see. How about Perrier?"

"Perry...?"

"You know, water."

"Water. No problem."

A short while later, the waiter brought her a plate of spaghetti, just as delicious as she remembered, and a glass of water, no ice, straight from the tap. This restaurant needed even more help than she thought it did.

"Oil," Angie called once more when she saw him stick his head through the swinging doors to see how his three customers were doing.

He walked over to her table. "Whatsa matter now?"

"Would you tell your cook that I think he's marvelous? Also, I'd like to help him put more choices on the menu."

"Why? He got da spaghetti right."

She braced herself. Now, she'd see if her plan would work or not. "I work for the government," she said, trying to sound bureaucratic. "I give cooking assistance to new restaurants."

The waiter stepped back. "You're from da gov'ment?" His eyes narrowed. "You don' look like you woik for da Man."

"It's a new program to help the small businessman," she said hurriedly. "There's been so much criticism that government doesn't help small businesses, that this administration came up with our little way to change all that."

He frowned. "What parta da gov'ment you from? You gotta badge?"

"You never heard of us, I'm sure. A small bureau—and no badges."

"So what's it called?

Good question. "Alcohol, Tobacco and Cookware."

"Oh. Dat sounds kinda familiar. Jus' a minute." He ran into the kitchen.

Earl skidded to a halt in front of the stove. "Ey, Butch! We got a retoin customer."

"Somebody came back for more?" Butch stopped stirring the spaghetti sauce and wiped his palms against his formerly white apron.

"Da dame. An' now she says she's from da gov'ment and she wants to help you cook better."

"Why does everybody think there's somethin' wrong with my cookin'?" Butch grumbled as he smacked his hands against the outside of his legs.

"Maybe sometime you gotta feed somebody somet'in' besides spaghetti an' meatballs," Earl offered.

"Vinnie says we ain't supposed to feed nobody nothin'— except we can't throw the customers outta here. That ain't kosher."

"But she's from da gov'ment. If we don' let her help, she might shut us down. Or call da FBI."

"Or worse," Butch muttered. "Our parole officers."

"And dey might look in da basement."

"We're stuck," Butch announced glumly. He felt for his long-gone shoulder holster.

"You t'ink we oughta tell Vinnie?" Earl asked.

"And put him in a worse mood? No way. We gotta keep this quiet. Tell him she was snoopin' around so we put her to work in the kitchen. That way, she'll keep busy and won't find nothin'." He frowned. "Anyway, ain't kitchens 'sposed to be a woman's place?"

"What if she hears noise from da basement?"

"We'll tell her it's rats. Women hate 'em. She won't have

nothin' to do with the basement."

"I don't know," Earl said. "My ex-wife usta say da only kinda rat she hated was da two-legged kind."

"She oughta know."

"Dat's right. She run off wit' No-Nose Nolan, an' he's a rat."

"Yeah, yeah. Look, we gotta stall. Tell her to come back in two days."

"I'll try, but I t'ink she's kinda stubborn. Like Vinnie."

"Naw. She ain't big enough."

Earl went to the swinging doors and tried to push them open. They wouldn't budge. He tried harder. They gave only a little. If anything it seemed they wanted to open inward, toward him. It was all he could do to stop them from smacking him in the face. He wasn't amused.

Carefully, he let go of the doors and stepped back. When they didn't open in on him, he curled his arms against his stomach and, leading with his left shoulder like the 49ers Fred Warner going in for a tackle, he leaped, both feet leaving the air, and hurled himself against the doors.

Angie decided the so-called "swinging" doors must be broken. They wouldn't open into the kitchen, no matter how hard she pushed against them. With her shopping bag on her arm, she grabbed hold of a door handle and stepping to the side, yanked the door open.

The waiter named Oil flew past her like a cannonball and headed straight toward the other customers. Angie had noticed that they'd been sitting waiting for their check. It was about time Oil began taking his job seriously.

She stepped into the kitchen, undistracted by the sound of breaking dishes behind her.

"Whaddya you want?" In front of the stove, a small, wiry

man wearing a disgustingly dirty apron bounded around on the balls of his feet. Angie figured he must have just burned himself on a pot.

"My name's Angelina Amalfi." She placed the shopping bag on the large butcher block. "You must be the cook here."

He stopped jumping and scowled at her and her bag. "You the Fed?"

"Let's not think about that." Angie looked around the kitchen in amazement. It was fully stocked with restaurant equipment and everything looked quite clean—probably well-scrubbed by the owner so that he could rent it out. "I'm here to help get you started. I've got lots of experience in restaurants. I even once worked at LaTour's, which was quite famous before it unfortunately shut down."

"I don't know no LaTours, El Tours, or LaTrines, and I don't want no Fed in my kitchen. I don't even vote."

"As I said, just forget about that. I'm afraid I don't know your name."

"Butch Pagozzi."

"Italian, just like me. I should have known that when I tasted your meatballs. *Parl'italiano?*"

"Huh?"

So much for consanguinity. "I want to compliment you on your spaghetti and meatballs. They're quite unique." She began going through the shelves of food. Little was there except a twenty-pound box of spaghetti, cans of tomato paste and a few containers of Italian seasoning. Hamburger meat was in the refrigerator, plus French bread—exposed to air and getting hard—and big cans of a variety of stews, chili, and strange processed foods no self-respecting restaurant would be caught dead serving.

"Where's the rest of your food?" she asked.

"I didn't wanna spend much money 'til we got some customers," Butch said.

"You're not going to get customers unless you spend money to buy the food to bring them in."

"Yeah, but we don't have no money to spend. So the customers get the spaghetti or they take a hike. It's a tough world, lady."

These boys were in trouble. "You really do need to have more on your menu than one thing." She began going through the spice shelves. They had a good supply of all kinds of spices. She looked with frustration at the shelf. There wasn't a single spice that could be giving Butch's sauce and meatballs their special flavor.

"It'll be easy for you to build an interesting menu on the base of the spaghetti and meatballs that you already have, you know."

Butch swaggered. "Sure. I know that."

"Good," she said, trying to hide her disbelief before going back to opening jars of spices and smelling them to see what was fresh and what had turned old and sour or flavorless. "What's your recipe for meatballs?" she asked nonchalantly.

"Nothin' special."

Damn. She hoped he'd just blurt it out. "You use ground beef, right?"

"Extra lean."

Extra lean? Angie didn't let her skepticism show. "And I suppose you put in salt, pepper, oregano, chopped onion, garlic, bread crumbs, and an egg to bind it?"

"I know how to make meatballs. I don't need no Fed—"

"But your meatballs are different. What else do you put in?"

He folded his arms. "Nothin'." His look dared her to contradict him.

"I'm not being critical. I'm interested. There's got to be something more. The taste—"

"Basil. Yeah, basil."

"Basil?"

"I put in a little basil. Always have, always will," he said with a pugnacious, smug smile.

Basil wouldn't do it. Basil would give a lightly scented herbiness to the meatballs, not the pungent, salty tanginess that had her so baffled. "And?"

"Nothin'." He fidgeted. "This is a real third degree, lady."

She'd just have to watch and find out.

"To show you how serious I am about helping out," she said, "I'll show you right now how you can double your menu with almost no additional work or expense on your part."

"I don't believe it."

"You don't?"

"No way."

From the shopping bag, she'd pulled out the shredded mozzarella cheese and French rolls she'd bought at the grocery. She spooned Butch's spaghetti sauce on the inside halves of a split roll and then halved three meatballs and placed them onto the bottom portion of the roll. She sprinkled mozzarella on top of the meatballs, then spooned on more sauce to melt the cheese. Angie put the sandwich together and, on a plate, sliced it in two with a triumphant flourish.

"Hey," he said. "It looks good enough to eat!"

"That's the idea."

One of the swinging doors opened all the way and hit the wall with a loud thud. Earl stood in the doorway. He held his hand to his forehead and blinked rapidly, as if he couldn't quite focus.

"Oil!" Angie cried. "What's wrong?"

"You better sit down," Butch said, taking his arm. "What happened?"

"I'm stronger'en I t'ought. After I knocked open da doors, I ran so fast, I hit a post and musta knocked myself out. When I woke up, da customers was gone—wit'out paying for da food. Dey stiffed us, da lousy crooks!"

17

"You've got to keep City Hall out of this case. As far as the press knows, she was a typist. Nothing more. Mumble when you say where she worked." Lieutenant Hollins got up from behind his desk, walked around to the front of it, and leaned against the edge. Paavo and Yosh sat facing him. They'd just completed briefing him on the Tiffany Rogers investigation. Hollins made it a point not to get involved in his men's investigations unless political heat was turned on. In this case, the heat was on high.

"Her friends and co-workers are at City Hall, and there's a good chance the guy she's been seeing is there as well," Paavo said.

"It's our only lead, Chief," Yosh added. "So far, the CSI unit can't even find a suspicious fingerprint to lift. The crime scene is clean as a whistle. She always met her boyfriend away from her apartment. We aren't sure where yet. We've got a few leads we're still checking."

"So you've got nothing except for a dead woman lying in her own blood on the floor of her own living room!" Hollins added.

"We have to follow wherever the leads take us," Paavo said.

"I'm not saying not to, all I'm saying is keep the press away." Hollins paced back and forth in front of his desk. "The Mayor and the Board of Supervisors want this murderer caught right now. This isn't the kind of publicity they want for themselves or the city. I mean, if someone who works for them isn't safe, who is?"

"Aw heck, Paavo," Yosh turned to his partner. "The Supervisors said they want us to catch this murderer fast. Here I was gonna take my sweet time."

Paavo couldn't help but grin.

"Cut the comedy, Yoshiwara." Hollins stuck an unlit cigar in his mouth and chewed. "This case is number one for you both, got it?"

"We are not dropping the Nathan Ellis case," Paavo said with an edge to his voice.

"Calderon and Benson can baby-sit it for you for a few days until you catch Rogers' killer."

Paavo bristled. "Nobody has to baby-sit our case. We've spent days on it."

"With City Hall involved, I don't want any hint that the Rogers case doesn't have your full, undivided attention."

"What about Debbie Ellis? She thinks her husband's case has our full attention." Paavo's eyes narrowed, a sign of his growing anger.

"Calderon will handle her all right."

Paavo and Yosh kept silent at that comment.

Hollins said, "Now, get out there and find Tiffany Roger's killer before City Hall comes down on all of us."

On her way to City College to teach her San Francisco History class at the extension—most of her students were senior citizens—Angie gave herself some extra time so that she could drive by Paavo's house to see if he was home. He'd been so busy with his latest murder case, she hadn't seen or heard from him for a few days. She hated the way their last date had ended, and she wanted to see him again.

His car wasn't in front of the house—his small cottage didn't have a garage—and his cat, Hercules, was sitting on the fence in the sunshine. Angie was quite sure Hercules spent his days heckling any dogs who went by on a leash.

When Paavo was home, Hercules was usually inside asleep after scarfing down a full can of 9-Lives. Once Angie brought him some fresh crab meat, shelled. He refused to eat 9-Lives for three days thereafter. Paavo made Angie promise she'd never do anything like that again.

She knocked on the door, but after receiving no answer, she continued on her way to City College. The class, as much as it was an asset to her students, was also to help her with her historical study of the city, a book she'd been working on for several months.

Writing the book might not have been interesting, but her class was a different story. In it, she didn't want to just look at the politics of the city which had been fascinating, decadent and corrupt—much like any other American city—but to view it from the point of view of the kinds of people who had lived there long ago. She wanted to talk about the San Francisco of longshoremen and teamsters, of gamblers, gold-diggers, and the Barbary Coast, of the only city to success-fully call a General Strike—the Left Coast home of the Wobblies.

As the class studied about each new ethnic group that moved into the city, she would cook up a small dish or two when the lesson began, and as each topic ended, she brought the class to a restaurant that specialized in the cuisine of that particular nationality. If you can't walk in their shoes, you can at least eat in their kitchen, was her motto. What better way to learn?

She brought her charges to Yuen's Gardens for *dim sum*, L'Etoile for bouillabaisse, Sorrento for manicotti, Speckmann's for sauerbraten, and Tommy's Joynt for a pint of the Guinness. It was expensive, but she didn't have a single drop-out—an achievement unheard of in adult education classes.

Pulling the Ferrari into the faculty parking area, she cut the motor and gathered up her books and lecture notes. As she got out of the car, she noticed a man walking her way. There was something strangely familiar about him. He wore a NY Yankees baseball cap and sunglasses, jeans and a blue parka. When he saw her watching him, he stopped walking, gave a half-smile and leaned casually against a black Beemer. It somehow didn't look like it was his car. In fact, he didn't look like a member of the faculty. Something about him made her uneasy.

No, she was being silly. Ever since she'd danced with that creepy guy at the Sound Works, she'd been seeing monsters in every corner. There was no reason for such paranoia. Heck, the poor guy was probably a new student here to check out the faculty, especially the female faculty. A schoolboy stunt. Nothing more.

She held her books tighter and hurried toward the school building, trying not to look his way.

18

"So tell me, Kirsten," Angie spoke on the telephone to the old friend she used to see quite a bit before her marriage, "you and Al have been married for almost two years now. How's it going? What do you think of it?"

"What do I think? What do you mean?"

"You know. Do you recommend it? Any problems I should know about?"

"Problems? What makes you think there are any problems?"

"I'm sorry. I didn't mean there were problems. I was just—"

"You heard about Alan with that woman, didn't you? They work together, that's all."

"No. I never—"

"I know what you're thinking! I didn't realize it had become common knowledge, already. But I'm glad you told me. You've always been my friend, haven't you, Angie?"

"No. I mean, yes, I'm your friend, but about Alan and that woman—"

"My God! Everyone knows, don't they? They must be going

everywhere together! Making a laughingstock out of me! Alan swears they're just working, but if so, how would you know about it? How would all my friends know? Work, *hah*! Thanks for telling me!" The phone went dead.

"Telling you? Kirsten, wait. Kirsten? Hello? Hello?"

19

He parked a block away from the house. It wasn't safe to park any closer. The judge had apparently noticed him sitting in his car a few times, and had begun to peer a little too closely, to grow a little too suspicious.

This was the morning. He had it all planned. Anticipation made his pulse race. He sat and waited for his breathing to return to normal, his pulse to slow a bit.

The first thing was to make sure no one noticed him. No one at all. He didn't want to throw up red flags before his entire plan—all of it—had succeeded.

His fingers tightened on the steering wheel. It was time to leave the car, to walk to the lush grounds along the Palace of Fine Arts, to stand behind the fir tree with the thick trunk and low, heavy branches, just as he had the past three days. There, he'd wait until the judge left the house to go on his morning walk along the Marina Green's waterfront path to Fort Mason for a cup of herb tea, and then walk home again. It seemed to be a health routine. It wasn't going to be very healthy for his wife, however.

He got out of the Honda and pulled the driver's seat forward so that he could reach into the back seat for his bouquet of roses. An SFPD black-and-white appeared at the intersection and stopped at the stop sign.

He kept his head down. He could all but feel the policemen taking him in, probably calling in the license plate on his car to the DMV. What'd they think they'd discover? That the car had been stolen? Maybe they would check the registration. Did they really think he'd be so stupid as to register it in his own name?

Not that it mattered. He knew all about the DMV, their computer system, and the cops. He knew it'd take a long time before the cops put two and two together. He'd be finished here by that time.

In the rear-view mirror, he watched the police car turn onto his street and slow down as it neared him. He waited, not moving, until he heard the sound of the engine as the car drove past. He glanced up, perspiration dripping from his forehead, and watched the car turn the corner.

They might have seen him. They should have. They must have. He breathed harder. What if they remembered something about him? Or his car? He had to be careful. His heart felt ready to burst from his chest. Patience, that's what he needed. It was necessary to be patient now.

It was a straight shot from there to the Presidio Parkway approach to the Golden Gate Bridge. By the time the cops went around the block, he'd be long gone. He jumped into the driver's seat, started the car and sped away.

Today, the old woman was lucky. But her luck wouldn't last.

Paavo sat in an overstuffed easy chair in Tiffany Rogers' living room. The morning sunlight streamed in from the window, bright and cheerful, in stark contrast to the ugly dark stain before him. The body and most of the evidence had been long removed, indexed, categorized, sliced and diced to be studied, analyzed and preserved.

Fingerprints, hair follicles, blood types, DNA, anything that could potentially be matched with a suspect, once one was identified, had been collected. The estimated time of death put it the evening before the first day she missed work—days before the police had been called. A six-inch military-style combat knife appeared to be the murder weapon. The roses strewn around her body and the single rose on her bed were from florists because the thorns had been trimmed and the stem cut at a fancy angle. Checking on florist shops, he'd learned there were more of them in San Francisco than he'd ever dreamed, including a flower market that was also open to anyone who wanted to get up early enough. He'd tried gathering information about customers who'd bought a dozen long-stemmed roses three or four days earlier, but after checking with just a few florists, he quickly abandoned hope of tracking down the killer through that means. The numbers were far too high, and a number of purchases had been cash transactions by men, as if they very suddenly found they needed to give someone a dozen roses. Paavo could understand that.

No vase had been found filled with water for the flowers. Nor was there a florist's box anywhere in the apartment. He couldn't imagine any woman leaving a dozen long-stemmed roses lying about to wither and die. Whoever killed her must have brought the roses with him.

A gesture of a lover? Of someone wanting to court her? If, even after receiving the roses, Tiffany had spurned the man's advances, could that have driven him to murder? She hadn't been raped, so it wasn't a sexual assault.

What kind of killer could have committed such a grisly murder and then stopped to pick up a florist's box and its wrappings? Those weren't the actions of someone who had just committed a crime of passion. They seemed more like those of someone who had planned to murder this woman.

He walked around, looking out windows and into closets, trying to get a feel for the place and what had gone on here.

The apartment Tiffany lived in was supposedly secure. There was a locked, steel front door, requiring the occupant to buzz the person into the building. Yet, time and again it happened with this type of security that after someone had legitimately buzzed in a friend, a trespasser would stop the door from relatching. They would hold it open about a half-inch, and once the legitimate caller was out of sight, the trespasser would enter.

The night Tiffany was killed, however, none of the other residents remembered having had a visitor or having let anyone in for any reason. A couple of people came in late that evening. They insisted they had been careful not to let anyone sneak in after them, but it might have happened.

Even if the murderer snuck past the front door, Tiffany would have had to open her door to him. Why would she? A single woman would worry about how some stranger had gotten into the building and up to her apartment, wouldn't she?

None of this made sense unless the man had been someone she knew, someone who had brought her the flowers, perhaps. She let him in, and then he killed her.

Neighbors up and down the block were questioned, but no one had seen a man carrying a box that could have held roses.

The police tried lifting prints off the buzzer to Tiffany's apartment, the front door handle, even the underside of her toilet seat, but found nothing, which meant the killer wore gloves or wiped off the prints. Again, the sign of premeditation.

In the meantime, a picture was emerging of Tiffany as a vivacious, ambitious young woman who had suddenly turned quiet. Everyone was convinced she'd been seeing someone who had warned her not to say anything about their relationship.

It also became clear that neither age, looks, or interests mattered to Tiffany in the men she dated. If they had money or power, preferably both, they were date bait to her. In the last two months she had found someone to date who was so special —for whatever reason—that she hadn't even told her best friend or her sister who he was.

Paavo had searched through Tiffany's desk and papers trying to find some clue as to who she had been seeing. There were few papers, no books, and her only reading material consisted of supermarket check-stand tabloids. She also had a single edition of the *Chronicle* dated nearly a week before she died.

Tiffany's sister, Connie, had agreed to meet Paavo and Yosh at the crime scene, arriving after the body had been removed. She was surprisingly strong in the face of the tragedy. Paavo learned she was four years older than Tiffany, had been married, now divorced, and was owner of a small gift shop in the city. It was immediately clear that Connie and her sister weren't very close, each having their own set of friends. While Tiffany was all about fashion and looking attractive, Connie was a bit overweight, with her hair, make-up and clothes nice, but she did little to make herself especially attractive.

She did a quick run-through of Tiffany's apartment. The wall hangings and bric-à-brac in the apartment were all inexpensive and not worth stealing. No one took the TV, and she didn't have a computer as far as Connie knew. Her most valuable possessions were her jewelry pieces. They found gold and diamond jewelry from Moulin et Cie, Sans Souci Jewelers, and her namesake, Tiffany's. She even kept the jewelry boxes, as if to prove the jewels weren't paste.

Connie told Paavo that the diamond tennis bracelet from Sans Souci Jewelers was new. It may have been from the new lover.

Sans Souci Jewelers was where the Fabergé egg thief had

killed Nathan Ellis. Could there be a connection between Tiffany's and Ellis' deaths? It seemed too big a leap, but Paavo would check it out.

He and Connie walked into the bedroom and looked at Tiffany's clothes hanging in the closet. He'd never paid much attention to women's clothes before, but since meeting Angie he'd come to appreciate the simple lines and small details that separated quality clothing from that which was simply expensive. Tiffany spent more than the average working girl on clothes, that was obvious, but she hadn't learned quality yet. The outfits were full of the kind of frills and ruffles Angie wouldn't be caught dead in. As far as Connie could tell, none of Tiffany's clothes had been taken.

Paavo placed the tennis bracelet from the Sans Souci Jewelers into an evidence bag.

The next day, he was at San Souci as soon as it opened. The owner, Philip Justin Pierpont, was in the store working the counter with one of his clerks. He hadn't yet hired a replacement for Ellis.

"Hello, Inspector," Pierpont said. "Any news on the killer?"

"We're still working on it. I've got something here I'd like you to check out for me." Paavo put on gloves before opening the Sans Souci box to disclose the bracelet. He would turn the box over to the CSU to try to find fingerprints, but from past experience with this sort of thing, he suspected it would have a lot of prints and most would be smudged or partial and tell him nothing. So he decided to check the jeweler's first. "Does this look familiar?"

"Quite. We ran a special on those for Valentine's Day."

"Is there any way you can check to find out who you sold this one to?"

"Of course. We didn't sell many of those. They weren't the best quality diamonds. Usually, if someone is looking for a diamond bracelet, they're willing to spend a little more money to get top quality stones even if the size is smaller than they originally wanted."

The jeweler took bent low and studied the piece. "We keep a record of all our merchandise." He put on his jeweler's magnifying glass, and carefully inspected the diamonds. "Yes, it's definitely one of ours." Next, he led Paavo into his office where he looked up the bracelet on the computer.

"Ah. Here we go. We sold five. Two to women in the city. One to a couple from Los Angeles, one to a man in the city, and..." He stopped talking as he studied the computer. "This is strange. I almost never see a transaction like this." He glanced up at Paavo.

"What is it?"

"We keep records of credit cards and checks. That's the way most customers pay us. But this bracelet was paid for in cash. We have no information on the buyer."

"If the transaction was that rare, there's a chance the clerk might remember it, right?"

"Absolutely. Except in this case."

Paavo suspected he knew the reason before he even asked his question. "Why?"

"The clerk was Nathan Ellis."

As Paavo took off his jacket and hung it on the back of his chair, he looked at the flurry of notes and messages left on his desk in his absence. He added to them the names of the Sans Souci diamond bracelet purchasers who'd used checks or credit cards, as well as the name of the clerk who had worked with Ellis the day the diamond bracelet cash purchase had been made. Except for early morning, Pierpont always had two employees in the store at the same time.

The clerk, Meredith Park, was off work that day. Paavo tried reaching her at home, but there was no answer. Next, he quickly disposed of the other bracelet buyers—all were able to give solid, easy-to-verify information as to what happened to the bracelet they'd bought.

He was going to try Park's home again when the phone buzzed.

"Smith here," he said.

"This is O'Rourke in Robbery. We just got a call I think you might want to check out."

"What's it about?"

"A jeweler. Said a small guy with a fake beard came in, held him up at gunpoint, and stole just one thing. When my Lieutenant heard what it was, he said I should call you."

Paavo could think of one object only that could cause the Robbery detail to think of him. "An imitation Fabergé egg?"

"You win the Big Banana."

Paavo stood. Hollins had given Nathan Ellis' case to the team of Calderon and Benson. But they were out working on another case at the moment. The possibility of a tie-in with Tiffany Rogers' murder existed, but also he remembered his interview with Debbie Ellis, how she begged him to find whoever killed her husband.

"I'll be right there," he said.

20

Angie sat in the family room of her parents' Hillsborough mansion with her father. He had a hockey game on the TV, a basketball game on the radio, and the TV remote control in his hand. Periodically, he'd flip through the dial to be sure he wasn't missing anything else. Salvatore Amalfi wasn't a sports fanatic by any means, but since his bypass surgery the year before, the doctors told him he had to back away from anything stressful. Since he'd already sold his retail shoe business, that didn't leave him much to stop doing. So, he started watching sports on TV.

Now, looking at him scowl, rant and rave about the Sharks play on the TV and the Warriors on the radio, Angie thought he didn't seem to be following orders.

She sighed and kept watching, glassy-eyed, while talk of power-plays, hat tricks and slap shots swirled around her. She couldn't have given the box score if her life depended on it. The more she thought about it, she wasn't even sure why she was here. All she knew was that she hadn't felt like spending a Friday night home alone hoping Paavo would show up.

Her single girlfriends, those few there were left, would be

out on dates, and she didn't want to disturb the married ones. Everyone seemed to have someone to belong to but her, she thought, indulging in a heavy dose of self-pity. So, she came to the place she did belong—home with her parents. She was always welcomed there.

Although, considering that her mother had gone off to bed with a book, and her father was engrossed in TV and radio, they, too, didn't seem terribly overjoyed at her unannounced arrival. She heaved a heavy, rueful sigh.

"*Che c' è*, Angelina? I haven't heard so many sighs since I took your mother to a Hugh Grant romantic movie when we were first married."

"It's not funny, Papà. I'm trying to figure out my future."

"Your future? That's no reason for such a long face. You're young, healthy, with a good education. You can do whatever you want. So... what is it you want?"

"Well... I haven't figured it out yet."

"This doesn't have anything to do with that fellow with the strange name, does it?"

"I'm not talking specifics here, Papà. In general. Marriage? Career? Both?"

"Since you haven't settled on a career yet, how can you think of giving up what you've never had?"

"It's not for lack of trying." She heaved another sigh.

"*Il poliziotto*—he's your problem, right? How serious are you about him?"

"I don't know."

"You aren't thinking about marriage already, are you?"

"I'm not sure. I mean, what is marriage?"

"It's a life sentence and you're too young for it!" Suddenly, he jumped to his feet, staring at the TV. "No! The Sharks just scored. I've been watching for two hours, the score one to nothing. Detroit's favor. The Sharks tie and I miss it!"

So much for her future. "Sorry, Papà. I'm going to bed," she said, standing.

He put down the remote, his dark eyes taking her in a long time. He was still a handsome man, tall and distinguished despite the shadows his heart condition had brought to the area under his eyes and the sallow color to his skin. "Don't be sad, *bambina*. There's so much in life for you to see and do and experience. Take your time. Life's a wonderful thing, Angelina. Now get out of here. They're going to show a replay."

She walked to his side, rested her hand on his shoulder and kissed his cheek. "Goodnight."

He touched her fingers lightly, and she left the room.

Before going into her bedroom, she stopped to say goodnight to her mother.

She knocked on the bedroom door. "Mamma?"

"Come in, Angelina," Serafina said. The bedroom was large, with an adjoining sitting room that overlooked a small creek, and a bathroom that was larger than the living room of Angie's apartment. The room was furnished with Italian antiques, the pieces lavishly carved and ornately finished in an off-white color with pink-cast faux marble, and trimmed in gold paint. It would have been gaudy except that it was so inherently Italian, it made Angie feel comfortable and secure.

Her parent's bed was king size, and the mattresses sat high off the ground. Serafina was sitting on the bed, propped up with pillows, and had tears streaming down her eyes.

Angie's heart nearly stopped. She could feel the blood drain from her face as she stared at her mother. "Mamma, what's wrong?" she cried. She ran to the side of the bed, stood wringing her hands, her mind swirling. Was it her father's illness? One of her sisters? Serafina? Not Serafina—her mother couldn't be sick!

Serafina dabbed her eyes with a lace handkerchief. "It's an old book. I meant to read it years ago, but I forgot about it. I wish I'd never started it. It's so sad. *Che terribile.* It's called *The Bridges of Madison County.* It's about a poor husband who goes away from home to help his family, and his back is no sooner turned than his wife has an affair with some drifter photographer! She doesn't even know the man!"

Angie took a deep breath to calm herself. "Mamma, I don't think that's the point."

"Not only that, Angelina—*Dio! Che disonore!*—this terrible wife... she's Italian!" Serafina tossed the book to the foot of the bed.

"It'll be all right, Mamma. Most people won't remember that about her, and probably won't even remember the book, or the movie, anymore. And she didn't act very Italian."

Serafina dried her eyes. "Maybe you're right. That story— that's not what marriage is all about."

"It's not?" Angie sat on the edge of the bed.

"It's two people building a life together. It's the union between the two that makes them strong and lets them survive whatever life throws at them."

"You really believe that, Mamma?"

"*Veramente.*" She took Angie's hand. "When me and your father were first married, he worked two jobs. Almost eighteen hours he was gone, six days a week. It didn't matter, though, to how we felt about each other. If anything, it made our love stronger because we saw how much we hated being apart. We worked hard so that we could make this time to be together."

"I know you did, I remember."

"And you know what's strange, Angelina, as much as I adored your father when I was a young wife, I love him even more now. When young, our love was the flame of a match— sharp and hot and bright. Now, it's like the fire of coals—dry and warm and solid—and will last until we are but ashes."

Angie nodded. "It's good to hear that."

Serafina looked surprised. "You didn't know?"

"I should have, shouldn't I?" She stood up. "I think I'll go back home tonight after all."

"You are home."

"I mean, to *my* home. I love you, Mamma."

"*T'amo*, Angelina. But before you go, will you hand me my book again? I tossed it way down there by my feet."

———

Angie arrived home about ten-thirty, and about a half-hour later came the knock on the door she'd been hoping to hear for the last few nights. She ran to the peephole and looked out.

"Paavo." She opened the door.

"I was hoping you were still up," he said.

She was still dressed. "I am. Come in."

He came in, closed the door behind him. "I felt bad about the way our dinner ended the other night," he murmured, his voice heavy with weariness and longing. "I just wanted to see you."

"I felt bad, too," she said, running her hands over his hair, damp from the night fog. She gazed up at him. "Can you stay awhile? Shall I put on coffee? Have you eaten?"

"No, to everything." He gripped her shoulders and held her back so that he could see her better. "It's late. I should let you get some sleep. But I wanted to see you, even if just for a few minutes, to be sure... I wondered if you'd still wanted to see me after the way I walked out..." He shook his head.

"You could have called me." The words blurted out, seeming to come from nowhere, even though she'd meant to be supportive. She'd have to backpedal rapidly.

"I tried a couple times tonight, but there wasn't any answer."

That was his excuse? "I was probably driving home from Hillsborough. I was going to stay at my parents' house tonight, but then changed my mind. You could have left a message."

Great, she thought, now I sound like a shrew. Of course he knows he could have left a message. She walked away, toward her petit point sofa. He followed.

"But it's you I wanted to talk to, not your phone."

She bit her lip. It was serious turn-over-a-new-leaf time for her with this man. "I know," she whispered, then, louder. "I understand."

"You do?"

He seemed shocked that she could be understanding. "Of course! You don't like voice mail and you're busy with your job. It's important to you. I can accept that."

His eyes narrowed, then he grinned. "Have you bought more ballet tickets?"

She couldn't help but laugh. "No, silly! I meant what I said. I understand."

"Well, all right, but..."

"But what?" She tensed.

"Nothing."

She studied him carefully. He'd come here to see her. He was tired, he was busy, but he came to her. The words of her parents, her friends, spilled over one another, adding to her confusion. Her voice was hushed. "I'm important to you, too, aren't I?"

He took her hands, his brow knitted, as he drew her closer and then wrapped his arms around her. He seemed genuinely surprised by her question and gave her a quick kiss before explaining. "Angie, if you weren't important to me, I wouldn't be here. "

"I'm glad." Then before returning his kiss, she smiled up at him and whispered, "You make me feel like a match."

"A what?"

Instead of answering, she kissed him.

21

The morning air was damp and thick with fog. A good day to die.

He waited until the judge left the house for his morning walk, then tinkered with a radar encoder until his universal remote unit signals meshed with those of the main controller of the garage door opener. Next, he put on a pair of latex gloves.

Checking carefully that no one was near, no one could see him, he aimed the remote at the garage door and clicked. The door unlocked. He sprang toward it, stopping it before it lifted more than a couple of feet off the ground. Then he dropped to the ground and rolled under it into the garage.

Quickly pulling the door to a closed position again, he lay still and waited for sounds of neighbors or passers-by who might have seen or heard him.

He listened, too, for sounds from the living quarters overhead, trying to hear them over the sound of his own heavy breathing.

All was quiet. He started to stand.

"Luke?"

He froze, his heart hammering at the sound of a woman's voice. "Luke, is that you?"

Sharp-eared old bat. There were stairs in the back of the garage leading up to a door to the house, probably to the kitchen. He darted to the bottom of the stairs and crouched down, expecting the wife to open the inside door to investigate further. But there was no sound of footsteps. No sound at all from upstairs.

She must have decided she was mistaken.

He crept up the stairs slowly, ready with each step for a loud creak to give him away.

The stairs were solid. Quiet.

At the door that led to the house proper, he twisted the knob, praying the door wasn't locked. His prayer was answered.

Slowly, he pushed the door open. The kitchen was large, yellow, with two walls of cabinetry and, over the sink, a window box filled with tiny plants in four-inch pots. The room was empty.

Where had the woman gone?

He shut the door behind him, holding the knob until the last moment. The latch made a tiny click. He pushed in the button in the center. If the old man came back that way, he'd find the door locked.

Not that it would matter. He'd be too late to save his wife.

She was in the house somewhere. From the kitchen door, he could see a hallway. The way these San Francisco houses were built, he knew it led to a living room and dining room in the front of the house and to the bedrooms in the back. Quietly, he moved toward the door, half expecting her to appear in the doorway with each step he took.

A loud whistle sounded. He snapped his head toward the stove. A teakettle.

Hurling himself behind the kitchen door, his heart racing,

he waited. But despite the noise the kettle made, he didn't hear the woman hurrying down the hall to turn it off.

She would come eventually, though. He could wait right here for her.

The loud kettle jangled his nerves. Perspiration formed on his forehead. He tried to remain there, without moving, to wait for her. It'd be so much easier that way. He covered his ears, needing to cut off the kettle's shrill scream. No! That wouldn't be safe. He had to listen for her.

Where was she? Could she be hard of hearing? She had heard noises in the garage, though, had called out her husband's name. *What in the hell is she doing that's more important than turning off her goddamn teakettle?*

Control. He needed control. He flexed his hands, his fingers. But the noise grew louder, shriller. Steam shot from the spout. It squeezed the air, choking him. He clutched at his throat. If he shut the flame under the kettle, would she notice? Would it alert her?

Where the hell was the bitch?

He'd have to find her, kill her, then turn it off himself. That was the only way to stop the noise that was making his head split, making it hard for him to think.

His hand against the frame of the kitchen door, he darted his head out into the long hallway. She wasn't there.

Keeping his back against the wall, he sidled along the hallway toward the living room. The room was empty, as was the dining area between it and the kitchen.

That meant she had to be in the back of the house, in one of the bedrooms.

Suddenly, he didn't mind the loud whistling of the teakettle. It masked his footsteps as he eased his way, once more, down the hall.

He reached the bedroom without her seeing him and peered inside.

She stood beside the bed, her back to him, wearing only a slip, hose and brown, low-heeled shoes. Her clothes had been neatly laid out before her on the bed. She picked up a pink blouse and put it on. He watched, mesmerized, as she proceeded to fasten the many buttons that lined the front of it. Next, she reached for a brown skirt and stepped into it, hiking it up to her waist, then spending a considerable amount of time smoothing the blouse and slip once more. Such a pity, he thought, so much trouble for no reason.

She button the skirt. As she worked the side zipper, looking down, giving it her full attention, she began to turn in his direction.

He pounced. She opened her mouth to scream, but his hand covered it, muffling her cries and forcing her back on the bed. He lay atop her, crushing her with his weight. She fought, kicked, tried to get away, to scream, but she was no match for him.

His blood pounded. His temples throbbed and a fiery redness built against his eyes. The incessant whistle in the background, the squirming of her body beneath him on the bed, heated him. He backed off a bit, closing his eyes as he let her struggle, enjoying the feel of her, remembering what it was like to have a woman writhe beneath him. Helpless. Captive. He opened his eyes.

But instead of beautiful Heather, beneath him was this old hag. Disgust raged at her. Filthy slut, tempting him that way, making his body do things he didn't want it to do with someone ugly like her. He pulled the combat knife from his back pocket. She'd never tempt him again.

He took the dried rose from the back pocket of his jeans and placed it on her pillow. It was smashed and dark, and most of the petals had fallen off, but he didn't think the police would care. They'd get the message.

He wiped off the knife on the blood-soaked bedspread, then took off his shoes. He didn't want to track bloody shoe prints onto the carpet. That would give the police too clear a picture. But he'd never heard of tracking sock prints before. Especially heavy woolen ones.

In the kitchen, he shut the gas off under the shrieking teapot, then went to the hall closet and took out the judge's trench coat and felt hat. Putting on his shoes once more, he walked out the front door, down the stairs and up the street to his car.

Paavo sat in the living room with Judge St. Clair. The judge was hunched in the center of the sofa, his hands covering his face. His trembling had stopped, but the slump of his shoulders, his bowed head, created about him an immutable sense of defeat and pain.

"Tell me exactly what you did after you found her," Paavo said gently.

The judge lowered his hands. His eyes were red-rimmed, his cheeks blotched from earlier tears. His mouth worked awhile before he could get the words past a tightened throat. "I didn't even have to touch her. I knew. I knew she was... But I did touch her. Her hand, her face. They were already cold, and her eyes..." He swallowed and waited a moment or two. His hands shook. "I took a bath towel from the linen closet and covered her with it. I know I shouldn't have, but the way he'd left her... She was always such a proper lady. I couldn't let her be found that way. I just couldn't. I'm sorry!"

Paavo put his hand on St. Clair's shoulder. "It's all right. Anyone of us would have done the same."

The judge nodded and tried to hold back his tears.

Paavo left him and went back into the bedroom. Homicide Inspectors Rebecca Mayfield and her partner, Bill Sutter, were the on-call team this week. But one look at the crime scene and Rebecca had contacted Paavo. It looked frighteningly similar to the way she had found Tiffany Rogers' murder.

"Did the judge know anything that might help?" Rebecca asked.

"It's hard to tell. He's in a bad way," Paavo answered.

"You're pretty sure it's the same guy, though?"

"It's got to be. The way he stabbed them, the rose on the pillow. Just one difference. This one was even more brutal."

22

Angie's third sister, Maria, looked up from the catalogues and files spread out on the floor and scowled. They'd never been close, and that look reminded Angie why.

Maria was the serious, religious one in the family. Everyone thought she'd become a nun. The family was shocked when she eloped with a saxophone player from Pier 17, a jazz nightclub on the Embarcadero. No one knew Maria even liked jazz.

Now, she acted as publicist for her husband, and had turned the name Dominic Klee into a household word for jazz buffs. They now owned the Jazz Workshop where Klee's Quintet played when they weren't touring. Maria straightened the catalogues into a stack and then turned her full attention on Angie.

"Did Papà send you here?" she asked, her eyes narrow. "He can't believe we're not starving."

"I didn't even tell him I was coming," Angie said.

Maria flicked her waist length, straight black hair off her shoulders to fall smoothly down her back. With no make-up, rows of silver bracelets and heavy, dangling silver earrings, she grew more exotic every day.

"So, what's this about, Angie?"

"I'm trying to learn about marriage," she said. She knew Dominic had to leave Maria and their son at home while he toured, and, in a sense, Paavo was gone a lot, too, because of the long hours he worked. Angie found his schedule, or lack of one, hard to deal with. "I was just wondering if Dominic being gone so much bothered you?"

Maria shrugged. "What can I say? It's his job. His life. It's what he loves, and I love him."

"But he's working in nightclubs. There's drinking, drugs, women throwing themselves at him. I mean, he's very... um..." Angie wasn't sure of the word to use around her religious sister.

"Sexy?" Maria offered.

"Well... yes."

"Don't I know it." Maria's face broke into a smile as she thought about her husband—a smile that Angie realized had nothing religious about it.

Her sister grew serious. "I trust him, Angie. I have to. For our marriage, it doesn't matter if he's home or away. I've found the perfect way to deal with it."

"Oh, good." Angie was desperate for answers. "How do you do it?"

"I pray a lot."

23

Angie sat at her tiny kitchen table and absent-mindedly stirred her morning coffee. The other night, before he left, Paavo had told her he had been working on the well-publicized case of the young typist from City Hall. That was why he and Yosh were putting in such long hours. It was also clear that he was irritated that Nathan Ellis' murder had been put on the back burner, so to speak.

She read the *Chronicle's* account of Tiffany Rogers' murder and the investigation. She also reread earlier accounts of the jewelry store killing.

Tiffany was just a year younger than Angie. She had been born and raised in the city, and had attended parochial schools here. For all Angie knew, their paths had probably crossed. Paavo had mentioned that Tiffany had a sister named Connie. Connie Rogers... that sounded familiar for some reason. But Connie was four years older than Tiffany, three older than Angie. Angie probably didn't know her, but maybe one of her sisters did.

No one seemed to have any idea why Tiffany had been killed. What if it had something to do with her family? Something that anyone who knew Connie might figure out? She could easily make a few phone calls. What harm could it do? It might help. And Paavo was so tired lately, working both this case and the jewelry store murder.

Why not help him?

She picked up the phone and called her sister Frannie. Connie and Frannie were just about the same age.

"Never heard of her," Fran said.

Undaunted, Angie tried her middle sister, Maria. Maria was irritated at such a dumb question. Angie should have known Maria wouldn't bother to remember anyone who hadn't gone to morning mass each day before class. Caterina and Bianca were probably too old.

That left her cousins. She started with Loretta, the one who owned *Herobics* and kept in contact with lots of people, doing all she could to make them feel guilty about not getting enough exercise. But Loretta didn't know Connie.

Then she tried her cousin Gloria, who was married and sang in a church choir. She didn't know Connie either.

She thought about her male cousins. Tiffany was quite attractive, so maybe Connie was as well. She knew exactly which cousin to call.

"Buddy, how ya doing?" she said. Buddy Amalfi lived in South City, the natives' name for South San Francisco. Years would go by without her seeing or talking to Buddy, but when they made contact again, it was as if they'd talked only yesterday.

"Hey, Angelina, long time no see."

"I've been busy. Listen, I've got a favor to ask."

"Ask away."

"I'm trying to find a woman named Connie Rogers. She's about your age, went to school here in the city."

"Connie... Connie... Connie. Sure, I remember her. Come to

think of it, I went out with her a couple of times in high school."

"I'm trying to find her. Do you know where she is?"

"God, I haven't seen her in nine, ten years. Maybe more."

"It's important, Buddy."

"Well, let me work on it. I still keep in touch with a lot of the old gang."

"Tell them her sister, Tiffany, was just killed, that should get them thinking harder."

"Her kid sister? Killed? What do you mean killed?"

"Tiffany was stabbed to death. She was a typist. It's been all over the papers."

"Holy! I'd heard some woman was stabbed. Good Christ! I didn't pay any attention to the name. Poor Connie. Okay, I'll get right on it."

Angie hung up and looked at her phone with a self-satisfied air. When she took an interest in something, she didn't fool around.

"I t'ought we'd be outta here by now," Earl said as he chipped at the cement wall with a hammer and chisel.

"We would be if you two bozos didn' waste all your time talkin' to the low life that comes in here. One more day, maybe two." Vinnie sat on an upside down wastebasket and puffed on his cigar as Earl worked. Butch stood at the top of the stairs listening for customers and keeping an eye on his kitchen.

"I didn't ask to talk to 'em," Earl protested. "I don't even like being a waitpoison."

"What's he talkin' about, wait poison?" Vinnie looked up at Butch.

"One of the customers told him waiter and waitress were

sexist," Butch said. "Now he thinks he's s'posed to be politically correct."

Vinnie looked at the ceiling. "Still payin' me back, ain't ya, God? Stuck me with these two. I hope you're havin' a good laugh."

He noticed Earl had stopped working to look at him. "So dig, already," he ordered.

"I t'ink we need a jackhammer," Earl said.

"God, he's dumb!" Butch muttered. "How we gonna find a jackhammer?"

"We could steal one," Earl reasoned.

Butch came down the stairs. "Sure. We'll go down to the corner store and swipe some cigs, a bottle of whiskey, a jackhammer..."

"Shut up, both of you," Vinnie said. "I'm thinkin'."

"That's a revelation," Butch grumbled.

"Shut up! I said!" Vinnie bellowed. "I got it. We're gonna get a big drill and use it at night when no one else is around."

"Except maybe some cops drivin' by," Butch sneered.

"I t'ink we should take toins standin' watch," Earl added. "Den, if we see a cop car we can holler down to toin off da drill."

"Holler? Over the sound of a drill?" Vinnie glared at Earl, then turned to Butch. "What's he got for brains?"

Butch just shook his head. "I think I hear a customer."

"You're sure?" Paavo asked. He stood in the office of Sans Souci Jewelers and faced the clerk who had been working with Nathan Ellis the day someone paid cash for the tennis bracelet.

"Yes, sir. That's all I can tell you." Meredith Park's steady gaze met Paavo's. "Tall, distinguished, Caucasian and between fifty and fifty-five, I'd say. Prematurely gray. Sort of okay, I guess."

"What do you mean, sort of okay?" Paavo asked.

"Let's say, he wasn't my type. Too slick—like a politician, maybe. In fact... No, I don't know." Meredith shrugged.

"Would you recognize this man if you saw him again?" Paavo asked.

"That's hard to say. There was something vaguely familiar about him, but I'm just not sure."

Paavo nodded. Distinguished, gray-haired, middle-aged. Given all he'd learned about Tiffany, the description sounded perfect for one of her boyfriends. The question was, who was he? What was his name? "If you think of anything more, let me know."

"I will."

Paavo turned to leave.

"Oh, Inspector. One other thing."

"Yes?"

Meredith Park turned shrewd, intelligent eyes on him. "It's probably nothing, but a couple days before Nathan was killed something peculiar happened. It's been on my mind. I didn't want to bother you because I doubt it means anything, but since you're here..."

"It's fine, Mrs. Park. Tell me."

"A woman came into the store asking about the Fabergé eggs. She was probably in her late thirties, early forties; five-feet-three or four; with long brown hair, dull and lopped off at the ends as if she'd cut it herself. Anyway, it was only a day or so after we'd put the eggs out for our Easter display."

"Yes?"

"So, out of the blue she asked if they were from the original Fabergé artisans in Europe. I said as far as I knew there was some connection to the famous studios—that's how they were allowed to use the name. Then she asked if the quality was at all the same. I said of course not, that original eggs were found only in museums."

"Go on."

"She asked if that were true of all Fabergé pieces. And I told her the real eggs were priceless, and even the smallest Fabergé pieces, these days, would be valued in the hundreds of thousands of dollars, if not more."

"So I've been told," Paavo said, not seeing why that mattered.

"Well," Meredith Park leaned closer, "when I told the woman that, she turned so pale I thought she was going to faint."

Paavo nodded thoughtfully. "If you see this woman again, I'd like you to call me right away."

"Will do, Inspector."

24

Angie walked into her classroom to find a cellophane-wrapped bouquet of long-stemmed red roses in the center of her desk. Could they be from Paavo? she wondered, although he wasn't exactly the flowers-giving type. Maybe he'd sent them because he'd been too busy to see her lately.

She searched the flowers for a card.

She hadn't heard from Paavo in a couple of days, not since his late-night visit. The city was astir in the wake of the murder of a retired judge's wife, and the papers made it sound as if all of Homicide was now working on these murders, with Paavo as the detective in charge. This was another one of those cases where she saw more of him on the local TV newscasts than she did in person.

The press speculated that the same crazed murderer who had killed the typist had also killed the judge's wife. They made much of the fact that both murdered women had connections to city government, which led them to dub the cases the Municipal Murders.

The Mayor and Board of Supervisors were furious at the

gory attention given to their administration, as if bad government had led to the murders. No matter how much political pressure they exerted on the press to stop its coverage of the murder investigations, the interest continued. Finally, they realized there would be only one way to end the examination—for Homicide to catch the killer. Paavo was in the middle of a firestorm.

Angie found no card with the roses. That was strange. Who would send her such beautiful flowers and not give his name? It had to be Paavo.

She quickly shuffled through the stack of papers the school's administration office had left in her mailbox. Information about some money raising events, a faculty meeting for the regular staff, a meeting to introduce the new third assistant vice administrator, and a card telling her about a late enrollee into her classroom, W.C. Lake. She flipped it over to see if it was a joke. She'd spent enough vacations in England to know their meaning of W.C., and tied with "lake" make her wonder. She put the card aside. Probably just some unfortunate American name.

"Does anyone know who brought me the flowers?" she asked the few students, retirees mostly, who'd arrived early for her class.

"A sweet young man. Rather shy," Lynette answered. "He said he was signing up for your class, but he couldn't stay today, and hoped you'd forgive him."

Something was strange about this. She'd had students who claimed to be sorry they'd missed class before, but none had been sorry enough to bring her a gift. Not even a posy of pansies, let alone expensive roses. Especially since this was just an adult ed class. No grades, no credit.

"Did he give his name?" she asked Lynette.

"I don't think so."

"He said you'd know him when the two of you finally met," Herman said, looking up from his notebook.

"He did?" Angie was more confused than ever.

"He seemed to be quite a fan of yours," Joan, another student added, then smiled. "I thought he was a bit smitten myself."

Angie tried to put aside thoughts of her mysterious, smitten student while she gave her lesson, but it was difficult. Particularly as the strong scent of the flowers permeated the front of the classroom.

The lesson dealt with President Warren G. Harding's visit San Francisco. He'd checked in at the St. Francis Hotel and had promptly checked out. Permanently. The public was told he'd died of influenza and exhaustion due to a tour through the Western U.S. and Alaska, but rumor had it that he'd been poisoned.

No one ever found out, to this day, what the real story was.

When the lesson ended, Angie began to gather up her lecture notes. She, Lynette and Joan were going out for coffee after class. Usually, Angie had some decadent chocolate dessert —but not during Lent.

"Roses, Angie?"

She knew that voice. Paavo stood in the doorway scowling at the flowers.

"They're from one of my students," she said, smiling broadly.

"They look a little wilted," he said as he approached her desk.

Spoils sport. But then, maybe he was jealous that he hadn't thought of giving her flowers himself? "It's the thought that counts," she said.

"Sorry. I didn't mean to pick on your student." He glanced at the two older women standing nearby, gawking at him and taking in every word he and Angie said. "I guess you're busy. I should get going."

"No, not at all. These ladies are Lynette and Joan, two of my students. They used to work for the government."

"Oh?" Try as he might, he couldn't make himself sound the least bit interested.

"We're retired now," Lynette said, a big, friendly smile on her face. "We were going out to have some coffee. Want to join us?"

"No, thanks. I don't think so. I guess I'll catch you later, Angie." He backed up a step.

"We'll make it another time," Joan quickly said to Angie. "You two young people don't need us. Right, Lynette?"

Lynette kept looking from Paavo to Angie and back. Joan jabbed her with her elbow. "Oh. Right!" she said, and they left.

"Sorry about that," Paavo said. Alone with her now, he walked to her side and tucked back a curl that had fallen too near her eye, then bent forward and kissed her quickly.

"It's okay," she said, feeling suddenly all but radiant at this unexpected visit. "You've been pretty busy yourself, Inspector. Lookin' good on TV, too!"

His gaze caught the flowers. "It's been no bed of roses."

She put her hands on his arms. "It sounds like you're getting a lot of pressure from City Hall," she said, concern in her voice.

He held her waist. "You could say that."

He wasn't the type to admit to more, no matter how ugly it could get. And she knew local politics could get very ugly indeed. "Where's Yosh?"

"He's gone home for a change of clothes and some home cooking. He also wants to make sure his wife and kids don't forget what he looks like."

"Did he drop you off?"

Paavo nodded. "He did. We saw your car in the lot—a Ferrari's easy to spot. I've wondered what you've been up to."

"Me?" She felt her cheeks burn as she thought about her conversations on marriage with friends and family. The whole thought of marriage and all the strange things it meant had put her mind in a muddle. She dropped her hands from his arms and turned away. "A little of this, a little of that. Nothing special." She stuffed papers into her briefcase.

He paused. "Nothing special? What about your roses? They seem pretty special."

"As I said, they're from a student."

"You've been pretty busy charming him, I guess."

"I wish I could say that, but I haven't even met him yet." She snapped the briefcase shut. He took hold of the handle before she did.

"Hmm, odd. Anyway, how about I take you out for a cup of coffee?" he asked.

She took a deep breath. "Shouldn't you eat and freshen up like Yosh? I suppose you have to go back to work?"

"In a couple of hours."

"Tell you what, let's go to your place so you can relax, change, shower, and feed Hercules. I'll make something for you to eat."

"You don't have to do all that."

"I know. And I know you don't expect me to. That's why I don't mind doing it."

He wasn't sure what to say. He wanted her with him, wanted to be together, but she had been acting so strange lately he didn't know what was going on. Just what did 'a little of this and a little of that' mean, anyway?

She picked up the roses. He wished she'd have left them. He wished he'd thought of bringing her flowers. He wished... a lot of things. He eyed the roses. From a student she hadn't even met? That made no sense. His stomach knotted. As they walked down the corridor, the smell of the flowers brought back to him the scent of death and blood.

She's carrying my roses. He smiled. *Carrying them against her soft, round bosom.*

His smile vanished when he saw the detective behind her, though. He'd almost forgotten about Smith. How could he forget? He was letting her distract him from his mission. Letting thoughts of her as a woman... as *his* woman... get in the way. He couldn't allow that.

He adjusted his glasses and leaned forward. He liked how gently she carried the roses. One of them touched the hollow of her throat. He could almost see it pulse with the warmth of her blood. Red blood, like his roses. Sacrificial blood.

How would it be to offer her blood instead of an old woman's or a young whore's on the altar of revenge? She was more innocent. Innocent like Heather. Hers would be the blood debt paid—no, not paid—there was no redemption to be had. On Easter his work as avenger, not redeemer, would be complete.

He followed the white Ferrari. She drove straight to Smith's house. It was becoming pretty clear that despite her blond fiancé, she cared about Smith, and that the feeling was mutual. That was all he needed to know.

She was as two-faced as all women. Despite himself, disappointment filled him. It was too bad he had to kill her.

Paavo's kitchen was always a challenge. Angie took a box of Kraft's Macaroni and Cheese from a shelf. Why would anyone waste money buying something packaged that was so easy to make? A little pasta, fresh grated cheddar, or even better, fontina, add some onion powder, salt, cracked red pepper, milk and butter—and of course, a little garlic never hurt anything—and it was ready.

Hercules let out a howl at the back door. It had to be intuition that told him when she was in the kitchen, Angie thought, as she let him in. The sight of the big, tough tomcat making little mewls and rubbing against her ankles made her laugh.

She scooped a small dollop of mayonnaise onto a saucer. "That'll have to do until I get back," she said. As soon as she heard the shower running, she hurried to her car and drove to the nearby neighborhood market.

She expected Paavo had been living on Dunkin' Donuts and fast foods and wanted to make him something substantial.

Using the key he'd given her to let herself back into his house, she hurried into the kitchen, gave Hercules a small salmon filet, and then put Paavo's French lamb chops into a marinade of red wine, vinegar, olive oil, bay leaves and peppercorns. She sauteed fresh garlic and red pepper flakes in olive oil, and added chicken stock. When it came to a boil, penne pasta went into the pan. Once the liquid boiled again, she put broccoli florets atop the mixture, covered it and let it cook until the pasta was done. As it cooked, she broiled the lamp chops and made a small green salad.

It was funny, she reflected, as she prepared the meal, but she had always thought she'd end up with an epicure, someone who enjoyed and knew good food and wine the way she did. Paavo wouldn't know a truffle from a mushroom, beluga caviar from trout eggs. Where had she gone wrong? Not only that, she didn't even care.

But then, the staff writer at *Haute Cuisine*, Marianne Perrault, dined with her husband at Buffalo Wild Wings. At least Paavo appreciated good food when he had the time to eat it.

"Angie, what's this? I didn't want you to go to all this trouble."

His face was shiny from his shave and shower, his hair slightly damp, and he smelled like Old Spice aftershave. She turned back to the pots and pans, forcing her thoughts back to cooking instead of other things he made her think of. He had to eat and go back to work even if she didn't. "It's no trouble," she said. "I enjoy it."

He wrapped his arms around her shoulders. "I enjoy you."

"Go sit down," she said. "You'll make me burn the food."

"If I wasn't half-starved, I'd try." He lifted the pot lid to look at the pasta and then checked on the broiling lamb chops. "Where did you get all this?"

"Ve haf our vays."

When the pasta was al dente and the broccoli crisp but tender, she drained the mixture, leaving a little as a sauce. She put pasta, broccoli, lamb chops and thin sliced, hot cherry peppers on plates and served them.

"How are your cases coming along?" she asked as she sat to eat. "Any luck yet?"

"Not yet." He tasted the penne pasta. "This is delicious."

"I thought you might like it. You seem to enjoy good food."

"Everything you make is wonderful."

She waited until he was more than half finished with the meal before she brought up his case. "The news is saying the same person killed both the judge's wife and the City Hall typist."

"So I've heard."

He went back to savoring each bite. She guessed she should be flattered, and maybe she didn't blame him for not wanting to talk about murder.

"What do you think of streaming movies for entertainment?"

He glanced up at her, surprised. "What *kind* of movie?"

"I don't know... I was going to ask you that."

"What's this about?"

"Nothing. Just curious."

He thought a moment. "Well, Yosh was singing the praises of *Kung-fu Killer* the other day."

"Oh, dear."

He chuckled at her stricken expression and went back to quietly enjoying the rest of the meal.

As they cleared the table, Angie said, "You know, Paavo, the press wants to link the Rogers and St. Clair murders, but Tiffany worked at City Hall and Superior Court is at the Hall of Justice, right?"

"True."

"I guess it's possible," Angie said, "even though the judge worked in one place and Tiffany in another that they came into contact with the same people—the same madman."

"We're checking on it, over and over again." Paavo put the pot and cooking utensils in the sink. "The most logical thing is that the two women knew someone in common. So far, though, we haven't found anyone at all. Not even a hint of a mutual friend."

"If there was a connection," Angie said, putting the spices she'd used back in the cupboard, "between the judge and Tiffany, why kill the judge's wife? Wouldn't the judge have been the most likely victim?"

"Exactly. The press hasn't bothered to ask that question. I guess they haven't figured it out yet. We're checking out Supervisor Wainwright, Rogers' boss, and everything connected with the office, but so far it's another zero."

"The city hall connection might be pure coincidence. A lot of people are involved with city government these days."

"I'll look at coincidence last."

Angie couldn't let Paavo's case go. "Tiffany was single, right?" she asked, filling a dish pan with soapy water. Paavo didn't own a dishwasher. "What about her boyfriend? Who was he?"

"She was seeing someone, but she wouldn't tell anyone who he was." Paavo wrapped the garbage in old newspapers and took it to the can in the side yard. "No one's volunteered any info," he shouted.

"That's suspicious," she called out to him. "Why wouldn't she say?

Back inside, he grabbed a dishtowel. "Her friends think he was someone important in city government. Probably married."

"No woman who's got an exciting, powerful new boyfriend isn't going to give at least a hint about him to someone. It's just not possible."

She could tell that Paavo was thinking about her words as he wiped the dishes until they squealed. He took every job seriously. "That's what's strange. If anything, she was a person to flaunt her successes, not hide them."

"See?" Angie said. "Who was she close to?"

"A couple of women at work and, to a much lesser degree, her sister."

"That's all?"

"Far as we know."

"You've got to be missing something."

There was a pause and Angie realized she had no business being critical when he'd been working so hard on his cases. She was about to rush in with an apology about her runaway mouth. He stared intently at her. "Yes. I know I am, and it bothers me." He put down the dishcloth. "As soon as I put out some food for Hercules, how about a lift down to the Hall since my car's in the parking lot. Yosh is probably there already."

She wiped off the rim of the sink and countertop. The kitchen was spotless. "I fed him already. Let me get my jacket." She headed for the living room for her jacket and purse.

He grabbed her hand as she rushed by. "Did I thank you for the dinner, Miss Amalfi?"

"Not properly, Inspector Smith."

"Then let me do so now, even if you do get flowers from strange men."

"I never—"

He took her in his arms and stopped her protests.

25

Three days later, Angie stood on the steps of Sts. Peter and Paul's Church where she'd gone to light a candle in memory of her grandfather on his birthday. This was one of those special, sunny spring days when the sky was a cloudless, brilliant blue. Against the colorful buildings of North Beach, clusters of easygoing people shopped or dined or played in the park and gave the area the busy, friendly Mediterranean flavor it was famous for.

Angie crossed Filbert to Washington Square and sat on a park bench. For a few minutes, at least, it was an afternoon to enjoy.

"I have a lot of experience with marriage."

Angie turned at the sound of the loud, gravelly voice. Directly behind her was a tall bush, and on the other side of the bush was another bench. She couldn't see who sat on it.

"I didn't know you'd been married," a slurred, younger-sounding voice replied.

"Can't even remember how many experiences with wedded bliss I've endured, son. I'm a marrying man, I am."

"You like it, do you?"

Angie pressed herself hard against the back of the bench to better hear what the "marrying man" had to say. Someone talking about marriage, and she didn't even have to prod him with questions or bribe him with treats!

"I do. Hey! See what I mean? The words 'I do' just roll from my tongue like butter on a hot cob of corn. The little ladies I was married to, though, they were a problem. Women have these hang-ups, you know."

"I didn't know that."

Anxious not to miss a word, Angie knelt on the bench and leaned into the bush behind it.

"Yeah. About stuff like having a job. Staying sober. Taking a ridiculous number of baths. They forget the ecstasy."

"I see."

"I had one wife, every time I'd hop into bed, she'd hop out. Now, of course, she just might not have felt worthy of the marital gift I was about to bestow. But for some reason, she used to say odd things, like I was overwhelming. I never understood what she meant, unless it was my charm. That was one of my shorter marriages."

"I can understand that."

"You know, son, the carnal seems to be another hang-up with women. I got a theory. Men and women are different and I don't just mean in the obvious way. I'm talking sex drive. I figure from the time a fellow knows it's possible, he's raring to go. But little ladies' sex drive peaks later. Probably posthumously."

Angie listened to the two guffaw over this a long time. Then the younger-sounding one said, "At least you understand them."

"I hate to disillusion you, but despite my vast experience, they're still a mystery to me. So much so, I'm not ashamed to admit, I'd just as soon pay for it. But you know something, even the pros feel unworthy of me. It's amazing. I've got to be one hell of a guy."

That did it. She *had* to see this wondrous marrying man. She knelt on the bench and grabbed hold of some branches from the shrub behind it and spread them apart. But the shrub still blocked her view. Leaning further forward, she grabbed more branches, a lot more, and was trying to separate them enough to see through them when she lost her balance and toppled head first over the bench. Holding onto the bush, she belly-flopped on top of it, causing the branches to sway under her weight and carry her to the back of the opposite bench. She looked right into the blood-shot eyes of two scruffy men. They jumped to their feet.

The older one, a seedy but still faintly debonair character in his shiny too-tight striped suit and bowler hat worn at a jaunty angle, proudly puffed out his chest as he smiled down at her.

"There, son. See what I mean? They're always falling for me."

***

Earl ran out of the kitchen and came to a screeching halt when he saw who stood near the entrance waiting for a table. "You back?"

Angie looked around to see if he could be addressing anyone else. No, she was the only one here. "Yes."

"Which table?"

"How about the same one as last time?"

He led her to the table and even held the chair out for her. She pulled a twig she'd missed earlier off the leg of her slacks and sat. He handed her a menu—the same Columbus Avenue Cafe menu with the name lined out.

She gave it back. "What's on the menu today?" she asked.

"T'ree t'ings."

"T'ree? I mean, three?" she said with surprise. The cook must have taken her advice and expanded the menu. "How wonderful! What are they?"

He squeezed his eyes shut, counted with his fingers, then opened them and looked at her. "Spaghetti wit' meatballs, spaghetti wit'out meatballs, an' a meatball sangwich."

She clasped her hands to her forehead. "I think I need to pay the cook another visit."

"He's busy."

Angie looked around the empty restaurant. "Give me a break!"

Just then another customer came in. A plain man, his black hair was long and scruffy, and pulled back into a pony tail. The color was so off it looked like a wig, or maybe a really bad dye job. He also wore thick, black-rimmed glasses that rode too high on the left and too low on the right, making him look like his head was perpetually cocked. The fellow was tall and surprisingly muscular looking. As she stared, there seemed to be something familiar about him, but she couldn't remember having met him before.

He smiled shyly in her direction. She smiled back. Did he know her?

"See?" Earl looked at her smugly. "What did I tell you?" He walked over to the new customer. "You wanna eat?"

"Um, yes. I believe so."

"Okay. Follow me." Earl led him to a table near Angie. "Here's da menu. I'd recommend da spaghetti an' meatballs."

Angie turned around to watch. The customer looked from her, to Earl, to the menu, then folded it shut and handed it back. "Sounds good to me," he said.

Earl went back to Angie's table. "You decided yet?"

"How about a new waiter?"

"It ain't on da menu. How 'bout spaghetti an' meatballs?"

She held her head. "Not today. I think I'll pass, in fact." She stood, picking up her purse. "Tell the cook I suggest he look into polenta. There isn't a restaurant around that does it really well. The trick is to mix diced roasted green chilies—mild ones—in with it. If he wants to try it, I'll help."

She was about to leave, but noticed that the customer had been listening to her conversation with the waiter. She didn't want him to get the wrong impression.

"Let me assure you," she said, "the spaghetti and meatballs are truly delicious. I'm just tired of them."

"Thanks. I'm glad to hear it. This is the first time I've eaten here. I'm new to the city."

"Well, welcome." She couldn't help staring.

"Is anything wrong?" he asked.

"I'm sorry. You look familiar."

He looked at her as if she were mad, then grinned. "I remind you of Ryan Gosling, maybe?"

Even his smile and attempt at humor didn't lesson the sudden uneasiness she felt. "Sorry, my mistake. Enjoy your lunch."

"It was nice talking to you." He gave her a friendly, almost puppy-dog smile. Placing his elbows on the table, he steepled his hands, and leaned forward, toward her. "Hurry back," he said.

26

District Attorney Lloyd Fletcher slowly leafed through the reports from the Crime Scene Investigators, the photographs and laboratory tests, as well as Paavo and Yosh's notes on interviews with Tiffany Rogers' co-workers, neighbors and family. When he finished, he did the same with the folder for Velma St. Clair.

"Frankly, I expected much better from you, Smith," he said.

Paavo wasn't surprised to hear a remark like that from Fletcher. Still, it stung. "The guy the judge used to see hanging around each morning hasn't shown up since the murder. We've got an idea of what he looks like. Also, we just talked to a kid, age thirteen, who lives across the street from Tiffany Rogers' apartment. He described a man with the same build, baseball hat, carrying a long, white box—sounded like a florist's box—the night Rogers was killed. The kid said someone let the guy into the building."

Fletcher ran his hand over his thick white hair as if to smooth it, except that every strand was already in place. "A tall, muscular white guy who wears a baseball cap. Let's see, that probably describes ten thousand or so men in San Francisco alone. Maybe twenty to thirty thousand if we take in the whole Bay Area. I'm not impressed."

"We're still working on finding Rogers' boyfriend. She has to have left some clue, somewhere, as to who he might be."

"You're wasting your time. Everyone said she'd gone out with the man for two months or less. The way she was killed couldn't have been by a former lover. And why would he have killed the judge's wife? No, you're barking up the wrong tree there."

"But with City Hall—or at least, City government—involved in both murders, plus the missing boyfriend, there are too many questions all pointing in the same direction. The key has to be right here. Someone close. And whoever it is might hold the key to the whole case."

Fletcher shot out of his chair, placed his hands on his desk and leaned forward. "Or you might be wrong. You might be ready to ruin a man's career because of an indiscretion with some bimbo who had the bad taste to get herself killed."

Paavo stared, taken aback by the vehemence of Fletcher's outburst. The man had a reputation for being pristine. If not, Paavo would wonder about his remarks. Despite his reputation, in fact, Paavo still wondered.

Fletcher straightened and tugged at his shirt cuffs as he paced in front of this window. "How much clearer can I make myself, Smith? You are not to involve City Hall, the Board of Supervisors, or anyone connected with City government in this case. These women were murdered by some psycho, and I'm not going to have you disturb any political types in this city more than you already have. Do you understand me?"

Paavo tried to tamp down his annoyance at the man's bossy arrogance. "City government is our one constant."

"Keep away from the Board of Supervisors. That's an order."

"Hello," Angie called to a pleasantly smiling woman standing by a display of ceramic swans as she walked into Everyone's Fancy, a small gift shop on West Portal Avenue. "I'm looking for Connie Rogers. "

"I'm Connie." The woman's expression turned wary.

"My name is Angie Amalfi. I came to give my condolences. My boyfriend is the homicide inspector working on your sister's investigation, Inspector Paavo Smith."

Connie's eyes teared, and she went back to rearranging some glass swans. "Do you always visit the families of your boyfriend's cases?" The disgust in her voice told how macabre a pastime she considered that to be.

"My goodness, no," Angie said. "I'm so sorry! It turns out that you went to high school with one of my cousins. We were talking about how scary it was that two women were killed in the city, and my cousin mentioned you were a friend. I was in the neighborhood, saw your shop, and decided to come in."

"Really?" Connie's expression told Angie she wasn't inclined to believe her. "What's this cousin's name?"

"Dan Amalfi. Everyone calls him Buddy."

For the first time, Angie saw Connie's caution lift. "Buddy! You're Buddy's cousin?"

"Yes," Angie said with a smile. "So you remember him, too."

"Yes," Connie replied as a splash of color appeared on her otherwise pale cheeks. "He was *so* handsome."

"He still is."

"I can imagine," Connie murmured, her demeanor suddenly turning introspective. "It's hard to remember, after what just happened, how happy we once were." She attempted to brighten. "So, how is Buddy? What's he up to these days? Married? Kids?"

"No kids. Divorced," Angie said. At Connie's look of interest, she added, "Not even after twelve years of parochial school could he keep his marriage together. A mistake from the start."

Connie sighed. "I know the feeling." She put the last swan in place. "I had twenty-six months of sheer hell."

It was on the tip of Angie's tongue to ask *why*. How could a marriage turn so sour so quickly? Didn't she know the man she married well, or had she ignored the faults that were there until it was too late? But, despite aching to know, she wasn't here to learn about marriage, she was here to help Paavo. "Buddy's marriage lasted only eight months."

Angie knew why his marriage failed. He and his wife had married right out of high school. They were young, horny, and both dumb in the way only teenagers in love could be about the real world and the mundane problems of making a home in it.

"So, Buddy remembered me when he read about Tiffany?" Connie asked. "I'm surprised."

"Your poor sister," Angie said gently. She wasn't here to discuss Buddy.

Connie rubbed her arms as if chilled. "My God, it's still such a shock."

"I'm surprised her boyfriend never showed himself." Not subtle, but to the point.

Connie lifted an eyebrow. "How'd you know that?"

Angie sensed Connie's wariness taking over again. "It was in the papers."

"Oh. Well, she did her darnedest to keep his name a secret, so I guess even after she's dead he'll make sure he keeps his name out of it, the rat!"

"Why do you call him that?" Angie asked.

"Why?" Connie looked at her as if she were crazy. "He killed her. I know he did!"

Angie's jaw dropped. "You do? You know who he is?"

"No, but I've got a brain—and I know my sister. She probably had him wrapped around her little finger. Maybe he was afraid she'd tell his wife, or his wife found out and threatened divorce and that she'd take every penny he had. Everyone says he had to be rich and powerful or Tiffany wouldn't have given him the time of day."

"Oh, I see," Angie said, disappointed. So, Connie didn't really know, she just guessed. "Well, you're right, he does seem to be a likely killer, although most politicians don't get their hands dirty directly. They get someone else to do their dirty work—plausible deniability and all that."

"Hmm," Connie said, "I hadn't thought of that."

"Say, since no one's in the store at the moment, do you want to take a break at the coffee shop next door? Fifteen minutes to sit down and talk? My treat," Angie said. "It'll probably do you some good."

Connie's face fell as she looked around the empty gift shop. "It seems most people don't want to come in to a store soon after learning there was a murder in the family.... So, yes, let's have some coffee. They make a wonderful lemon meringue pie there, as well."

The two were soon seated with oversized lattes with chocolate and cinnamon sprinkled on top, and large slices of lemon pie with three inch tall meringues. Connie asked Angie a little about herself, and Angie used the opportunity to talk a lot about her experiences in the culinary world.

"So you're basically trained as a gourmet cook, looking for a job in that industry," Connie said, "and you're dating a homicide detective? That sounds like a strange combination."

"It is," Angie said. "Believe me."

"How did you two meet?" Connie asked.

Angie shook her head. "It's a long story."

"Hey, I haven't had a customer all day," Connie confessed. "I have time."

Angie told her about her job at the *Bay Area Cooks* TV show and how her life came to be in danger, keeping the gory parts to a minimum out of deference to what Connie was going through with her sister's death. She also attempted to make some of it light and even funny—such as the exploding dishwasher—even though it wasn't at all humorous at the time. But soon, the two were chuckling and talking together like long-time friends.

"I don't really want to talk about your sister's situation," Angie said after a while, "but there's one thing that just bugs me."

"Really?" Connie said. "What is it?"

"I know whenever I, or one of my friends, meets a guy we like, we talk about him incessantly to at least someone. How did Tiffany keep this guy such a big secret?"

"I don't get it either." Connie's lips wrinkled, and she shook her head.

"Everyone keeps saying he was a big shot," Angie added, "but what if Tiffany was actually ashamed of him? That would be a reason to keep quiet, don't you think? I mean, I talk about Paavo all the time. I talk about what he says, what he does, even what he thinks—at least, when he tells me. And this is despite my family being completely opposed to me going out with a cop—or, I should say, everyone is except my mother, who likes Paavo. But the rest of them, well, you know how families can be."

"Do I ever. Mine is the same way. You should have heard everyone when me and Keith got divorced. You'd think it was all my fault. But tell me about Buddy?" Connie asked suddenly. "Was the family angry when he got his divorce?"

Angie was eating up Connie's increasingly obvious interest in Buddy as Connie grew more relaxed around her. "The family was more disappointed than angry. But, you know Buddy. He could charm the scales off a toad. Everyone got over it fast enough."

"That's Buddy." Connie heaved a sigh. "Say hello to him for me, won't you?"

"Of course."

"In fact, if he's not too busy, he should come by the gift

shop. We've got great gifts. But, tell him, he doesn't have to buy anything. I'd just like to say hello." As a wistful smile filled Connie's face, Angie could see that the woman actually was quite pretty. She was 'hiding her light,' as the old saying went.

"I'll do that," Angie said. "And I suspect he'd like to drop by very much."

Connie put her elbow on the table and rested her chin in her hand, a faraway look in her eyes. "We dated a couple of times, if you didn't know. Once to the movies, and another time to Charlie Markowitz's party."

"Buddy mentioned it," Angie said.

"He remembered?" She sounded pleased.

"Yes. Anyway, I was just thinking about Tiffany—"

"Poor Tiffany." Connie straightened. "Every time someone mentions her, it's like an electric shock all over again."

"Did she ever talk about what it was that attracted her to the man she was dating, or what they did together—I mean, where he took her on their dates?"

Connie removed her elbow from the table and sat up straight, back to reality. "Well, I doubt she was ashamed of him, so forget that theory. It was clear to me he had money, and for sure, him being rich was the kind of thing Tiffany valued. She never named the places he brought her to, but she always threw out things like, 'He took me to a big fancy restaurant in Marin where he wouldn't be recognized.'"

Angie's eyebrows popped up at that piece of information. "How interesting. That means his picture must have been in the newspapers or on TV."

Connie shrugged. "That's what I figured. Of course, San Francisco is small in many ways. Look how easily you found me."

"That's true. I'd suspect, since he felt okay about going to Marin, he worried that established San Franciscans, not tourists and commuters, might recognize him. That means he's just a local big fish."

"That's how it sounded."

"How did she refer to him?"

"As her friend. That's all. Anyway, I guess I really should be getting back to my shop. I think I'll close up early and go home. Thank you for coming by, Angie. I really enjoyed our talk."

"I'll walk you back," Angie said. "My car is parked just outside it."

As they reached the shop, Angie noticed a display of Fabergé style eggs in the window. She seemed to remember Paavo mentioning something about them in connection with his jeweler's case, but she couldn't remember quite what. "Aren't those lovely," she said.

"They're made by modern Fabergé artisans. Some places sell ugly knockoffs from China, but not these. They're hand-made, but nothing like real ones which are all but priceless. Still, they make a nice Easter gift for the person who has everything."

"I guess so. They aren't cheap, are they?"

"No, but there's so much significance in eggs and Easter, I actually do sell a few of them each year."

"I'd like to buy one to give to my mother at Easter. I know she'd like it."

"You don't have to buy anything, Angie," Connie said. "I'm sure my customers will be back soon."

"No, really. My mother loves things like that, and I know she'd appreciate getting a gift—she always cooks a big meal at Easter for the family, and I think she'd enjoy someone giving her something besides more food or yet another bottle of wine."

Connie nodded. "Okay, if you're sure."

They went into the shop and Connie beautifully gift wrapped Angie's purchase. As she did, she murmured, "Tiffany loved those eggs." Her eyes welled up, and suddenly she was in tears. She reached into her pocket for a wadded up tissue and wiped her eyes. "I'm sorry. I just remembered that one of the last things she said to me was that she would ask El to buy her one, and now...."

Angie could scarcely believe what she'd just heard. "El? That's his name?"

Connie shook her head. "No, not really. She said "El" as in *el amigo*. That's what her pal Manuela called him—her friend, the friend. Tiffany just used El for short."

"So, you don't think El is the letter of his name?"

"I never thought about it."

"Did you mention this to Paavo?"

"No. Frankly, it just popped into my head now." She put the package in a bag and handed it to Angie. "Anyway, here's the present. I do hope your mom loves it. And, please, don't be a stranger, Angie."

There was something about Connie Rogers that Angie found she liked—a completely unpretentious genuineness she didn't find too often in the culinary world with its arrogant chefs and food critics. "I'm sure I'll be back," Angie said. "It was great to meet you."

27

The Coventry Hotel was in an old, unprepossessing building with a brass name plate so small it could have been a mail slot. As such, one was unprepared one for the elegance behind the wood and glass front door, the lush sofa in red and gold brocade, and matching striped chairs set on Persian carpets under a massive crystal chandelier. Mahogany and faux marble antiques finished the old world ambiance of the lobby. The rooms promised to be every bit as elegant.

Paavo faced the manager, a slight, balding man, every bit as haughty and sophisticated as the furnishings. "We found your matchbook in the victim's apartment. We're wondering if she was ever a guest."

James Sneed studied the photo Paavo handed him, then gestured for the desk clerk to join them. "Tiffany Rogers, you say?"

"That's right."

"She doesn't look familiar to me at all. If I may be so bold, she doesn't strike me as the sort who would be one of our regular clientele. We run a highly respected hotel."

"I'm sure you do."

The desk clerk reached their side. "Inspector Smith, this is Arthur Mills. Do you recognize her, Arthur?"

"Not at all."

The manager handed back the photo. "Sorry, Inspector."

Paavo tucked it in his breast pocket. "Do either of you work nights?"

"Our guests are rarely here *only* at night," Sneed said.

Paavo repeated his question.

"No."

"What time does your night shift report? And also, I'd like to take a look at your guest register for, let's say, the past eight weeks."

Paavo went through the guest register carefully, but saw nothing at all that jumped out at him as odd. Not even any repeat names. He gave the material back to the manager. "Everyone who stayed in this hotel is listed here, is that correct?" he asked.

"Well... not exactly," Sneed said.

"What do you mean?"

"The city rents a suite here at all times. They keep it for special guests because it's nearly impossible to find superior accommodations in this city on short notice. In summer, the suite is filled constantly. That's not the case this time of year. Several of the, er, dignitaries of the city have access to the suite —keys, in other words. They come and go as they please."

"They don't have to check in and out at the front desk?"

"We ask them to. But we know they don't all do so."

"Do you have a list of people with keys?"

"We only issued one—to the Mayor's office. But I know other people use the suite because the maids have told me they've seen different people entering or leaving on occasion. Of course, the height of propriety is always observed."

"Of course," Paavo said. "Thanks for the information."

Angie telephoned Paavo that evening. "I'd like to go with you to Mrs. St. Clair's funeral tomorrow afternoon," she said.

There was a long pause. "You know how much I enjoy having you with me, Angie," he began, "but—"

"My father knows Judge St. Clair. But he shouldn't go, his heart, you know. It's not good for him to be around murder victims. I'll represent the family."

"I'm not going there as a social gesture."

"I know. You do your thing, and I'll have enough etiquette for both of us."

"What's the real reason you want to go?"

"No real reason, other than going for my father. And seeing you won't be terrible. By the way, I met Connie Rogers today."

"You *what?*"

"She's an old girlfriend of my cousin, Buddy. In fact, she's still interested in him, if I'm any judge."

"Where did this cousin suddenly appear from?"

"What's that supposed to mean? I've got a lot of cousins."

"It means that it's pretty convenient that your cousin's love life involves the family of my murder victim."

"You are *so* suspicious, Inspector. Look, the Rogers sisters, both Tiffany and Connie, and a number of my relatives, including me, are all around the same age, and we all went to Catholic high schools in the city. It's natural at least one of them would know her. How many Catholic highs do you think we have here?"

"Obviously, not enough to keep you out of my cases."

"Before you complain, let me tell you about 'El'."

Angie told him about her conversation with Connie. After leaving Connie's, Angie had phoned her district supervisor and made a pest of herself until the office secretary emailed her a list of each department head in city government, their deputies and their mid-level managers.

Once home, she concentrated on the department heads. Tiffany liked men with money and power. She wouldn't have bothered with a mid-level manager, and the deputies were also iffy. Angie found four top level people whose names started with L. The Chief of Police and a member of the Board of Supervisors were both named Lawrence, the District Attorney was named Lloyd, and Llewellyn was the chief of the Department of Sanitation. Besides them, the mayor's executive officer was named Luis.

Now, she needed to see how these men looked and acted, to see if any of them might seem the sort of man Tiffany could be interested in. Since it was likely that they knew the judge, they might be at the funeral. It was a good place to check them out.

"Hold everything, Angie. First of all, how do you know El is the first name? Why not the last?"

"I admit, it's a guess. But all the women I know refer to their boyfriends by their first names. Maybe it's a Catholic school thing, but using last names is usually a joke."

"Before you go rushing off with this, let me talk to Manuela. If she's the one who came up with *El Amigo*, as Tiffany said, to check men's initials would be a waste of time."

"I knew you'd help!" Angie said.

He seemed to make a strange guttural sound before hanging up the phone.

Paavo picked Angie up at her apartment and they rode in his old Mustang to the church where Velma St. Clair's funeral would be held.

"I talked to Manuela," he said as he drove.

"What did she say?"

He frowned. "That she knows nothing about 'el' and never used the term 'el amigo.'"

Angie smiled, that meant the term was purely Tiffany's. "All *right!*"

A large crowd stood outside the church talking in hushed tones, and an even larger crowd was inside.

Paavo circled the outside group, then did the same indoors, to get a sense of who was here. Angie followed, trying to get a glimpse of her list of "L" names.

"Tell me, Paavo," she whispered, holding his arm, "which one is your boss, Lawrence?"

Paavo put his arm around her waist, speaking quietly into her ear as he looked over the crowd. "It wouldn't matter if the Chief of Police had ten L's in his name, he didn't date Tiffany Rogers."

"How do you know?"

"His wife would kill him."

"Some men can be pretty sneaky."

"Not from their wives, or not for long," Paavo said. "That's him. Blue suit, gray hair. That's his wife in the green suit. I've known him for ten years, Angie."

"Hmm." Angie nearly bore a hole through the man trying to figure out if he looked like someone Tiffany might have dated. "His eyes are shifty," she announced.

Paavo turned her to face in another direction. "Forget him."

"Do you see any of the others?" she asked. "I know what Supervisor Coglin, Larry Coglin, looks like, but I haven't seen him here. Isn't it suspicious that he wouldn't come?"

Paavo frowned. "Could be. Lloyd Fletcher, the D.A., is the tall, white-haired fellow near the judge." Paavo thought about his strange conversation with Fletcher, and how the man had insisted that he not pursue finding Rogers' boyfriend. That it could ruin a man's reputation and not lead to the killer, anyway. Could Angie actually be on the right track here?

"I've seen him before. He wants to be mayor, I hear."

"So they say."

"And the others?"

"I don't know the Chief of Sanitation. You're on your own there. And I don't see the Mayor's XO."

"X—, oh, the executive officer. All you government types talk in letters. Say, I wonder if the L isn't an initial for a name at all, but a job? An L? What job could that be?"

"No government job just has one letter. Bureaucrats are always too long-winded. You know that."

"Considering his fling with Tiffany, how about Ladies' Man?"

"That'd be LM."

"You're so precise, Inspector. Let's find the... what did you call him? The XO."

Paavo noticed a delivery man hovering nearby holding a bouquet of roses up in front of his face. If he never saw a rose again, it'd be too soon. All the flowers should have been up by the casket already, though. Why would a delivery man—

"Oh, look, Paavo!" Angie leaned close against him. "There's someone new at the door talking to the mayor. Good looking, too. Could he be Luis the XO?"

Paavo faced the doorway. "That's him."

"Let's go over there. I want a better look at him."

"Wait."

"What?"

Some strange feeling caused him to turn back to check on the delivery man. Paavo let go of Angie and slowly started walking toward the casket. Near the side exit, he saw a bouquet of roses lying on the ground.

He scanned the room quickly, then hurried out the exit. It led to a side alleyway. He ran down the alley to the street, to find another crowd milling about, getting into and out of cars and talking. He saw far too many of them wearing gray slacks similar to the delivery man's.

The man's upper body seemed to be clothed in beige, a sweater, most likely. But his face....

All Paavo could remember was the sight of the roses.

28

Paavo picked up the crime lab report, read it once quickly then threw it down on his desk. "No good news, I take it," Yosh said.

Paavo handed it to him. "No prints could be found on the rose display, not even on the vase they were placed in. It had to have been him, standing right there, listening to me, laughing. Damn! I looked right at him."

"Hey, you weren't the only one. I missed him, too. I mean, you expect to see flowers being delivered to a funeral."

"It makes me wonder if that's how he got into Tiffany's apartment. What if the guy the kid saw entering the apartment building with flowers wasn't someone she knew, but just some delivery guy? She probably would open the door for him."

"Could be," Yosh agreed.

"She didn't want the flowers to die. Instead, she did."

Paavo felt a sudden chill as he remembered the roses one of Angie's students had delivered to her—a student she said she'd never met.

"What's wrong?" Yosh asked.

He shook away the feeling. "Nothing. It takes a real scum to use something like roses for such ugliness. By the way, who would you say is the biggest gossip in Homicide?"

"Benson wins hands down. Why?"

"I'm curious about our friend the DA."

"Careful, Paav."

"I know."

Yosh picked up the DMV report Paavo had been reading and scanned it quickly. "Damn! I thought we had him when those patrolmen wrote down the green Honda's license number. Now, I see the car's registered to a dead man."

"I asked for a bulletin to go out on it, anyway. I'd like to talk with this ghost driver."

"A hundred bucks and you can buy any kind of I.D. you want on the street anymore," Yosh said. "They make things tougher for us all the time."

"Ain't it the truth," Calderon muttered as he walked into Homicide, scowling harder than usual.

"Hey, buddy," Yosh said. "How's it going?"

Calderon winced. "Another robbery."

Paavo and Yosh jumped up and crossed to his desk. "Another fake egg?"

"Who would have thought this city would be so lousy with phony Russian eggs? That was the fourth robbery. Some weird little guy with a fake beard and black wig. Not hard to spot, I'd say. Maybe I should transfer to Robbery and help solve their cases? Those guys need lots of help if they can't nab someone going around looking like a bearded Charlie Chaplin."

"In other words, no new leads on Nathan Ellis' murder?"

"I followed up on what the clerk at Sans Souci told you— the one who said some woman was asking a lot of questions. Seems a woman who looked like her was at this gift shop the day before the attack."

"Good work," Yosh said. "It sounds like the thief is a woman."

"Not so fast," Calderon cautioned. "To see how valid it was, I went into five jewelry stores that weren't robbed, gave the same description and asked if a similar woman had been in those stores the day before. They, too, said yes. In other words, women in fancy stores that sell fake Fabergé eggs, will often ask jewelers about them. What else is new?"

"Great," Yosh said. "Who knew those things were so popular?"

"I don't think they are, but I know someone who would know," Paavo said. He picked up his cell phone and called Angie. She picked up immediately. "Quick question," he said. "Have you ever seen fake Fabergé eggs that are sold around town, I—" He listened as she told him all about buying a beautiful red and gold one at Connie's gift shop. "Okay, thanks. See you soon," he said, then hung up and looked at his co-workers. "They're a rare gift item, but desirable enough that she bought one yesterday."

"Okay," Yosh said. "But I think the reaction of the woman the San Souci clerk spoke to wasn't normal, no matter how often women ask about such things."

"I guess we could track all the women who show interest in the eggs if we didn't want to do anything else for a few weeks."

"We've got until Easter, a little over three weeks," Paavo said. "Then the eggs mostly disappear from shops, and so does our murderer."

"We'll get him, or her," Calderon said, showing more energy than usual.

"Let's mark the city map with the stores that were robbed, as well as those where a woman has gone in to ask about the eggs." Paavo said. "Look for a pattern."

"With little Easter bunny stickers," Yosh said.

"One pattern," Calderon said, "is that the robberies, so far, have happened on Tuesdays. It's nothing I'd count on, though. Easter, good God! Who'd have thought Easter would bring out the wackos? I thought people weren't religious anymore?"

Just then, Bo Benson walked in. "Excuse me," Paavo said, "But I've got some gossip to catch up on."

―――――

"You've got to do it, Connie," Angie said. The evening before, while watching a mystery on TV, she suddenly came up with a brilliant idea. If "El" wouldn't come to them, they would go to "El." She now faced Connie across the counter of Everyone's Fancy.

"I don't feel right about it." Connie took her feather duster and a rag and began bustling about her shop, wiping away dust and rubbing fingerprints off display cases. She was at the carousel horses as she tried to shut out Angie's arguments.

"Don't you want to know who was dating your sister? The police haven't figured out who he is, but we might be able to. And there's a chance he knows something about whoever killed her. Including the possibility that he killed her himself."

"And the judge's wife?" Connie asked, dusting faster.

"So the killer's a psychopathic government bigwig. Wouldn't be the first time."

Connie wielded her Windex bottle. "It was random, Angie. It had to have been. Some serial killer. It'd be just like my sister to pick up with a Ted Bundy type."

"Paavo doesn't think it was random. He thinks there's a reason those two women were chosen. We just don't know what the reason is yet."

"I don't know, Angie. I hate to do anything that might mess up the investigation. Besides, I think my sister really fell for this guy. It wasn't like her not to brag about whoever she was seeing, but she kept quiet about him. Could be because she loved him."

"All the more reason to find out who he is. The investigation is stalled. Paavo's own boss is trying to stop him from talking to City Hall." She paused to chew her lower lip. "Gee, I wonder what Lieutenant Hollins' first name is? I'll have to ask Paavo—if I can manage without him bellowing at me about it."

"I can't imagine Inspector Smith bellowing at anyone," Connie said.

Angie shrugged. "I seem to bring out the best in him. Anyway, I know my idea won't mess up anything. You can close the store for a couple of hours for a good cause, can't you?"

"I don't know. It's close to Easter and Passover. I'm selling a lot of little gifts."

"Speaking of gifts," Angie said, "I heard someone's been going around the city stealing Fabergé style eggs. You might want to get them out of the window."

"You're kidding. Who'd want to steal such a thing?"

"Nobody knows, but Paavo called me yesterday to ask if they're popular gift items. And I know he's investigating a case where a jewelry store clerk was killed by the robber. The store is one I know, and they kept jeweled knickknacks, like the eggs, along with expensive jewelry. So, I simply put two and two together."

"Oh, no!"

"Oh, yes. Homicide calls it the Easter Egg Murder. Let's carry them in the back, then get out of here. Okay?"

"I give up. Let me move the money to the safe first. Could you lock the door, Angie?" Connie waited by the cash register.

Just as she was swinging the door shut, a strange looking little man, dressed in black clothes, wearing a wig and fake beard, appeared before her, looking very much as if he intended to come into the store. "Sorry, you'll have to come back later," Angie announced, then shut the door in his face and flipped the sign to Closed.

The two women drove in Angie's Ferrari to Tiffany's house where they spent some time going through her closets. Most of the belongings would be given to charity or sold off. Finally, they found the perfect outfit.

An hour later, they went to Tiffany's hairdresser, who was only too happy to oblige despite a salon filled with customers. A very big tip helped.

"Actually," Connie said, looking in the mirror, "I look pretty good, don't I?"

"Very good," Angie said with a critical eye. The light blond color and short, stylish hairdo was a definite improvement over Connie's mousy-brown side part and fringe of bangs. Next, with help from the manicurist who also did make-up, her eyes looked bigger and bluer than ever, and they even managed to contour her cheekbones. Tiffany's red lipstick, her Tiffany's long, dangling earrings, and a pair of spike heels finished the transformation.

"Let's go," Angie said with a burst of excitement. Connie looked uncertainly at her, but nodded.

They started out at City Hall. Up on the second floor, they went to the Mayor's office. The reception area was large and elegant, decorated in an eighteen-century style reminiscent of the White House.

A receptionist smiled pleasantly as Angie approached.

"I need to see the Mayor," Angie announced.

The gray-haired woman reached for her appointment book. "Do you have an appointment?"

"No, but it's very important."

She gazed up at Angie. "What is it regarding?"

"East and West Pakistan."

"Pakistan?" She blinked rapidly several times behind her

bifocals. "There hasn't been an East Pakistan in decades. Haven't you heard of a country called Bangladesh?"

"I know, and that's the problem. I'm part of the Coalition to Reunite All Pakistans. The acronym is unfortunate, but it does not reflect on our cause! Our group believes the City of San Francisco needs to be involved in this. We are the city that knows how! We're in the forefront of *all* important movements, and this, I assure you is a most important movement."

The receptionist stood. "I'm sorry, miss, the Mayor is out."

Angie squared her shoulders and smoothed the front panel of her red Ellen Tracy suit—the kind business women called a power suit. "I'm not leaving until I speak to someone in authority. This means a lot to the people of this city."

The woman frowned, but said, "Let me get the Mayor's executive officer." She disappeared into the side room.

Yes! Angie thought. The XO himself.

Luis Hernandez came out of his office. He was the epitome of charm as he smiled broadly, extending his hand in greeting, his gold Rolex and diamond pinky ring flashing, his expensive Ralph Lauren suit fitted to emphasize each bulging biceps, triceps and deltoid. "Mr. Hernandez," she shouted as they shook hands, "how nice of you to see me."

He halted, surprised at her outburst, and looked around. At just that moment, Connie appeared in the hallway at the entry to the mayor's suite of offices. She turned her back to the door and looked over her shoulder, as if someone had called her, then she continued on, wobbling slightly.

Angie saw Hernandez eye Connie, saw his gaze do a rapid up-down as if admiring her good looks, and then turn back to Angie. He seemed calm and unflustered.

"What can I do for you, Miss, er—?"

"On second thought, maybe Pakistan is better off as two countries. I mean, maybe it's not even a San Francisco issue, although that's hard to imagine. Thanks for your time, Mr. Hernandez."

As he gaped speechlessly at her, Angie hurried out of the office. She grabbed Connie's arm and the two of them hurried away from the Mayor's chambers.

"Nothing at all," Angie said.

"These heels are killing me," Connie said unhappily, as she tottered beside Angie.

They found Lawrence Coglin's office down the hall in the Board of Supervisors chambers. Angie, once again, left Connie in the hallway.

Angie stepped into the office, leaving the door open wide behind her. "Is Supervisor Coglin in?" she asked.

The secretary, a young woman with hair that had been teased and moussed to incredible heights and eyeshadow applied with a trowel gave her a withering look. "Yes, but he's busy at the moment."

"I just want to see him one second to give him this petition." She held up a large manila envelope stuffed with papers.

"I'll see that he gets it." The secretary took hold of the edge of the envelope.

A small tug of war ensued until Angie pulled it back and clutched it to her chest. "I've got to give it to him personally. I represent two thousand constituents. Two thousand *voters*! It'll just take a minute."

"What is it regarding?"

"PG & E."

"Utilities?"

"Does the supervisor want to irritate two thousand voters?"

"All right, one moment."

In a minute Lawrence Coglin himself, all smiles, came out of his office. Tall, with thinning brown hair, bushy eyebrows, wearing horn-rimmed glasses and otherwise nondescript—the sort of man no one would ever notice if he didn't have a title before his name. "Hello, there, I'm Larry Coglin." He swooped down on her and gripped her hand in one of those knuckle-crunching handshakes that politicians seem to think makes them appear sincere rather than boorish.

"I represent the people of the Marina District," Angie said.

"Marina?" He glanced at his secretary, then back to Angie. "My area is the Sunset."

"It is?"

From the side, she saw Connie go into her same routine of slowly walking by, turning her head away from the Supervisor as she looked over her shoulder, then continuing on. Coglin noticed her, but didn't bat an eyelash.

"I thought you were our Supervisor. My mistake. I'm so sorry to have bothered you."

He smiled. "Well, if you ever move, keep me in mind."

"Sure thing!" Angie said, as she backed out of the office then turned and hurried to Connie's side. "These people are either completely cold-blooded and insensitive, or innocent."

"Well, they *are* politicians," Connie said. "Are you sure we want to continue with this?"

"We can't stop now," Angie said, hurrying away from the Board of Supervisors' chambers. "We can forget the Chief of Sanitation. He's on a month-long junket to Paris to observe French public toilets."

Connie followed as best she could in Tiffany's stilettos. The two ran down the long staircase and out the door to the Civic Center parking lot, jumped into the Ferrari and rode the few blocks to the Hall of Justice.

"This is going to be harder," Angie said as she ushered Connie past the metal detectors and into the building.

"Maybe we should just forget it," Connie said. "These guys aren't fools."

"Don't worry," Angie said encouragingly. "Anyway, I think it's a terrific idea. Your lipstick needs a touch-up."

"But it's your idea." Connie obediently took a peek in her compact.

"That's what I mean. Let's go."

They rode to the DA's offices on the third floor. Angie went up to the receptionist. "Is Mr. Lloyd Fletcher in?" she asked.

"I'm sorry, he's in court this afternoon," the lanky black man said politely.

"Court? Which courtroom?"

He checked his calendar. "Courtroom C."

"Which floor is that on?"

"This one. On the opposite side of the building."

Angie and Connie had to walk past the elevators to reach the courtroom. "I don't like this one bit!" Connie whispered fiercely. "I'm sorry, Angie, but I'm leaving." She turned to the elevator bank and hit the down button.

"You can't leave." An elevator bell bonged and the up-arrow lit. "The elevator is going up. You don't want it, anyway." She took hold of Connie's arm and tried to steer her away.

"I'll wait." Connie dug in her heels and tried to pull her arm free. "I'm not going to the courtrooms!"

"You've got to," Angie insisted, tugging at her.

The elevator doors opened as the two battled.

Angie suddenly dropped her arm. There, in the elevator, his mouth open and his eyes bulging, stood Lloyd Fletcher.

Angie gasped.

Connie turned around and stared straight at Fletcher.

The D.A. stared back. The color leeched off his face. As if taking on a will of their own, his eyes slowly went from the stylish short haircut—cut and dyed exactly as Tiffany's had been, to the make-up exactly as Tiffany had worn it, to the form-hugging pink dress that was Tiffany's, to the pink suede pumps, then his eyes jerked back to Connie's face. For a moment, the two women thought he was going to pass out. He mumbled an apology and hurried off the elevator.

Angie and Connie jumped onto it. As soon as the doors closed Angie whispered, "That was *him*! Did you see the expression on his face?"

"Oh, my God." Connie leaned back against the elevator wall, her hand against her heart. "He looked at me as if he'd seen a ghost."

"He looked like a ghost himself! He's the one. He's got to be. My idea worked!" Angie squealed. They looked at each other, shrieked, held hands together and hopped about in a little victory dance. On six, the elevator doors opened. A group of lawyers peered in at the dancing women and decided to wait for the next one.

Angie pushed the button for four. "We're going to go see Paavo," she said. "Right now."

Both Paavo and Yosh were staring as if they couldn't believe their eyes. Seconds before they had been in the midst of the tiresome task of going over, once again, the interviews with Judge St. Clair's neighbors when a commotion burst into the Homicide office. Angie flew in, her face aglow with excitement, made a beeline for Paavo and grabbed his hands. He barely had time to register how beautiful she looked when his attention was caught by the woman tottering behind her on a pair of pink shoes with heels higher than the San Francisco Yellow Pages.

She looked so much like Tiffany Rogers, it was unnerving.

Behind her came the Homicide's administrative aide, trying to grab the wobbling woman, whether to support her or hold her back, he wasn't sure. Angie let go of him and, for some reason, got involved with the other two.

He stared at the blonde and quickly realized two things.

First, that the three women were all talking at once. Second, what Angie had done.

He stood and held his hand up. "Stop!" Miraculously, Homicide's aide let go of the blonde, who he now recognized as Connie Rogers, Angie stopped trying to pull Connie away from that aide, and Connie kicked off her high-heeled shoes.

"Hello, Miss Rogers," Paavo said.

The admin aide looked baffled.

"It's okay, Elizabeth," he told her. She hurried back to the relative sanity of her desk.

"We did it, Paavo!" Angie rushed at him and took hold of his hands again. "I can't believe it, but we did it! We found out—"

"Angie," he interrupted, placing his hand against her back and steering her toward an interview room. "Let's not disturb everyone."

She looked around to see that the four inspectors in the room had stopped work and were staring at her. She smiled hesitantly.

Yosh hurried over to join them.

"Hey there, Angie," he said. "How ya doin'?"

"Top of the world, Yosh."

Yosh carefully took in the other woman. "Connie Rogers," he said, and then his eyes narrowed. "New hair color, I see. New style, too. It looks quite nice."

Connie's cheeks flamed. "Thank you."

The four entered a small, soundproof interview room and shut the door, Paavo and Yosh sat on one side of the metal table, Angie and Connie on the other. Angie had the distinct impression she and Connie were on the wrong side of the table here.

"Lloyd Fletcher," she announced proudly. "He took one look at Connie dressed up this way and I thought he was going to pass out. He's got to have been Tiffany's boyfriend."

"Do you know what's going on, Paavo?" Yosh asked.

Paavo folded his arms. He had to do it—the urge to dole out

corporal punishment for such a childish stunt was overwhelming. "I'm afraid I've got a good idea. You two didn't parade Connie in front of every man whose name began with an L, did you?"

"Why not?" Angie asked. "Anyway, we only had to check out three of them since you insisted the Chief of Police couldn't have been involved and the Sanitation boss is out of town."

There was a short silence then, carefully pronouncing each word, Paavo said, "What do you mean by 'check out'? You can't just go waltzing up to those men and say you want to see them."

"Maybe some people can't," Connie said, then cocked her head toward Angie.

He fought a strong desire to unfold his arms. "Don't explain. I don't want to have to arrest her."

"It was all perfectly legal," Angie assured him. "These men are politicians, after all. Anyway, no one batted an eye but Fletcher. He's our man."

"He's been involved in the Rogers and St. Clair murders because of City Hall. He's seen photos of Tiffany. You might only have seen him reacting to the fact of the resemblance."

Angie rolled her eyes. "No. You and Yosh reacted to the fact of the resemblance. His reaction was much stronger. More... more visceral."

"It's true," Connie said, nodding vigorously. "You wouldn't believe the expression on his face, the way he stared at me. It was creepy."

"They might be onto something," Yosh said. "You can't say Fletcher's been cooperative and Benson told me everyone says he's been acting peculiar lately."

"There you go!" Angie cried. "Now, I've just got to—"

"The man's the District Attorney, Angie," Paavo said firmly. "You've got to do nothing, and *especially* do nothing that might cause him to realize you two set him up."

"I know, I know. It's police business."

"That's right. I'll talk to him."

"Talk? There's got to be a better way," Angie said. "I mean, what could you say? 'Seen any dead girlfriends lately?'"

Connie winced.

Angie was horror-struck. "Oh, Connie, I'm so sorry! I didn't mean to be so disrespectful."

"It's okay, Angie. At least *you're* trying to be helpful."

Angie saw Paavo's and Yosh's irritation at Connie's slap at the police. At times, even *she* recognized when she'd gone too far. "Let's go, Connie." She grabbed Connie's arm and hustled her out of there. "See you around, fellas."

29

He ducked behind the Volvo wagon parked on the Jones Street hill as a car drove by, its headlights sweeping the area before it. The nearest parking he could find for his green Honda was a red zone two blocks away.

He didn't want anyone to see him there, outside the garage to the apartment building where Angelina Amalfi lived. The garage door was locked, but all he needed was for one person to come home. Just one. That person would use a remote control to open the door, and he'd slip in before the garage door shut again.

He'd tried to rig up his remote to open the door, like he did at the judge's house, but this security system was much more sophisticated. It'd be a chore to break, and why take the time when this way was so easy? Tenants were careless. A good reason to take advantage of them.

He'd already waited there two hours, ever since midnight, for someone to drive into the building. The fog had come in and the air was damp, but he wasn't cold. His body felt neither warmth nor cold, he was beyond such mundane things.

If no one came home tonight, he'd be back tomorrow. What did a day or two matter?

He ducked again as another car turned onto Jones Street and started up the hill. This one slowed. When it reached the garage, it turned onto the driveway. He scrunched down further behind the Volvo, waiting. He heard the garage door squeal open. To his surprise, the area became flooded with light as the garage's interior lights came on—a safety precaution. In a moment, he heard the revving of the car's engine as it moved slowly into the garage.

He hurled himself forward, against the outside wall of the building, hoping the shadows would keep him hidden. Crouching as low as he could, he darted through the opening, flattened himself against the inside wall, then scrambled quietly for a dark corner, out of the garage lighting.

He waited. The garage door stayed open for what seemed like an eternity until, finally, he heard it rumble and emit a high-pitched squeal until it shut with a thud. The people who'd driven into the garage, a man and a woman, got out of the car and walked to the elevator. He watched the man insert a key into the elevator, then the two of them got on.

The elevator, too, was secure. No problem. He didn't like elevators—he'd had enough of being trapped in a cage to last a lifetime. He'd take the stairs. She lived on twelve, but he could make it up that high easily. He'd worked out in prison, knowing the day would come when he'd have to rely on his strength, his body, to get him what he wanted. He went in the ultimate nerd: brainy, skinny and a wimp. He came out buffed up, handsome, and even more brilliant than before. A laugh bubbled up inside him. He loved irony.

When all was quiet, he took out his keychain flashlight and went to the car that just drove in, used a jimmy to unlock the door and then lifted the remote control opener off the visor.

That was to make it easier if he ever had to come back. It was cold out there on the street.

He then searched for the door to the stairs. He found it, just a little ahead. Someone had even stenciled "S-T-I-A-R-S" on it. Thoughtful, if illiterate.

Gripping the doorknob, he turned it. It didn't open. He tried again. The door was locked.

He looked around, flashing his small light at the walls, floor, ceiling. These people thought they were so clever, making the garage secure. But that meant everyone in this building who used the garage had to always remember their elevator key, or the key to the stairwell. If they didn't, there was a phone so they could get the doorman from upstairs to come down and let them in. How many people, though, would want to call and make themselves feel foolish? How many....

He spotted a tall cigarette tray in front of the elevator, a metal cylinder with a bowl of sand on the top. The elevator was probably a "no smoking" zone. Now, if some clever resident, knowing that not everyone remembered all their keys all the time...

He tipped the ashtray and flashed his light on the ground underneath it. He didn't see anything at first and was ready to give up when the glint of metal against the gray concrete floor caught his eye. Sure enough, it was a key.

He snatched it up. But he had his doubts about using the elevator. If someone else got on, he couldn't explain his presence, and would have to kill the person. But how many people would be riding the elevator at two a.m.?

His heart pounding, he got on and pushed the button for twelve. As the door clanged shut, his body broke out in a sudden, cold sweat. He kept his finger on the "Close Door" button, in hopes that would trigger the mechanism to keep the doors shut and travel non-stop to twelve. The elevator lurched, then started climbing.

He reached under his jacket, and his hand closed around the handle of the combat knife as the elevator neared the lobby. This would be the most likely spot for someone else to get on.

He kept his eyes, without blinking, on the floor indicator. The lobby light was lit... would it stop?... then the 2 light came on. He breathed easier.

3... 4... 5...

No one would be going between floors this time of night. He was home free.

6... 7... 8...

The elevator lurched to a stop. He stared at the floor indicator: 9. What was going on?

The doors open and a small child, wearing pajamas with little cowboys on ponies, stared up at him.

What the hell? His teeth gritted and his fingers tightened on the knife.

"Tommy!" A woman's voice shrieked. "Tommy, baby, what are you doing out of bed? Don't you dare get on there!"

He tried to make himself small, pressing his shoulder hard against the side, where the woman couldn't see him. His heart raced. If the kid got on and then his mother, he'd do what he had to. He couldn't have witnesses. But then he'd have to be fast with the Amalfi woman, which was too bad. He had planned to take his time with her, to enjoy her first. He scowled as hard as he could at the boy and in a deep, hushed whisper, said "Boo!"

Tommy's eyes widened, and he turned and ran to his mother.

He punched the close door button over and over until the doors finally shut. He leaned back against the wall, trying to breathe and get his heart back in his chest.

On twelve, the doors opened.

The hallway was well lit. There were only two doors on the floor. 1201 and 1202. He turned toward 1202.

This would be the hardest part of the whole thing. If Angelina had a normal apartment door lock, he'd be able to get inside in about a minute with his credit card. If not, he'd have to try to get the door pick to work. He'd had it explained to him time and again in prison, and had practiced a lot, but it took a calm, cool hand. He would have been fine, except for that damn kid. Now his nerves were shot to hell.

He took out a plastic card and slid it between the door and the jamb. Holding it almost sideways, he shoved it in further, so that it bent around the door, then angled it downward until it touched the latch. Carefully, he worked the card until the latch caught. At the click of the door's latch, and he gave it a little push. The door opened.

The apartment was pitch black. He stood by the door, listening for any noise over the sound of his heartbeat and his own heavy breathing.

He thought again of the woman he'd held in his arms on the dance floor.

He'd make her his own tonight. Before he killed her. He remembered lying atop the old woman as she'd struggled. How he'd reacted to the friction of her body against his. Just the thought of what he'd almost done with her had made him throw up later that day.

With Angelina, though, it'd all be different. She wanted him. She'd smiled at him. Even at the restaurant, she'd smiled and been friendly. He'd saved himself for her, just as he'd once saved himself for Heather.

As his eyes adjusted to the darkness, he could see a few shadows in front of him. He eased forward, expecting to find a chair or table blocking his path. Since the apartment remained quiet, he took out his flashlight and flicked it on, and gave the room a quick perusal.

The sight of his bouquet of roses on her coffee table

brought a smile to his lips. He picked one up, gently lifted it to his nose, then smiling, ripped the petals from the stem.

He tossed the rose aside when he spotted the cell phone on the coffee table. He shut it off.

The kitchen was to the left of the living room, and just beyond it had to be her bedroom. He shut off the flashlight and headed for the room.

The air in Angelina's apartment didn't smell the way he'd expected. There was a staleness, a masculinity to it. That had to mean she spent even more time than he thought entertaining men.

Now it was his turn to be entertained.

He stood in the bedroom, trying to make out her figure in the darkness. He inched toward the bed. What if she had her fiancé with her?

He hadn't thought of that before. That would change all his plans.

He saw the form of one person, only, on the bed. He smiled.

As he watched, thinking about her, he felt himself grow hard and relished the power it gave him. He knew exactly what he was going to do.

Still holding his knife, he went to the bedside. Feeling for the edge of the covers, he slowly eased them back. She lay on her side, facing away from him. Stretching his hand out, he let just one finger lightly touch her shoulder. He'd expected the feel of a nightgown, some lacy, fancy thing. Instead he felt bare skin. It shocked, yet thrilled him and he snatched his hand back.

He lowered his zipper slowly, the metal teeth sounding as loud as machine gun fire in the quiet apartment. She didn't stir. Then, clutching the knife tight, he placed one knee on the bed, leaned over her. "Don't move," he whispered as he then pressed his hand to her face concentrating in the darkness on finding her mouth, stopping her screams.

But her face was too big... too scratchy... even bristly...

He yanked back his hand.

"What the—?" a masculine voice cried.

He slammed the knife down onto the man.

The man screeched, arms and legs flailing in a tangle of bed sheets. He stabbed again, and the man gasped, then fell silent.

30

The first thing Paavo saw as he stepped off the elevator was the pool of blood on the plush carpet between Angie's and Stan's apartments. Angie had phoned him and told him someone had broken into Stan's apartment and stabbed him. Stan had managed to call 911 and then crawl across the hall and knock until she opened the door. Paramedics and the police were with him.

Both apartment doors stood open. Paavo's heart contracted painfully at how close such horror had come to Angie's quiet, elegant home. He glanced quickly into Stan's apartment. A patrolman had secured it until the Crime Scene Investigators and the Crimes Against Persons Detail arrived. He looked over the apartment, at the trail of blood from the bedroom to the front door and into the hall. Then his gaze fixed on a rose petal lying on the ground, and to the bouquet on Stan's coffee table.

He went cold. Roses. Another knife attack and roses. But this time... a man was attacked? It didn't make sense.

He glanced over the room quickly once more. Robbery didn't seem to be the motive here. His eyes returned to the roses. Could it be a coincidence? Lots of people had roses, after all. Deep inside something told him, no, this was no coincidence. But then, what was it?

He hurried into Angie's apartment. She was speaking quietly with a patrolman. Her hands, arms and face were bloodied. Although he knew she hadn't been hurt and that the blood had to be Stan's, seeing her that way made his legs feel like jelly. He had to reach her, to hold her, but each step seemed to take forever. She turned, and their gazes met.

In a moment, she was in his arms and he held her tight against his chest. He saw no tears, but her face wore a scared, hollow look that tore at him.

The patrolman walked up to Paavo, ready to question him when he pulled out his badge. "Smith, Homicide."

"Gribbs. Central." The policeman gave a questioning glance from Paavo to Angie and stepped back.

"Are you okay?" Paavo asked Angie, even as he ran his hands over her to assure himself that she was.

She nodded, then took a deep breath. "I was asleep when I heard a loud banging on my door." She shivered and Paavo helped her to the sofa. "I looked out the peephole, but couldn't see anything, then I heard someone moan. It was Stan, Paavo." Her voice broke. "It was awful." She put her face in her shaking hands. Paavo hugged her closer.

He looked at Gribbs. "Did you see the wounds?"

Gribbs nodded. "The cuts looked pretty deep. High, on his shoulders, front and back."

"I've got to go to the hospital," Angie said, then glanced down at her blood-stained bathrobe. "I've got to get dressed."

Paavo helped her walk toward the bedroom. Her legs were wobbly as her adrenalin diminished and the shock of finding her friend that way began to settle in. "I'll drive you there when you're ready," he said.

"Paavo, do you think that patrolman will let you into Stan's apartment? I need to find his parents' phone number. Hopefully, he's got it written down somewhere and not just on his phone."

"I'll see what I can do."

"Why, Paavo?" she looked up at him.

"Why?"

"Why would anyone want to hurt Stan?"

While Angie dressed, Paavo phoned Yosh and asked him to get over to Stan's apartment. It wasn't a homicide, yet, but it was connected to the two they already had. He'd stake his life on it.

He then put on gloves and hurried to find Stan's parents' phone number. A cancelled check from his father—a generous check—had it. He told the uniform guarding the crime scene that Inspector Yoshiwara would be on his way to take over the investigation.

Once Angie and Paavo arrived San Francisco General, Stan was already in surgery and they were directed to the waiting area. As they sat and waited for the doctor to let them know how Stan came out of the surgery, Angie gradually calmed down and Paavo asked the question he'd been wondering about since his quick glance in Stan's apartment.

"Did Stan tell you who gave him the roses?" Paavo asked.

"Roses? I didn't know he had any."

"Okay."

"Is it important?" Her brow was scrunched with worry.

"It's nothing." He kissed her forehead as she rested her head on his shoulder. She was exhausted by the whole experience, physically as well as emotionally. He'd ask her more about the roses later, when she was more focused.

It was seven a.m. before they got word that Stan was out of surgery and in intensive care. He'd lost a lot of blood, but nothing vital had been hit. With any luck, the prognosis was excellent, but he wouldn't be in any condition to talk to anyone for a day or two.

Paavo brought Angie back to his house. She was exhausted and could sleep there while he went to work. Something was going on that was very, very wrong, and much too close to Angie to suit him. He worried about her being alone in her apartment, and couldn't help but wonder if the attack on Stan had been anything to do with Angie walking around with a Tiffany Rogers look-alike. But that didn't make any sense. Or, did it?

31

Angie sat at a table in Wings of An Angel, drinking a cup of coffee and trying to pull herself together after the horrible night she'd had. Paavo had left for work before she woke up and had left a note telling her to stay in his house and wait for him. But thoughts of Stan plagued her, and she decided she needed to think about something other than being frightened.

She vaguely recalled Paavo's question at the hospital about roses, but everything had been in such a muddle she wasn't sure. Still, even today, she didn't remember Stan mentioning roses, although it seems he had said something about a strange delivery man. What was it? *When* was it?

A customer walked in—the man with the weird hair, lop-sided glasses and the puppy-dog eyes she'd met a couple of days earlier. Earl showed him to a nearby table.

"You're crying." Puppy-dog eyes stopped as he passed her, his voice soft. "Is there anything I can do? Anything I can get you? Some water, perhaps?"

She shook her head. "I'll be fine. Thanks."

Earl pulled out a chair and waited impatiently until the

customer sat. But as soon as Earl left the table, the stranger immediately turned in his chair and faced her again. "Would you like to talk about it?"

She wiped her eyes with her handkerchief and shook her head.

"I'm sorry." He folded his hands. "I didn't mean to pry."

"You didn't really," she said. "A friend of mine was... was hurt last night. He's in the hospital."

"How terrible! I'm so sorry. Will he be all right?"

"The doctors say so."

"Was it an accident?"

She sat up straight in the chair. The man was probably simply trying to be nice, but there was something about him she didn't care for. "No. He was attacked by someone. Some monster of a human being."

His eyes showed surprise. "Maybe it was a mistake?"

"I don't care what it was. Whoever did it was evil, horrible!"

He reached for his water glass.

"Miss Angie," Earl stepped up to her with a piece of pound cake. "Me an' Butch was hopin' dis might make you feel a little better. It's to go wit' your coffee. I tol' him how your friend was hurt an' dat you went up to da church dis mornin'. He said you was a good woman."

"I don't know about that, but thank you both. You're very thoughtful."

"You must be a regular here," the customer said, interrupting again. "Miss ... Angie, is it?"

Earl stepped between the two tables. "Miss Angie don't wanna be distoibed. Is dere somet'in' you wanna eat or not?"

"Uh, yes. I do."

Earl handed him a menu. "I'd recommend da spaghetti an' meatballs."

The stranger handed the menu back. "Fine."

Once Earl was back in the kitchen, the stranger smiled at her. "My name's Carter, by the way."

She nodded and went back to reading the newspaper she'd brought in with her. *The North Beach Shopper* was new, a local advertiser that was given away door to door and left on sidewalk racks. She wondered if they would be interested in having a food column.

"I see you reading a neighborhood paper. I live near here myself," Carter added. "It's sure nice to have an inexpensive restaurant nearby."

"Yes, it is." She tasted the pound cake. As she suspected, straight from a grocery store shelf to her plate. Well, at least Butch and Earl had tried. She'd come here for nothing more than to spend a moment pulling herself together before calling Paavo and telling him that she was doing fine and was going back to her apartment. The attack on Stan had affected her deeply, but she understood that Paavo needed to concentrate on his cases and couldn't do it if he felt he'd have to hurry home to play nursemaid to her. The attack wasn't on *her*, after all. She had to get over the shock of Stan being attacked. It was just that there were people in this world you never expect anything bad to happen to. Stan was one of them.

"Do you live nearby, Angie?" Carter interrupted again. "You seem to come here a lot."

"Not far."

"Maybe we're neighbors?" He gave her another of his puppy-dog smiles, yet his eyes had a hardness to them, a knowing glint at odds with the affable slackness of his mouth and jowls.

Something about the shape of his lips, the tone of his voice as he said her name was disarmingly familiar. Why? Where could she have met him previously?

They'd talked here once before. That must be what she was

remembering. She tried to shake off the sudden uneasiness she felt.

"I know all my neighbors," she said, making it clear the subject was closed.

"Oh, but..." He glanced past her, then turned around, suddenly finding the need to study his cutlery.

Peering over her shoulder, she followed his gaze to see Earl frowning fiercely at Carter. Earl walked over to her. "Miss Angie, I t'ink Butch could use a little help," he cocked his head toward Carter, "if you'd like to come back into da kitchen."

"I'd love to."

"Just in time," Butch said as she entered. He stood over a large kettle with a wooden spoon. "I'm tryin' some polenta like you suggested."

Angie looked at the huge pot of golden polenta. He'd made enough to feed half of Italy. "Good. We'll use just a small batch of it to start. Did you roast any peppers?"

"They're in the oven right now."

Angie opened the oven door and found six large Fresno chilies. They had softened nicely. She took them out and easily peeled off the hard, outer skin.

"You don't hafta let dat guy bug you none," Earl said, dishing out some spaghetti and meatballs.

"I don't want to be rude to your customers, Oil."

"What oil?" Butch asked.

"Him." Angie pointed.

"Earl?" Butch asked.

"Earl?" Angie repeated.

"Yeah, Oil," Earl said. "You was pronouncin' it jus' right, Miss Angie."

She nodded. "Ah. I see. Anyway, I can handle that guy Carter."

"He's a bad egg, Miss Angie." Earl stated. "You keep away from him when I ain't around to look after you, okay?"

Butch hurled himself at the back door. "'Ey, Vinnie, get up here quick," he yelled. "You gotta come hear this!"

"Who's Vinnie?" Angie asked, stirring the polenta. "And why is he in the basement?"

"Yeah, Butch," Earl said. "You're so smart, tell da lady what's he doin' in da basement."

"It, uh," Butch looked at the door to the basement then back at Angie, "it ain't a basement. It's an apartment. We stay down there to save money on rent."

"Oh? How clever. Restaurants are expensive to start up, that's for sure."

"What's all the yellin'?" Vinnie stepped into the kitchen.

"This is the Fed we was tellin' you about," Butch said. "Angelina Amalfi, meet Vinnie Freiman."

Vinnie frowned as they shook hands. "You called me to meet a Fed? Thanks, Butch. Just what I always wanted to do."

"Yeah, well, wait 'til you hear Earl. He's protectin' her from the other customers."

"Yeah?" Vinnie looked from Earl to Angie. "But if she's a Fed, maybe the other customers need protection from her?"

"I just don't like da looksa dat guy," Earl protested.

Angie mixed the pepper and polenta in a bowl. "You think he's some kind of crook?"

"Takes one to know one," Butch muttered, whereupon Vinnie stomped on his foot. Butch yelped.

Earl poured a glass of red wine and put it on the tray he was preparing.

"So," Vinnie said to Angie, "you teachin' Butch here how to cook?"

"I know how!" Butch grumbled.

"He's not bad," Angie said. She put some of her polenta and pepper on a plate, heaped grated Romano cheese on top, then spooned some of Butch's special spaghetti sauce over it and handed the plate to Vinnie. "Try it."

He took a spoonful. "Hey, this is good."

"What a screwball! Didn't I tell you dat guy's no good?" Earl came back into the kitchen, the tray still full of food. "Here I do all dis woik an' he takes off wit'out eatin'. He shoulda tol' me he was tired a waitin'."

Paavo walked into Homicide and tossed his notebook on his desk. Frustration was evident in every step he took.

"I guess it didn't go so well," Yosh said.

"No. St. Clair couldn't pick out anyone in the mug shots who resembled the guy he'd seen outside his place. We doubted he could. Sometimes I don't like being right."

"I'm not having any luck either," Yosh said. "The car registration form, listing the dead guy as the owner, was filled out a few weeks ago in San Francisco. We tried to lift prints off the form, but it's been through too many hands. A handwriting analyst is looking over the writing, for whatever that's supposed to be worth."

"It'll give the Chief something to say at the next briefing, 'Police bring in handwriting expert to help solve vicious murders.' Why does the public think some quack can do it better than us?"

"Because superstition is easier than hard work."

"Good point."

Paavo picked up the drawing the police artist did based on St. Clair's description. There were no distinctive features shown —only a baseball cap shading the eyes, aviator sunglasses to cover the cheekbones, a straight nose, full lips, and a heavy jaw.

The guy was apparently around six feet, muscular arms and shoulders, but slim waist and hips. Sounded like someone who worked out.

He could stop by a few gyms and pass around the artist's sketch. A long shot, but maybe worth a try. There were a lot of those places, though. And would someone with such a clunker of a car have money for expensive gyms?

He could concentrate on inexpensive ones. Start with the Y, maybe? Where else? Heck, the cheapest places he knew of with workout equipment were prisons.

Prisons. An ex-con? Hanging around a judge's house, attacking a judge's wife? Possible. Very possible, in fact.

What if Angie was right about the D.A.? Fletcher and Tiffany's boss, Supervisor Wainwright, were friends—Paavo saw them at The Court House bar together. And Tiffany got the job through "connections." A judge and a D.A. Interesting. Could there have been some trial, some case, they were both involved in?

But it wasn't the D.A. or the judge who were killed. It was their women. Was that the connection? Or, was it a coincidence?

Damn. Much as he hated to think it, right now, a criminal case, a trial, was an obvious connection—if one existed—with the two men. He didn't have anything else to go on. And he never did like coincidences.

He tried reaching Angie again. When she didn't answer her cell phone, he called her landline. No answer. Where could she have gone? And would she tell him this time where she'd gone, or would she give him more of her mysterious non-answers?

He tried the hospital. Stan hadn't awakened yet.

Paavo put down the phone in frustration. It was going to be another one of those days.

Myron Liu had worked in the computer center at the Hall of Justice for nineteen years, starting as a clerk and working his way up to the prime programmer in the department. He should have been made supervisor last month. Instead, he was passed over, again. This time for a woman brought in from San Francisco State University who didn't even know the police administration's computer system. He was sick and tired of it.

He watched Homicide Inspector Smith walk into their shop. He rose from his desk to help, when Ms. Smart-stuff stood up and gave him a look that told him to sit the hell back down and get to work.

He'd been helping Homicide for fifteen years. No one was better at filling their requests than him. Now, she was going to cut him out of this part of his job as well. What was up? Did they want to fire him?

He kept his head down as Smart-stuff came up to him a couple of minutes later.

"Here's a request from Homicide that I want you to get right on." She slapped a form on his desk. "I want a computer printout of every case that Judge Lucas St. Clair and attorney Lloyd Fletcher were involved in together."

"When Lloyd Fletcher was D.A. or even before that?" Liu asked.

"I said *all* of them, didn't I?"

He nodded. "You want complete SF records?"

"I want it as complete as you can make it!"

He lowered his gaze once more. "Really? As complete as that?"

"You *do* understand English, don't you?"

His cheeks burned. "I'll start the search immediately."

"Good."

Clenching his teeth to stop himself from telling his boss exactly what he thought of her, he began the development of a search program that accessed court databases throughout California, from tiny Yolo County, to the City and County of Los Angeles.

He looked over what he'd done. On second thought, she'd said she wanted it as complete as he could make it. He changed "California" to "U.S." Yes, Ms. Smart-stuff, he thought, I *do* understand English. I can make this search very complete indeed. He just hoped Inspector Smith wasn't in too much of a hurry.

32

"I'm sorry, Mindy," Angie said. "I didn't think you'd be so busy at seven-thirty at night."

She sat in the living room of Mindy Dunleavy, one of her closest friends in high school. Mindy dropped onto the sofa after putting the kids to bed. "Sorry about that interruption," Mindy said, "but I don't get the kids down early, I don't have any time to myself. They won't go to sleep yet, but at least they're in their rooms and not underfoot."

"This way, you have adult time for you and Collin, right?"

Mindy looked at her and gave a wry grin. "Yeah, right."

"Do you expect him home soon?"

"He is home. He's down in his 'man cave' watching TV. Or sleeping. Why? Did you want to see him about something?"

Angie tried not to show her surprise. Mindy and Collin had been inseparable in high school and married shortly afterward. Angie and had always thought of them as the perfect couple.

"No, not at all. I'm here to see you."

"I'm sorry." Mindy said, pushing her curly hair back from her face. "I don't know what got into me. What was it you wanted me to help you with?"

"Well..." Angie cleared her throat, suddenly having her doubts whether this was the right time to ask her questions.

"Yes?"

"I'm curious about marriage, and that made me think of you and Collin. You two were always so much alike, with a lot in common. It made me wonder if that's a key to a happy marriage?"

Mindy gave a hollow laugh. "Me and Collin?"

"Yes."

She scrunched her face, thinking. "I guess we were alike, weren't we? We shared everything once."

"Exactly. Isn't that important?"

"I don't know, Angie. For the last few years, we've seemed to grow more and more apart. Without shared interests, there isn't much else between us."

Angie was shocked to hear that. "I'm sorry. I didn't realize."

"Oh well, we might work it out. Who knows? There are times that marriage is really good—even mine and Collin's." She glanced at the clock on the mantle, ticking the minutes by. "But there are other times, Angie, think of it this way: the kids are in bed, the house is quiet, and your husband isn't paying any attention to you. That's when you feel the need to get out. To feel alive again. I mean, here, I cook, clean, and keep the house. It gets really boring sometimes, you know? Actually, pretty much all the time."

"I can imagine," Angie said sadly, as a mounting despair over what Mindy was really saying hit her.

"Sometimes, I need to go out. Alone, you know? There's got to be more to life than these four walls." Then she gave Angie a sly smiled. "And sometimes, there is."

33

Angie was skittish as a feral cat, Paavo thought. From the time he picked her up at her apartment to go to the hospital to see Stan, she'd been giving him sidelong glances and other strange looks.

Usually, Angie's thoughts and emotions were shown in her eyes clearer than on any bulletin board. He'd gotten used to those big, brown eyes looking at him with openness and love. It felt strange after the unconcealed wish-you'd-drop-dead glares he got every day doing his job, but welcome.

Now, though, Angie seemed subdued—for her—around him, almost wary, uneasy, and he didn't know why. She had tried to talk about their relationship the night he had dinner at her apartment and the phone call from Yosh stopped her. She hadn't brought it up again. That worried him. Was this the beginning of the end? He hated the way his stomach clenched when he thought that, hated how bleak the prospect was of days ahead without her to brighten them.

He found himself studying her almost as intently as she studied him.

He wasn't sure where he'd gone wrong with her. No, that wasn't true. In fact, he was quite sure where. Too much work. Not enough time for her. Maybe he hadn't told her clearly enough how he felt about her. Hell, before he'd met her, he'd never told anyone at all. Even saying as little as he did, had been difficult for him. To say he *thought* he might be falling in love with her, which he figured could be what he was feeling, had been to him, a big step.

And so he watched her drift away from him, not in the way she acted, but emotionally.

He should have known better than to care. The bigger fool, he.

They reached the hospital.

Stan was still groggy from the attack, the operation and the massive doses of pain killers he'd been given.

"Angie," he whispered, his mouth twisting into an anesthetized half-smile. "Thank you."

"Thank God I was home, Stan." She kissed his cheek and took his hand in hers.

Could it be Stan? Paavo wondered, watching the two of them gaze at each other. She'd always admitted to being fond of him. They even went dancing the other night. She'd said it hadn't meant anything, but maybe, on reflection, it had meant a lot more than she'd wanted to admit, perhaps not even to herself.

He took in Stan's flat, dull, boring expression as the two of them talked. She couldn't possibly be in love with Stan. He couldn't have misjudged her—or Stan—so completely. Could he?

"Paavo is in charge of the investigation," Angie had said.

"Homicide? Was I killed?" His eyes were half-shut. "I feel like I was."

Paavo could see he was in no shape to answer many questions yet, but he had to try.

"Bonnette, your attack was similar to that on two women who were murdered," Paavo said. "Do you understand what I said?"

"Yes. I think," Stan murmured.

"A judge's wife and a City Hall secretary. Did you hear of those murders?"

"Hear? I don't... remember."

"Tiffany Rogers," Angie added helpfully.

"Tiffany Rogers and Velma St. Clair," Paavo said. "Do you know either woman? Have you heard of them?"

"I don't think so," Stan shut his eyes. "I can't seem to remember..."

"Stan, think now," Paavo enunciated carefully. "Pay attention. Do the names Lucas St. Clair, Judge Lucas St. Clair, or District Attorney Lloyd Fletcher mean anything to you?"

Angie caught Paavo's eye at the mention of Fletcher's name. As she realized he had accepted her theory she gave him a brilliant smile, looking so much like the Angie he knew and loved, he felt a mixture of hope yet despair at all he might be losing.

He forced his attention back to Stan, but Stan was sound asleep.

Angie sat at a table by the window of Wings Of An Angel, reading her script for the TV show she would audition for the next day. Thank goodness they'd finally called her. After all, she might have had other irons in the fire if they'd waited much longer, something a lot better than a show on a predominately Farsi station, too. On the other hand, considering the butterflies in her stomach with this audition, if it were any bigger, they'd have to carry her out to the TV cameras on a stretcher.

"I was hoping I'd find you here again."

A shadow fell across her script and she looked up to see

Carter standing in front of her. "Oh, it's you," she said. Earl's warning rang in her ear.

"It's good to see you again, Angie." He slid his hands in his back pockets. "You make this restaurant special."

Earl ran up to Carter. "You back? You gonna stick around dis time and eat?"

"I intend to."

"We don't like guys who order food den skip out on us. Dat's a warnin', bud. You can sit over dere."

"Oh..., well..." He looked expectantly from Angie to the empty chair at her table and back, but when no invitation was forthcoming, he went with Earl to the next table.

Two other tables had customers, two women at one and a man at the other. Angie was glad to see that a few other people had begun to discover the restaurant. She had brought in some lace curtains she no longer used and helped Earl hang them this morning before the place opened. They added a nice touch. She also gave him a brochure from a restaurant supply house for some red and white checkered tablecloths and red napkins, and suggested old-fashioned wooden chairs to replace the aluminum ones. The 'fifties decor just didn't work for her at all.

Earl took Carter's order, then stopped at Angie's table on his way to the kitchen. "I forgot to ask, how's your friend doin', Miss Angie? Da one who got stabbed."

"Much better. Thanks, Earl."

"He know who stabbed him?"

"I don't think he ever saw the man."

"Yeah? Dat's too bad. You call da police about it?"

"Of course!"

"Yeah, I shoulda figgered dat. Dey know anyt'in' about it?"

"Not yet. Actually, my boyfriend's got the case. He's a homicide inspector."

"I didn't know your boyfriend was a cop. A cop and a Fed. Man, you two must have to follow laws about kissin'."

"Not quite," Angie said with a laugh.

"So, what's homicide doin' wit' a stabbin'?"

"It's similar to a couple of other big cases he's got."

"Busy guy, huh? Guess you don't see him much."

"Not only that, he's got a third case, too. One where someone's been going around the city stealing faux Fabergé eggs. In one robbery, a clerk was killed. You better warn the jeweler next door to you if he's selling those eggs."

"Man, someone got killed 'cause of some kinda egg? What's dis world comin' to? I gotta tell Butch. He's got a dozen of them."

"Wait," she called him back. "It's an art piece shaped like an egg. Some of them open up and there are delicate porcelain figures or jewels inside."

"Yeah? People buy dose t'ings?"

"They certainly do. A friend of mine works in a shop that sells them. I was thinking that she and I should make a prominent display of a bunch of them, then hide in the back room, and when someone tried to steal them, we'd call Paavo to make the arrest."

"Sounds kinda dangerous, Miss Angie, for a couple gals."

"Not if you join us, Earl," she said, teasing him. His expression, though, remained serious.

"I don't t'ink so. But I'll ask Vinnie. He's got da brains in da gang—I mean, group."

She noticed the man sitting alone suddenly took a pager off his belt, looked at it, then stood, tossed money on the table and hurried away.

"I was joking, Earl," Angie said as she watched the man with the pager. She guessed he was a doctor or something, since they were about the only ones who still used pagers. "You know, I think that's what we need. A silent pager. We need to put bugs inside a bunch of those eggs. Then, when the thief strikes, we could get it to beep silently and follow him to his hiding place—if they work that way. We'd catch him."

"Dat's a good idea. Maybe you oughta be a crook."

Angie's eyebrows rose at that comment. Then, she turned back to her latest idea. "Only problem would be where to get such devices."

"Excuse me," Carter called, sliding his chair a bit closer to Angie's table. "I couldn't help but overhear a bit of your conversation. I'm a licensed electrician and I know some people who've been developing a prototype of a device very similar to what you're talking about."

Angie didn't like eavesdroppers, even if they might be helpful ones. It seemed a little too convenient, and this guy a little too pushy, to suit her. "That's all right. We're just speculating here."

"It's a very sound idea, you know."

Sound? What was he? A punster?

"I can see your skepticism," he said hurriedly. "But I really do know what I'm talking about, and I can access a lot of items not generally available. Take this." He reached into his shirt pocket, pulled out a small plastic case and opened it. Inside was a tiny metal chip that looked like a wristwatch battery. "It might not look like much, but with it, I can break into very sophisticated voice and text messaging systems—and can make copies of every text, email and even faxes being sent to the number I'm tapped into."

"You can?" Angie studied the chip, unsure if she ought to believe him or not. But why would he lie about such a thing?

"It's easy once you figure out how to do it. "

"Dere's always guys wit' big ideas, Miss Angie. You can't trust 'em."

Carter ignored Earl and kept right on talking. "There's another device that works like a reverse paging system. I install them in luxury cars all the time. They can also be used in dogs, cats, even kids, although we don't do any of that yet. Suppose your car is stolen, or your child is kidnapped. You follow the beep, which is silent since you don't want to alert the thief or kidnapper, and it'll lead you to it."

Angie thought she might have heard about something like he was describing. "That's impressive," she said.

"My friends are working on a microchip that does the same thing. The chips should go for about a hundred dollars a pop."

"That's all?"

"The biggest part of the cost with cars is the installation. You don't want anything a thief can see and easily remove. Also, the ones for cars are a lot more powerful than the one I'm talking about for you. They're good for hundreds of miles. These microchips, on the other hand, have a radius of about ten miles. But that could cover going from the place where stolen to a fence who'll pay cash for them inside the city."

"Interesting."

"Yeah, until da car t'iefs and dose udders figger out howta break da signal."

"But in the meantime, Earl," Angie said, her mind racing with possibilities, "I wouldn't mind learning a little more about them."

"By the way, waiter," Carter said, now moving his chair to Angie's table, "I'd like another glass of wine."

———

"Dat guy's gotta go," Earl muttered, pouring some house wine into a glass.

"What guy's that?" Butch asked, checking on the Italian

sausage he was now offering with spaghetti, polenta, or in a sandwich.

"Da one always hangin' around Angie. He's back."

"I think *you* wanna be the only one hangin' around her," Butch said. "She even has you puttin' up lace curtains like some little househusband. You two was really cute this mornin'." He snorted with laughter.

"Where's Vinnie? He downstairs?"

"Naw. Now she's got him buyin' chairs an' tablecloths. He's afraid she'll get suspicious if he don't. He don't want no suspicious Feds now that we're so close."

"We're close, huh?" Earl asked, turning a hang-dog gaze on Butch.

"Yeah. Tonight might do it." Butch kept his head bowed, not wanting to look at his partner. He checked on his sausages. Angie taught him to fry them in water instead of oil to make them less greasy. They were browning nicely. His mouth down-turned, his voice low. "It'll be nice to not have so much work to do alla time. Just sit around and count our money."

Earl's bottom lip pushed out, his eyes downcast even as he nodded. "Yeah. I'm really lookin' forward to it." Earl pushed the swinging door open a little way and eyed Angie talking with Carter. He shook his head and faced his friend again. "You, too, Butch?"

Butch raised his chin. "Sure. Me, too. Why not?" He swallowed hard and looked around his kitchen. "You don't think I care about this place, do you?"

"Heck no, Butch. Me, neither."

"I don't think this is something you should get involved in, Angie," Connie Rogers' worried frown annoyed Angie. Her plan was perfectly safe.

"I'm not getting involved. It's a test, that's all." She moved the miniature glass swan to the back of the display counter and the turtle to the front. Swans were out this season. "He's an electrician. He knows about such things. Tomorrow, I'm meeting him at the restaurant and buying one from him."

"But what if it doesn't work?"

"Then I'm out a hundred dollars and feeling duped. It won't be the first time," she answered. "Anyway, I want to buy another of your faux Fabergé eggs, but I'll leave it here in your shop. As soon as I get the device, I'll put it in my egg. Then, you bring it to your apartment when you leave the shop at night and I'll try to track its movement from my place. Since I don't know where you live, it'll be a great test. Then, if it works, I'll tell Paavo. The police can bug about five or ten eggs in the city, and take all the others out of the stores, and when the thief strikes, they'll follow the beeper and catch him. It's so simple a child could do it!"

Connie frowned. "If it's as easy as you say, why don't the police use this pager-thing already?"

"Because it's a prototype. Not available yet."

"I don't like it. I mean, I have to admit, you had a good idea about me dressing up to look like Tiffany, weird though I felt doing it. But I don't know about this creepy sales guy."

"He's harmless, I'm sure," Angie said.

"Look, I'll admit I had my doubts about you," Connie said. "You do come on kind of strong, if you don't know it. But now, I actually like you. I don't want to see you do anything dangerous."

"That's nice of you to say... I think. But, look at it this way, if Paavo doesn't have to think about the jewelry store murder, he'll spend more time trying to find Tiffany's killer."

"But I thought Tiffany's case already had his full attention."

"It has, but you know him. He's got all the Easter egg murder information stored in his head. Whenever he hears anything about the case, he gets involved in it all over again. What will it hurt to try? Have confidence, Connie, my friend!"

"Why should I? You've got more than enough for both of us." Connie said and then gave a sigh of resignation.

34

"Quiet on the set! Take *eleven*? I mean, take eleven!"

SNAP!

Angie took a deep breath. Looking straight at the camera she tried her best, under sweltering lights that hung inches from her face, to smile instead of cry. What she wanted more than anything was to wipe away the perspiration dripping from her forehead. But that would smear her quarter-inch-thick TV make-up. Considering that the make-up artist's idea of female beauty was a face that resembled a Barbie doll, that might not have been a bad idea.

The director, cameraman, and assistant—the only ones there besides her—were hidden in the darkness, while she stood in a two-by-four-foot area with a sink, range, and butcher block counter, wearing a once gorgeous Oscar de la Renta blue dress with the sort of understated simplicity she'd thought would look elegant on TV.

It did, before she began to drip with perspiration and flour. Behind her, cardboard had been painted to look like kitchen cabinets and a window overlooking a giant sunflower-filled garden, reminiscent of the road to Oz. Maybe that's where she was, come to think of it.

"I've put two cups of flour and two cups of mashed potatoes into this bowl," she said, smiling broadly as she tilted the bowl toward the camera. Her head bobbed up and down so that she could look at the camera and not drop the bowl, as happened back in the fifth take, or maybe the sixth.

"Now it's a matter of mixing the two together so that they form a sticky pasta dough for your *gnocchi*. Remember, even though it's spelled to look like 'ga-no-chee,' it's pronounced 'nyohk-key.'" She smiled again.

"Watch those smiles! Television is serious business," growled the director who clearly fancied himself the Federico Fellini of cooking shows. He'd already interrupted her during take four to explain that this was a cooking lesson, not a lecture on Italian pronunciation or an advertisement for cosmetic dentistry. Takes one, two and three hadn't made it to the insults stage. But after that, things had gone from bad to worse.

Stiffening her shoulders, she put the bowl with flour, a mashed potato, and some water under the mixer, hit the On button for the heavy tongs to whir and jumped back out of the way. At take six the director had upset her so much that she failed to add the water so when she turned on the tongs dry flour shot all over the studio, burying her and the set in a cloud of white dust. She still had some in her hair. So much for her $200 styling job. Instead of sexy blonde highlights, she had aging white globules.

The next take had ended because they hadn't gotten all the flour off the camera—or the cameraman—and it looked like she was cooking in the middle of a snowstorm. A sneeze ended take eight. The video camera died on take nine. And an attack of giggles from the director's assistant ruined take ten.

But now the mixer whirred nicely. When the dough looked to be the right consistency, she stopped the tongs, grabbed a dollop of the mixture, pulled and tugged at it, and then broke off a tiny piece and tasted it.

"Fine. Now we're ready—"

"*WHAT do you think you're doing?*"

"Testing it."

"You're not supposed to play with the product with your fingers!" The director stormed into the lights to face her, waving his hands in the air. "And we certainly don't advocate eating raw dough on our program. *Tell* the people what it's supposed to look like, Miss Amalfi, so that they can see for themselves if it's ready."

"But you can't tell by just looking."

He got down on one knee. "Pretend, Miss Amalfi. This is television, after all."

She wasn't in the least amused by this man's histrionics. "Fine," she said.

He got up and went back to his chair. "Let's start from this spot."

In the dark, someone snickered.

"Three, two, one. Take twelve."

SNAP!

"See how the flour and potato have combined to form a dough. Once that's done, it's time for you to make the gnocchi. Here's a simple way to do it. Take about a half cup of dough." She grabbed a small handful of it. "Then roll it into a long tube, about a half-inch around. After that's done, lay the tube down on a cutting board and cut it into two-inch long pieces. See these cute little tubes? That's the way you need to make them. Then, you take that lovely cut-glass bowl that's been either sitting in your dining room or was still at your mother or grandmother's house, probably doing nothing but gathering dust, and you carefully turn it upside down." She picked up the cut-glass bowl from under the counter, showed it to the camera, and—

"Stop! Right there! Hold everything!"

The director marched over and planted himself in front of her, his arms crossed over his chest.

She gave him a cold stare. "Yes?"

"You think this is some kind of joke, don't you?"

"Not at all."

"You think that because you don't like the name *Angelina in the Cucina* that you can come here and make a laughingstock out of this show!"

"What did I do?"

"If you tell people to take that damn bowl and put it on their heads, you're out of here, lady. Do you understand?"

"All I'm doing," she explained calmly, "is trying to show my audience the best way to make the gnocchi." She turned the bowl upside down and placed it on the camera. "You take one little tube of rolled dough," she said, demonstrating as she spoke, "and put three fingers along the tube, then press down in the center and *r-o-l-l* it along the cut glass. This way, you get a hole in the center of the tube, and indentations from the cut glass make a pretty pattern. You can also roll it along a cheese grater, but that's tacky for television, and dangerous for your fingers if you press too hard."

"I'm not going to have you stand here and tell people to poke their fingers into pasta and roll it on the outside of bowls! Television is art, Miss Amalfi. Not play school!"

"But if you don't form the *gnocchi* properly, the center will be doughy and heavy and taste horrible! That's what's wrong with gnocchi served in restaurants. A lot of it is like eating paste."

"Do it some other way!" he bellowed.

Angie got down off the platform with the phony kitchen. "I'll do it right, or not at all. After all, I know what I'm doing, which is more than I can say for you!"

The director's face turned a lucid shade of purple. "How

dare you! You're nothing but a *clumsy, chaos-creating kitchen catastrophe!*"

"I'll bet Giada De Laurentiis never had this kind of trouble." She picked up her bowl, gave a harumph and marched out of the studio.

———

He sat on a stool in the basement telephone closet just off the garage of Angelina's apartment building and studied telephone company landlines in the apartment building. *If only I could show you, Angelina—my Angelina—how truly brilliant I am, you'd be even more impressed with me.*

The lines were marked to the different apartments, but to be make certain, he used the cell phone he'd lifted from an unlocked Lincoln Towncar in the garage. He phoned directory assistance. Her landline number was listed under A. Amalfi on Green Street. So old school, he nearly laughed aloud. He dialed the number.

"Hi. This is Angie. I can't answer your call..."

Smiling, he attached her phone wire to a large metal box and turned up the volume control to listen to the rest of her message. The very sound of her voice was enough to make him all but delirious with wanting her. Sitting with her at lunch had been an exquisite torment.

Her answering machine beeped, waiting for his message. When none came, it waited patiently for a few seconds, then not so patiently shut itself off.

But not completely. His phone trap blinked knowingly at him, telling him it was on and working. Listening, invading her apartment. Her privacy. Her.

———

"It was horrible, absolutely horrible." Angie stood in front of Paavo's desk and burst into tears.

He jumped to his feet. He'd rather face a murder suspect any day than Angie crying. "What is it?"

"Oh, God. They were so mean, so...so *evil!*" Her sobs grew louder. "He even called me a kitchen catastrophe!"

The other detectives were watching. Even without looking their way, Paavo could feel their grins, their knowing glances at each other, their curiosity as to what Angie was involved with now.

He hustled her into an interview room, grabbing a handful of Kleenex from Inspector Mayfield's desk as he went by.

"Here." He handed Angie the tissues and shut the door. "Tell me what's wrong."

Angie wiped her eyes. "I'm sorry. I didn't mean to carry on like this, but I tried so hard. I wanted everything to be so perfect. I even cut my fingernails for the *gnocchi*, and now..."

He sat down, pulled her onto his lap, and put his arms around her as she curled up against his chest. "Does this have anything to do with your audition this morning?"

She nodded.

"It didn't go well, I take it."

She shook her head, wiping the tears that had started once more.

"Wasn't this your first audition, Miss Amalfi?" he said keeping his expression serious, his tone professional.

She glanced at him. "Yes."

"Do you know how many times even the biggest TV stars had to audition before they got a show?"

"No."

"Well," his voice grew soft and gentle, "I have it on good authority that Paul Hollywood went through dozens of auditions, and no one would touch Julia Child for years. Some say

Paula Deen wore out an oven before anyone would put her on TV."

She gave him a half-smile. "You're just saying that."

"Would I lie? Nobody expected you to be perfect the very first time you tried it."

She used more Kleenex. "I did."

"I know." He kissed her. "Did they tell you specific things they didn't like?"

"Just about everything."

"But some things more than others."

She had to think about this. "I guess so."

"Good. That's a place to start. Think about what they didn't like, what you can do to change or improve what you did, and then get out there and try again."

She dropped her gaze. "I couldn't do that. I feel like such a fool."

He lifted her chin and looked into her teary brown eyes, trying to gauge the extent of her disappointment. "You're no fool, Angie. You're clever and beautiful. If you want it enough, you'll probably be on TV someday, and then there'll be no stopping you. You can be anything you want."

Her arms circled his neck, and she pressed her forehead to his. "I wish I believed in myself half as much as you believe in me, Paavo." Then she raised her head again and sighed. "I know I try to talk big, but sometimes I feel like such a fraud."

He stroked her back. "You're no fraud, either. Not at all. The only problem you have is being impatient. Have patience, and believe me, you're going to do just fine."

"Do you really think so?"

"I know so."

She hugged him a long while, her eyes teary for another reason now. "What would I do without you?"

"Probably quite well."

"Never!"

He helped her to her feet and stood up beside her, glancing at his watch. "Why don't we get out of here and have a late lunch? I think a nice dessert in particular will make the world a much brighter place for you."

"Oh dear, it is late, isn't it? I... I can't. It's Lent."

"Forget the dessert, then."

"Well, I'd like to, but I'm... busy."

"Oh?" He frowned. "Something important?"

"No. I mean, yes. My... my mother. I promised Serafina I'd meet her. I'd better get going."

"I see."

"Maybe dinner?" she suggested.

He hesitated. He knew he could get away for a while now, but by tonight, he wasn't sure. "I'll know better later. I'll call."

"Hmm. Maybe you'll get some help in one of these cases soon," she said with a sudden cat-that-swallowed-the-canary smile. What could she be thinking about?

"It would certainly help." Especially help us, he wanted to add.

"Hopefully, I'll see you tonight." She gave him a kiss that scorched, then slipped from his arms and headed out the door, waving a cheerful goodbye to the men in the office. He knew he was going to be in for a lot of ribbing about this little visit.

35

Paavo went to the computer center and asked for his printout. The new supervisor told him the job was still running.

"What do you mean, it's still running?" he asked. There's never been this kind of delay before.

"It's a big job," she said huffily.

"You're kidding. It should be one of my smallest requests. Something's wrong."

She gazed pointedly at him. "You want us to be complete, don't you?"

"Where's Mr. Liu?"

"Myron has gone home." The supervisor picked up a stack of printouts and loudly rapped their edges against the desk top to straighten them. Also, Paavo figured, to let him know he was being dismissed. "I'll handle this," she said curtly.

"I want those printouts now."

"That's impossible."

"Then get Liu here."

"You can't order me around like that!"

He stared at her. He didn't bother to reply. Or to leave.

"All right." She sniffed. "I'll phone his house. But I'm not guaranteeing anything."

A half hour later, Myron Liu contacted Homicide.

"I'm at my computer, Inspector," he said to Paavo. "Tell me exactly what you need, and I'll get it for you right now."

"I want a list of any cases that Judge Lucas St. Clair and D.A. Lloyd Fletcher worked on together, in any capacity at all. Got it?"

"Yes. Give me five minutes."

"I'll be right down," Paavo said.

Angie stood with Earl near the entrance to Wings Of An Angel.

"Now, you sure you ain't gonna be alone wit' dis guy?" Earl asked again.

"I promise." She smiled. It was kind of cute seeing him act the Dutch uncle with her.

"I don't even like you doin' business wit' him."

"Shhhh! Here he comes."

Carter walked into the restaurant. A hard look flashed across his face when he saw Earl, but it softened immediately as his gaze met Angie's. In that instant, as she noted his quick cover-up, all her own misgivings about the man revived. She was glad she was meeting him here and nowhere less public.

This was a business transaction. Nothing more. And she wanted it over with.

They sat at a table, Earl hovering nearby.

"This piece needs to be hidden in the egg," Carter said, showing her a tiny round piece of metal. "Then you take this monitor,"—he patted a black box with colored lights on it—

"and it homes in on the pager. It blinks green as you get closer and red as you back away."

He carried the chip to one end of the restaurant and demonstrated how the monitor worked. Sure enough, the red and green lights blinked as he moved forward and back. She nodded sagely.

"Put the chip in the egg," Carter went on, "then take the control home and hit this reset button. When—if—the egg starts to move, the control box will blink."

"That seems easy enough," Angie said, deliberately giving a cool, businesslike edge to her voice.

"It is. But how about I come along to make sure it works?"

"That won't be necessary. Here's your hundred dollars." She gave him cash. "Thank you."

"Shall we have some wine?" Carter suggested. "A little something to eat?"

"Miss Angie," Earl said, "Butch is waitin' for your lesson about da rigatoni."

"Thanks, Earl. I'm sorry, Carter. Goodbye." So saying, Angie turned and hurried to the kitchen, Earl hustling along right behind her.

———

The computer listing had fourteen names on it. They were all dated seven to fifteen years ago—between the time Fletcher became an assistant district attorney for the city and St. Clair's retirement. Paavo glanced over the names, then handed the list to Yoshiwara.

"Let's see," Yosh said. "Darrin Alonzo, Dan Barrett, Wesley Carville, Manny Dain... lots of names here, pal. How do you want to handle this?"

Paavo frowned. None of the names meant anything to him. "Do you want the first half of the alphabet, or the last?"

Before pulling the criminal records for his half of the names on the list, Paavo drove over to the hospital and questioned Stan, still heavily medicated, but able to mumble a few words. Paavo could just make them out. Stan hadn't seen his attacker, but somehow he knew the man was muscular.

Paavo asked about the roses. Stan couldn't remember anything about them, not who had sent them or why. That was strange—how often did a man get flowers from an unknown person for an unknown reason? He'd ask again later.

As he walked back to his desk in Homicide, from the corner of his eye, he caught the city map on the wall on which Calderon had posted the Fabergé egg robberies. To his surprise—maybe because he was thinking about a different case—he saw a pattern. One he'd missed before.

He jumped up and hurried to the map. Could it be? It was too simple, he thought. But on the other hand, why not?

The first robbery—the one during which Nathan Ellis had been killed—took place on the Geary bus line. Witnesses at the time said they saw no one running, no car coming by to pick up the murderer—nothing. One of them had "joked" that the only thing that had stopped in the area was a muni bus. Sure, Paavo and the other cops thought, they could see a killer riding a smelly bus with food wrappings, undefinable crud and wads of gum all over the floor as his getaway car.

But now, looking at the map, he saw that the stores robbed were all on the Geary bus lines. The next robbery had been a bit farther west. Number three robbery was further west again. The fourth jumped quite a distance westward to the Richmond district, again on the Geary bus line, and some five blocks before the city's Russian immigrant community, centered around a large, beautiful Russian Orthodox church.

In fact, if the pattern held up, then on Tuesday—today—

the next robbery would be somewhere on the Geary bus line even farther west of the spot where the last one occurred. Also, all the robberies either took place soon after opening in the morning, or in the evening, near closing time.

A wild thought struck, and Paavo phoned the Holy Virgin Cathedral office and asked when they held services. Daily, eight in the morning and six at night.

That meant morning service ended about nine a.m. Since it took a city bus nearly an hour to get from 26th and Geary through traffic down to the Sans Souci jewelers, a bus riding thief would arrive at ten a.m. when the store first opened.

Two robberies had occurred between ten and eleven in the morning, and two between four and five in the afternoon.

The idea of a church-going thief was too crazy. Paavo didn't know if he believed this idea of his or not.

Quickly, he did a search on his phone for gift shops and jewelers near the Orthodox church, and started phoning. One shop, the Volga Jewelers, was on the bus line near 34th Avenue. He phoned, and they carried Fabergé replicas.

He tried to reach O'Rourke in Robbery, but O'Rourke was out on a bank hold-up. He glanced at the clock. Quarter to four. It was a long shot. But in case he was right, he didn't want to blow it.

He was almost out the door when he hurried back to his desk and made a call to Angie. There'd be no dinner date for him this evening.

"Hi! This is Angie. I can't answer your call right now..."

He nearly hung up. But then he remembered her irritation at the way he wouldn't leave her a message whenever he called. He might not have a chance to call back.

"Angie. It's me. I can't come by for dinner. Something came up. I want to see you, though. Maybe I can meet you later. Call anytime. I'll be here most of the night."

He hung up feeling like a tongue-tied teenager. The

message probably made little sense. God, but he hated those machines.

"I can't do it tonight, Angie," Connie said.

"But I've got the paging device right here." Angie put her purse on the counter at Everyone's Fancy and pulled out the black box and the small chip. "I bought the egg from you, remember? In case it got stolen and we couldn't retrieve it."

Connie frowned. "I'd like to help out. But... maybe we should give the police more time. I don't want to mess them up."

"This won't mess them up. It's between you and me."

"Well, the thing is, your cousin Buddy called me. We met after work yesterday for coffee, just a short visit, but hit it off really well. Tonight we're going out for dinner. I don't know what time I'll get home."

Ah ha! Angie thought. That explained Connie's languid, off-in-the-clouds demeanor today. She was acting like a woman in the throes of newfound passion. Despite her and Buddy both having had bitter experiences with love and particularly with marriage in the past, they'd sought each other out and were ready to try again. Angie mentally added this bit of news to her marriage survey.

"How exciting!" Angie cried. "I'm so glad to hear it. Well, we can always try another day."

Connie looked relieved. "Here," she said, handing Angie the wooden box with the egg inside. "It's almost Easter. Why don't you take it home and enjoy it the way it was meant to be. The police will do okay with this one. Trust them."

"I do trust them." Angie took the box. "But sometimes I think they need a little nudge, that's all."

Paavo drove down Geary Boulevard. He had just passed 34th Avenue when he saw a small, bearded man slipped into the Volga Jewelers. Bingo! He double-parked, flashers blinking, drew his gun and hurried toward the shop.

Two women had just stepped out of a restaurant in front of Paavo. "Police! Stay back," he said. They ran back inside.

He kept his body against the wall and slowly leaned forward to look into the shop from the big storefront window. The frightened looking jeweler was lifting a Fabergé egg into a paper bag. The robber's gun was drawn.

Paavo waited until the thief had the paper bag, his gun no longer pointed at the owner as he backed from the shop. Paavo crept up behind him. "Police!" he shouted. "Drop the gun."

The thief froze. The jeweler ducked behind his counter.

"Drop it *now*. Raise your hands and turn around," Paavo demanded.

The gunman let go of the gun and it fell to the floor. He turned slowly and, facing Paavo, then, arms in the air he carefully placed his hands on his head and removed the wig and then removed the fake beard.

When the wig was gone, shoulder-length brown hair, streaked with gray, fell around a ravaged, tear-stained face. The thief was a woman.

"It's not my fault," she said, arms still high. The woman was of medium height, with a frail build. She looked to be in her early to mid-fifties.

Paavo pulled her arms behind her back and slipped handcuffs on her. As he did so, Officer McMahon from the Richmond Station showed up in response to Paavo's earlier request.

Paavo turned the thief over to the officer to read her her rights.

The jeweler, a wiry little man, walked up to him, his hand

extended. "I'm Gregorovitch. Thank you for coming so quickly. When I got your call, I couldn't believe anyone would really want to steal such a thing. Then, when I saw the gun..." He shook his head.

"You did well," Paavo said, shaking his hand.

"I didn't want to hurt anyone," the thief cried. "I wouldn't have hurt him. I was just trying to help myself. Those eggs aren't worth much, you know. Just a little. This isn't even a felony, is it?"

"Armed robbery is a felony," Paavo replied. "And so is murder."

"Murder!"

"What's your name?" Paavo asked.

"Claudia Zelenin."

"Address?"

"93 Presidio Terrace."

He glanced up at the posh address, but she was too busy crying to notice. "Do you live with anyone?"

"Alone. The house was once my parents'. It's mine now."

"Occupation?"

"I don't do anything," she replied. "The house is all I have left. It takes every bit of cash I can put my hands on just to pay property taxes."

"I see. It's tough." Paavo managed to keep a straight face. The house was worth several million.

"That's why I needed the Fabergé eggs." She glanced up at him with clasped hands, her eyes pleading. "I had a Fabergé once, you see, a real one, but it was stolen. It was a family heirloom, brought from Russia when my great-grandfather escaped from the Bolsheviks. And then, it was stolen from me!"

"You had a real Fabergé egg?" He had read enough about them to know how impossible that was. They were museum pieces.

"Yes. I was so stupid, I let someone come into my house,

into my heart. I showed it to him." Suddenly she began to sob. "I would have done anything for him! Anything! But he just wanted my money and valuables. Even he didn't think it was real, and probably fenced it. I suspect it's in a fine jewelry store now, with the owner having no idea of its true value. I've been looking for it ever since. Don't you see? I'm the victim here!"

"No, Nathan Ellis is the true victim."

She stared at him, her tears gone now. "I didn't mean to shoot. He lunged for the gun and it went off," she cried. "It wasn't my fault! None of this is my fault!"

Paavo nodded to Officer McMahon to take the woman to City Jail and book her.

He had wanted to know why the thief had killed Nathan Ellis, why fake Fabergés were so important that anyone would take a young man's life for one. It amazed him still, the foolish things people could do when in the throes of newfound passion; and the even more foolish things they did afterward.

He took a statement from the owner, then left the store and hurried to his car, still blocking traffic.

As much as he was glad he'd caught the Fabergé egg thief, and probably the murderer, something about what the woman had said to him niggled in the back of his mind.

He hurried to his desk, to the files about cases both D.A. Fletcher and Judge St. Clair had waited for him. He knew that Yosh's list had nothing that fit a potential murderer at this time. He went through his own list of men the two had jailed:

Alonzo and Hurley still in jail. Forget them.

Alexander, vehicular manslaughter, out six months.

Barrett, dealing heroin. Out for four years. Seemed to have gone straight.

Callahan, in and out a half dozen times for robbery, drugs, pimping. Latest release, last December. Career criminal.

Carville, second degree murder. Out since late February. Model prisoner, no priors.

Dain, in for rape, skipped out on parole three months earlier. Still not located.

Paavo moved Callahan and Alexander to his highly doubtful stack. Career criminals and drunk drivers rarely turned into sexual psychopathic killers. Barrett had been four years straight. A maybe. That left Carville and Dain as probables. Dain would be his sole likely candidate if it wasn't for the timing of Carville's release. Carville got out just a short while before the first murder was committed—around the same time as the fake car registration was submitted, in fact.

Also, Carville was the only murderer on his list. Carville... something about the guy's name.

Paavo was sick of pussy-footing around these political types. He was going to get to the bottom of this, now. He called up a photo of Carville, printed it, and rushed down to his car.

As he drove away, thoughts of the foolish things we do for love reverberated in his mind.

"Smith! Who the hell do you think you are coming to my home? I told you already you're taking this thing too far," Fletcher said. He stood in the black-and-white marble foyer of his mansion, holding the carved solid oak door only half-way open.

Paavo put his hand against the door and pushed. Fletcher backed off and let him enter. "Where do you want to talk?" Paavo asked. "In the living room? Or, would you rather someplace private, away from your wife, for instance."

Fletcher's eyes narrowed. "I have nothing to hide. But I don't want to upset her by any crazy accusations. Let's go into the den."

They entered a room that was paneled in rosewood, lined with library shelves. An oversized desk with a leather top stood in the center of the room, a straight-back chair behind it and two matching leather wing chairs in front.

Paavo dropped his files and mug shots on Fletcher's desk, then sat in one of the wing chairs. "This isn't a game, Fletcher. I want some straight answers and to hell with your political ambition."

"I don't have to listen—"

"I've got a list of all the trials that involved you and Judge St. Clair. I'll be going to St. Clair's house next to see what he can remember. You can join us if you'd like, or we can go over the case right here."

Fletcher glanced at the printout. "I don't know what you're talking about."

Paavo stood and began to pace. "I've been looking at a connection between two women—one involved with a judge, the other potentially with a D.A. What does that sound like to you, Fletcher? It sounds like a trial case, doesn't it? A case that you might have tried back when you were an Assistant DA, and St. Clair presided over."

"What are you getting at?"

"I'm trying to find out if I'm on the right track with this, or if I'm a hundred-eighty degrees off base. I need the truth about you and Tiffany Rogers."

"I've already answered that."

"I need your help, Fletcher. I need to find out who's behind the killings, especially if I'm right about the motive. Think of it, Fletcher. What other cops or A.D.A.'s worked on this same case? What other women is this guy after? Is your wife safe? And then, when he's done with the women, will he stop there? What if he decides this revenge isn't enough and goes after you next? To kill you the same way he did Tiffany Rogers."

Fletcher paled and sat down behind his desk. "You aren't making any sense."

"Come on, man. I've got to know for sure if you were seeing

Tiffany Rogers, because if you weren't—if you *really* weren't—I could be heading down a blind alley that could be fatal to someone. You've got to tell me, Fletcher. Is hiding a liaison with Rogers worth the life of another woman? Is it worth your own life?"

"This doesn't concern me." His voice was unconvincing.

"If I'm right, and it was your woman he killed first, you might be the first man to get nailed by this guy," Paavo said.

Fletcher rubbed his forehead. "I love my wife, Smith."

"Then you'd better be telling the truth, because if you're not, and this psycho has something against you and those you love, she's in danger."

He gazed up at Smith, his eyes hooded. "I get it," he whispered, then louder, "All right. I was involved with Tiffany, but I'd better not hear a word about this anywhere!"

"I can't guarantee that, Fletcher."

"Damn it, Smith! This could ruin me, and you know it."

"Is being mayor so important to you?"

"It's the only thing that's important," he shut his eyes, "now that Tiffany's gone." He looked up at Paavo. "I did love her, damn it. It doesn't mean I feel anything less for my wife—Sally and I have had thirty-two years, wonderful years, and three fine sons." Tears filled his eyes. "But Tiffany made me feel young again. Important. She was the one who helped me decide to run for mayor!"

Paavo waited for Fletcher to regain control.

The D.A. clenched his fist, his head bowed. "You're on your own from here on out, Smith. Get the hell out of my life."

Paavo stood. "You should have told me about you and Rogers days ago, Fletcher. For your sake, it had better not be too late."

Despite the late hour, Julian Bosch agreed to meet Paavo at the Parole Office. Paavo had been calling for two days and every time was told Bosch was out or holding an interview and couldn't be disturbed. He'd never returned one call. Tonight, Paavo had reached him at home and insisted on a meeting.

Now, Bosch was waiting in his office when Paavo arrived. He was a small man with a florid complexion, heavy glasses and a nervous tick at the corner of his eye. "I'm sorry I hadn't returned your calls, Inspector," he said. "But if it concerns Wesley Carville, I knew it couldn't be anything urgent."

Paavo went into the small, sterile office and sat in a high-back government-issue chair. "Why do you say that?"

"Because Mr. Carville is one of my easiest cases. He's a well-educated man, Inspector. He'll do extremely well on the outside. I've already got a number of job interviews lined up. Just waiting for him to give me the word."

"Why hasn't he?"

"He's still got the money he earned while he was in prison. He's not ready to be tied down to a 9 to 5 job yet. We see this all the time. Free at last, you know. But he'll come around. Why are you interested in him?"

"I'm investigating a murder."

"And you think Carville might be a witness?"

"I think he might be a suspect."

"Impossible."

"That's what I need to determine. May I see his file?"

"Of course. Here are his records. You'll see he was a model prisoner. No trouble at all. And he's the same with me. A joy to work with. And that's really rare, let me tell you." Bosch shuffled his papers and smiled proudly, as if to take credit for Carville's spotless record.

Paavo started at the back of the file. The write-ups were from wardens, for the most part, from the time Carville entered prison. He read through them. The man worked hard, rarely spoke to anyone. Spent all his time in the electronics shop. No doubt about it. He was a model prisoner.

"What's this?" Paavo asked, noting a cross-reference to case C53794.

"Probably some situation Carville was involved with earlier."

"Did you check it out?"

"Those annotations are a waste of time. It's old, for one thing. I concern myself with my clients' current cases, not something that may have happened long ago."

Paavo nodded and kept going. He copied down Carville's current address—a cheap Tenderloin rooming house. "Is there anything at all strange or different, or in any way troubling, about this man?"

"Nothing. Absolutely nothing," Bosch stated emphatically. "I wish all my people were like him."

With a sweep of his arm he cleared the table of his Tenderloin hotel room of cockroaches and set up his tape recorder. Whistling softly to himself, he picked up his phone and tapped into Angie's answering machine. He hit the code for the machine to play its messages.

The first message was from her mother, wondering how her baby daughter was doing. The second was from her sister, Bianca. Bossy bitch. Next came one from some producer, wondering if she'd like to try her audition again.

He shrugged. She wouldn't be around for it. Too bad.

Then he heard one from the cop. He sat forward in his chair, flipped on the record button of the tape recorder, and hit the replay code for the answering machine. This was even better than he'd hoped for.

Next, he dialed Homicide.

"Inspector Calderon here," came a gruff voice.

"Inspector Paavo Smith, please," he said.

"Just a minute." Calderon must have put his hand over the mouthpiece, but Wesley could hear the muffled conversation. "Paavo around? He's got a call... Be back soon? No? Not 'til late? Yeah, okay. I got it."

He didn't need to hear anything more. He hung up the phone.

36

"Seth and I used to fight all the time," Frannie said as she put an egg and some skim milk in a blender. Angie's fourth sister looked almost radiant as she awaited the birth of her first child.

"I remember your fights," Angie shouted over the loud whirring sound. "I think the whole neighborhood remembers. You two weren't exactly quiet about it."

Two years ago, Frannie married Seth Levine, a young architect. One month after the wedding day, she was back home seeking special dispensation to divorce. Seth came seeking *her* two days later, and she went with him. Their truce lasted three weeks before they were at it again. Serafina threatened to put a revolving door in Francesca's bedroom.

"Ever since he found out about the baby, though," Frannie said, "he's been different. It's as if he finally realized that marriage means family and responsibility." She switched off the blender, dipped her finger in the mixture, and licked it experimentally. "It's as if he figured out what it's all about."

"Doesn't it worry him?" Angie asked, glad she could stop hollering. "You know, the commitment?"

Frannie poured the milk into a ten-ounce glass, then used it to force down a giant vitamin pill. "It does. There are times I think he gets scared by what's happening. I know I do."

"You do?"

"Look at me. I'm big as a house. I feel ugly, awkward, and sexy as an orange peel. I'm quite sure Seth's going to run off with the first halfway decent-looking woman that smiles at him. But you know what?"

"What?"

"He says I look more beautiful to him now than ever. I guess it's not really beauty he's talking about, but something deeper, something that comes from the heart. Seth and I are closer than ever before. I guess that sounds weird."

"No, I understand."

"What about you and Paavo?"

"I don't know, Frannie. The more I learn, the more confused I am. He's no marrying man, that's for sure. I'm lousy at compromise, impatient, and sometimes a little too emotional. We have nothing in common, spend too much time apart, and rarely see eye to eye. Is that a recipe for a happy marriage?"

"Does it matter?"

Angie thought about Frannie's question a moment. Then, with a big smile, she jumped to her feet and gave her astonished sister a hug. "Obviously, not in the slightest."

37

P aavo finally tracked down file C53794 in Oakland. At first, on being told by Criminal Records that the mysterious number found in Wesley Carville's file wasn't in San Francisco's numbering system, he thought he'd hit a dead end. But then he remembered reading that Carville had lived for a while in the East Bay.

The file was waiting for him when he reached Oakland's Homicide department. He sat down in an empty interview room and began to read the reports. Carville's parole officer had been right about one thing—the case was old. But he was dead wrong about something else. It was important.

The case had begun twelve years before with a missing person report in Berkeley. It involved a young woman named Heather Rose Fredrickson, a senior at the University of California. She had disappeared.

Hundreds of people were questioned—everyone who had ever known the attractive, friendly coed. Wesley Carville, a graduate student working on a Ph.D. in electrical engineering, was among them. Heather's friends had said she'd complained of someone following her, showing up wherever she went, but she never told them who he was. Or whether, in fact, she even knew who he was. Wesley Carville had never become a suspect in the disappearance.

Two years after Heather's disappearance, Carville had been found guilty of electrocuting his landlord, who didn't live on or near the Oakland property, but in San Francisco. Carville was known to have gotten into heated arguments with the landlord over the years, but he swore he had hadn't touched the electrical wiring in the man's San Francisco home. But because of Carville's background, a case was made that the death wasn't a simple accident, that someone—and Carville was the only suspect, plus sufficient evidence had been found against him— to conclude he had rigged the wiring to electrocute the landlord.

Carville was convicted of murder and sent to prison.

Two years after that, the landlord's widow sold the badly rundown one-bedroom house in West Oakland where Carville had lived. The new purchasers wanted it completely remodeled, and their workmen discovered a human skeleton bricked into a wall. Dental records showed it to be the remains of Heather Rose Fredrickson.

No cause of death could be determined, and no evidence was found to prove that Carville had murdered her—except the obvious. The house had stood unoccupied over two years since he'd lived there and theoretically, anyone could have hidden Heather's remains there. But that was just legalistic maneuvering. It was clear from the way the reports were written, the homicide investigators knew who had killed Heather. Since the man was already locked up for murder, they didn't pursue another trial.

But now, as prisons filled up and judges and D.A.s tended toward leniency even with "second-degree" murderers, Carville, a "model prisoner," was released.

Paavo shut the file. The coed had disappeared two years

before Carville was imprisoned. If he murdered her, he had lived with a corpse buried in the wall of his house that entire time. Presumably, he'd become intrigued with her, stalked her, then killed her and kept her near him. It was a sick perversion of love.

A sudden chill gripped Paavo. Carville... an electrical engineering student at U.C. Berkeley, and a dead landlord who resided in San Francisco. Something in that fact seemed to resonate for him. Something... from long ago.

———

Holding the door to the telephone closet open a tiny crack, he watched the white Ferrari pull into the parking space in the garage.

She got out of the car. His little one. His love. He longed to smother her with roses. She always liked roses.

He almost snatched her then and there, it was that tempting, that hard to watch her walk away from him once again after he'd waited so long, that painful to watch the elevator doors open and swallow her up inside them.

But too much could go wrong. Too many people down here. His original plan was a better one. Much better. In fact, brilliant.

She'd ultimately come to him—if not one way, then the other. He could be patient. After all, the longer the anticipation, the sweeter the fulfillment. Still, his heart pounded, and he felt a sheen of perspiration on his forehead.

He waited until the elevator had time to reach the twelfth floor, then he dialed her number. He was a patient man.

———

Angie unlocked her door to the steady ringing of her landline. After visiting Frannie, she'd gone to visit her parents and to have dinner there. She wanted to talk about the menu for Easter dinner with her mother, and go over what she should bring or make at the house.

It was after ten when she got home. Her parents always used her landline as their first resort; they still hadn't completely embraced the cellphone world. Her mother must have changed her mind about the menu. She ran to catch it before the answering machine clicked on.

"Hello?"

"Angie?"

It was a man's voice. A familiar voice. "Yes?"

"It's me. Carter."

She nearly hung up. "What are you doing calling me this time of night?"

"I hope I didn't wake you."

"No. What do you want?"

"I left out a part that belongs in the pager. It's an important part. The device won't work without it. I need to give it to you now. Tonight."

"No. I don't need it. My plans have changed. I have the egg here."

"There? That's even better. I'll come to your place. I charged you a hundred dollars for something that doesn't work."

He was making her nervous. "Forget it, Carter. You can give it to me at Wings. Or give it to Earl. He'll see that I get it."

"But I have to install it. It won't take long. Five minutes."

"I'm sorry. I'm going to bed."

There was a pause, and he spoke again. Very, very slowly. "I know where you live."

"No, stay away!" She slammed down the phone as hard as she could. Shaking, she stared at it, daring him to phone back.

In her mind's eye she saw a face. But not *his* face. Not Carter's. It was the face of the man at the dance. Reese, his name was.

Reese, without the beard, without the mustache... They were the same man!

No. She rubbed her forehead. Impossible. And yet ...

A man sitting on the fender of a BMW at the college. A student, watching her...

He had the same broad-shouldered, muscular build. It had been hard to see his face, though, because of his dark glasses and baseball cap.

A baseball cap... glasses...

There was someone else...

Stop this nonsense, Angie! Stop it! She sat down, her knees suddenly too weak to hold her. Was she going mad, or was there really someone stalking her?

She had to call Paavo.

She was reaching for the phone when she noticed the blinking "1" on her answering machine. One message. She pressed Play.

"Angie. It's me." Warm relief eased over her and she felt better, safer, just hearing Paavo's voice, but why hadn't he called her cellphone? "I can't come by. Something came up." Static crackled over the connection made it difficult to hear his words as he continued speaking. It must have been a bad cell connection, she thought, that must be why he used her landline recorder. "Another murder. I have"—the static suddenly cleared—"to see you. I can meet you"—heavy static—"at Coit Tower." The static cleared once more. "I'll be here all night."

Coit Tower? Now? Why would he want her to go there, of all places? An image of the tower flashed across her mind. The beautiful shaft of white standing in lonely splendor at the top of Telegraph Hill. Sure, the area teemed with tourists by day and on summer evenings, but on cold, foggy nights like this one...? There'd be no one there.

Why would Paavo want her to meet him at an investigation? He never had before. In fact, he'd tried to keep her away from his work. But he said he had to see her, that he'd be out all night. It didn't make sense.

And why the static on his phone? Something was weird.

She decided to call Homicide and see if anyone there knew what was going on.

No one answered in Homicide so the night operator for the Hall of Justice picked up her call. She didn't leave a message.

A shiver went down her spine as she thought of Carter's call. He said he knew where she lived.

Suddenly, she wanted nothing more than to get out of her apartment. She should be safe in it; she had a deadbolt...

But with Stan in the hospital, she was alone on this floor of the building.

She used her cell phone to call Paavo, and as usual, his phone went straight to messaging. "Call me as soon as you get this," she said. "I'm coming to find you." That did it. There was no way she was staying here like a sitting duck, waiting to be scared to death by that man. She wasn't even going to take the time to change to something nicer than her Armani jeans and Cole-Haan loafers, but put her phone, keys, and wallet in the pockets of her warm leather jacket, and ran out the door.

Coit Tower wasn't very far away. If she couldn't find Paavo there, she'd go straight to his house and wait for him. That way, if Carter did go to her place, he wouldn't find her. She'd tell Paavo about him. One meeting with an angry Paavo and Carter wouldn't dare to frighten her again. He wouldn't dare to even *think* about her again.

Damn Carter for making her afraid to be alone in her own apartment! She wished she'd listened to Earl.

At the San Francisco Hall of Justice, Paavo decided to go down into the belly of the building, to the archives. The secretaries and file clerks had gone home long ago. But while he had read summaries of Wesley Carter's case, he wanted to see the details, and he didn't want to wait until morning to read them.

First, he tracked down the report on Wesley Carville's arrest for the murder of his landlord ten years earlier. Although the small, run-down house Carville rented in was in Oakland, the landlord had lived and was murdered in San Francisco, so the SFPD had jurisdiction.

Paavo opened the file and turned to the first incident report. The name of the reporting officer leaped out at him— Matt Kowalski. He knew that ragged scrawl well, almost as well as he knew his own handwriting. He stared at it a moment, then rubbed his forehead, and searched for a place to sit.

Matt and he had been rookies together, and then partners for a short while as patrol officers at the Richmond station that encompassed the Sea Cliff. Paavo was promoted first, and went to Northern, but Matt was right behind him. Eventually, they both wound up in Homicide and became partners again. More than partners, they were best friends. And then, Matt was killed in the line of duty.

As Paavo carefully read through the pages of the Carville arrest, he remembered a call he and Matt had taken about an accident at a house in Sea Cliff. The caller had said a man had been electrocuted while working on his house's wiring.

When he and Matt went out to the house, he noticed that the ground wire had been disconnected, and an electrical boosters had been attached to the house wires. Only because Paavo had worked on some electrical circuitry while in the Army did he recognize that something strange was going on. He and Matt contacted Homicide to investigate. The next day, Paavo received word of his promotion to Northern station. He hadn't learned, until now, what had come of the electrical wiring case.

Paavo put down the file. Fletcher, St. Clair, Matt. Fletcher's and St. Clair's women had received roses, and ... a chill went through him ... Angie had also received roses from an unnamed student. He felt his blood drumming in his ears, his breath quickening.

Stan, too, had received roses, but didn't know who they were from, or why. Apartments 1201 and 1202. Easy to confuse. Stan had told Angie something about a peculiar delivery man.

He rubbed his temples. What he was thinking was impossible. Outlandish.

Hurrying back to his desk, he picked up the phone and called Matt's widow, Katie.

He apologized for the late hour. But she'd been a policeman's wife for eleven years. She understood. "Forget the apologies, honey," she said in the saucy, brusque manner she had. "What can I do for you?"

"By any chance did anyone send you roses recently?"

"Roses? Me?" She laughed, a rich, hearty laugh. Matt used to say he fell so hard for Katie because of her laugh. "I'm not ready to be courted yet, sweetheart. And everyone knows it. Why?"

"Just wondering if anyone strange has shown up at your door lately. That's all. It was a long shot on a case I'm working on. I don't even know why I called. I shouldn't have bothered you."

"It's no bother." Her voice turned serious. "But since you mention it, there was someone strange. He gave me the creeps, in fact. But it had nothing to do with roses."

"Tell me."

"I'm sure it's nothing, but the guy was a *Chronicle* salesman. He had some sort of two-for-one offer. I told him I wasn't interested, but he insisted my *husband* would want the paper.

Finally, I got so angry I told him my husband was dead, and I shut the door. He really upset me, though."

"What did he look like?"

"It was hard to tell because of his baseball cap and sunglasses. He had a mustache, dark brown hair, about six feet tall, muscular build. Like someone who worked out."

"Thanks, Katie. You've been a big help."

"Take care of yourself, Paavo. Love you, honey."

He hung up the phone. A *Chronicle* salesman asking about Matt.

The salesman that the judge had complained about.

A single, days-old copy of a *Chronicle* at Tiffany's.

And the copy of the *Chronicle* Angie left at his house the other night.

"Good Christ," he whispered.

38

___

No murder investigation going on here, Angie thought as she reached the circular parking area in front of Coit Tower. Just a couple of parked cars, and they stood empty. The thick fog made it hard to see into the bushes beyond the blacktop. Angie slowly drove along the edge of the parking area, trying to see into the shrubs as she went by.

Near the road that led away from the Tower and back down Telegraph Hill, in the mist she could somewhat make out a tall, broad-shouldered man standing among the shrubs. When her headlights reached him, he lifted his arm, waving in a "follow me" gesture and moved further into the tree-filled shrubbery. He disappeared into the fog.

She told herself it must be Paavo, wanted to believe it was him, yet his stance, the angle of his shoulders, wasn't quite right. Was it someone else... or was something seriously wrong?

She rolled down the window. "Paavo?"

She agonized over what to do. Perhaps it was him and it was just the fog refracting light from the headlamps that made him appear different.

It had to be him. She'd heard him on the answering machine, telling her to meet him here. And now he'd waved for her to follow.

The fog seemed thicker now, making it more difficult to see. She rolled her car closer to the place where Paavo, or whoever it was, had stood, and tried to see where he'd gone. What exactly was back there in the trees? A thick mist covered her windshield and the wipers only streaked it. If he didn't answer, she would phone and text, and if he didn't answer, she was leaving. But first, she tried calling one last time. "Paavo!"

Suddenly, an arm reached in and pulled up the button to unlock her door. Startled, she turned, and in the instant it took for her to grasp what had happened, her door was yanked open. She stomped on the gas pedal, but felt someone grab the back of her jacket, felt herself being pulled her from the car as it lurched forward. She landed hard on the pavement and when she opened her mouth to scream, something smashed against the back of her head.

The world shattered, then went black.

***

Paavo hammered out Angie's phone number.

"Hi! This is Angie. I can't answer your call—"

He slammed down the receiver and phoned the hospital. Expecting a nurse to answer, he was surprised when Stan picked up the phone.

"This is Inspector Smith. I didn't think you'd still be awake."

"The damn pain killers are wearing off," Stan complained. "I ache, but at least my head's not in a fog anymore."

"I'm trying to find Angie. Have you seen her or talked to her tonight?"

"She came by this afternoon. That was it, though."

"Did she say what she had planned for this evening?"

"No."

"Okay. Sorry to have disturbed your rest."

"Wait, Inspector. Didn't you ask earlier about some roses?"

"Yes."

"They weren't connected to the attack on me, were they?" Paavo heard a slight tremor in Stan's voice.

"I'm pretty sure they were. Why? Do you remember who sent them?"

"I thought *you* sent them."

"Me? What are you talking about?"

"I ran into the delivery man down in the lobby and—stupidly—I diverted them to my apartment. My God, man, you've got to do something!" Paavo's hand tightened on the receiver as he listened to the anguish in Stan's voice. "The flowers weren't meant for me, Inspector. They were meant for Angie."

Angie felt her head being stroked and petted. She kept her eyes shut, squeezing them tight, not letting him know she was awake.

Slowly, she began to sort out her perceptions. Her mouth was gagged, and she was breathing deeply through her nose, the fear of her air being cut off causing her near panic. Her arms had been pulled back and her hands tied behind her back. And her whole head pounded mercilessly.

The gag cut cruelly into her flesh, preventing her from screaming. She trembled, terrified.

"Awake, my love?"

Carter!

"I didn't want to hurt you," he whispered, still stroking her hair. "You trusted me. You trusted my love. You should always trust me, Heather, and be true to me."

She realized her head lay in his lap, and that she was stretched across a short, upholstered bench of some kind. It smelled of stale tobacco, rotting food, a rancid, musty, dust-filled odor. He ran his thumb over her eyebrow, tracing it, gently at first, then harder and harder, as if he were trying to rub it from her face.

He was mad! Her heart beat so hard she was sure her entire body was pulsating from it, but he didn't seem to notice. She ached to open her eyes, to try to get away from him. But as scared as she was, she was even more afraid of letting him know she was awake.

Suddenly, his tone changed. "Wake up, bitch! I don't have all night! I didn't hit you that—"

He broke off at the sound of an auto going past them. "Damn. We'll have to find someplace else. Someplace where we won't be interrupted. We need to have a long time together, don't we? It'll be like it used to be between us, Heather." He traced his finger over her ear, her jaw, her chin, then wrapped his hand around her neck. "Just like it used to be."

After his talk with Stan, Paavo noticed he had a voice message. He listened, baffled to hear her say she was going to meet him —but she didn't say where. He tried phoning, but she wasn't answering her phone. He left a message, and then tried her landline, leaving another message.

Contacting the Richmond station, he asked for a patrol officer to go by his house immediately, to see if she was there. Word quickly got back to him to say his house was empty. The officer said he'd keep watch and call Paavo if anyone showed up.

With the siren blaring, he drove to her apartment, telling himself the whole way that she wasn't in any danger.

He'd prayed she'd be here. That when he knocked on her door, she'd open it, her big, brown eyes widening in surprise. Then she'd smile and fling herself at him. He loved the way she did that. No one else had ever seemed half so happy to see him.

In front of her door, he knocked. No answer. They'd exchanged keys—a sign of friendship, she'd told him; a sign of her trust in him, he believed.

He unlocked Angie's apartment door and went in. Its emptiness surrounded him, making him feel a sudden chill.

The apartment was empty.

He saw a box on the coffee table and a strange metal device beside it. The box had the name Everyone's Fancy on it —Connie Rogers' shop. It was a Fabergé egg. Why would Angie have it? And the metal device? What in the world was it?

What had she been up to?

He went through the kitchen, living room, bedroom, into the den, looking for a note or message that might give some clue to where she'd gone. Nothing.

He hated to do it, but he phoned her parents' home. Her mother answered.

"Serafina," he said. "This is Paavo. I'm trying to find Angie. Is she there, or has she talked to you this evening?"

"Paavo, *caro mio*. What's wrong?"

He didn't want to alarm Serafina, but he didn't have time to waste. "It's nothing to worry about. But I need to find her."

"I wonder why she didn't tell you where she's gone? Did you two argue again?" Her tone was accusatory.

"No. Nothing like that."

"Paavo, *caro*, you've got to figure out what to do. *Mia bambina,* she loves you so much. And you love her. You're a smart man, you need to use your head about this, so you don't have to telephone her Mamma in the middle of the night asking where your sweetheart is."

"Serafina, please," he interrupted, desperately hoping that this was just a stall before she put Angie on the phone. "Do you have any idea where she might be?"

"No, *poverino*. She left here at nine and said she was going straight home. "

He shut his eyes, then drew in a deep breath. "Okay. If she contacts you, tell her to get hold of me immediately."

"All right, *caro mio*. I'll phone her sisters and see if she's gone to one of their houses. If I find her, I'll have her call you. By the way, it's almost Easter. You come here with Angie for dinner, okay?"

He didn't have time to say anything but "Yes, thanks," and then hung up.

He went back into the den, took Angie's appointment calendar from her desk drawer and opened it, flipping to that day's date.

The page was empty. Where now?

He looked around her apartment again, feeling helpless, furious and scared. It was eerie being here without her bubbling through the place, filling not only the rooms, but all the dark places of his soul. He had to find her.

Carter pushed her off his lap and stepped out of his car. As soon as she was alone, she opened her eyes just a little. She was on the floor, wedged between the front and back seats of a tiny automobile.

She heard a door open and felt the car list as he got back into it. Then she heard him crank the ignition switch.

Her eyes were open now. She lay on her side, her legs bent.

She was still gagged, her hands tied behind her back, and the throbbing of her head had grown worse.

Where did he plan to take her? The newspapers were full of stories about women driven to remote spots, raped and murdered. Fear paralyzed her, tempting her to give in to whatever he planned in hopes of preventing more terror, more pain.

But something inside her wouldn't give up. Not yet.

As if some new thought had occurred to him, Carter suddenly reset the hand brake between the front bucket seats. She squeezed her eyes shut as she heard him shift in the seat.

"I'm making them pay, Heather. I'm making them all suffer like I did when they took me away from you. When they separated us. And you know what, Heather? Even our house is gone now, too. I know how unhappy you were, with the leaky roof, the heater that never worked. That goddamned landlord. I took care of him for you. I fixed him good."

She felt him grope for her, then his hand touched her hair and he began stroking it. "At least you're here with me again. Just like before." He shifted more and the small car rocked. "Come here to me, Heather."

His hand gripped her hair and pulled upward. She couldn't stop her cry of pain, and her eyes flew open to see his face looming over her. He pulled harder, making her eyes smart as she scrambled as best she could into a kneeling position.

She looked out the window to see nothing but fog and in the mist, Coit Tower. So she hadn't been out long. The car was small, old, with a stick shift—a green Honda. Where else had she seen it?

"You're not Heather." He spat the words, letting go of her. "You're the one with the cop! Thought he was so smart just because he knew all about electricity. No one would have investigated— they'd have accepted that it was an accident, except for him."

She shook her head, needing to convince him she was

Heather. She'd be safe if he thought she was Heather. He loved Heather.

He leaned closer, his face only inches from hers. He smiled. "After I kill you, my vengeance will be over, Angelina. The men who hurt me, who took me from Heather, will have lost their women, too. Isn't that sad?" He chuckled.

Again, she tried to shake her head, to persuade him he was wrong. Despite trying to be brave, though, a tear formed at the corner of her eye. He lifted it onto his finger then put the finger in his mouth. "Heather did that, too," he murmured. "She cried when I told her she was going to die. But it was for her own good. She wanted to leave me. I tried to tell her it wasn't safe out there. She wouldn't listen. Finally, I found a place to keep her very, very safe." He ran his hand over Angie's face, touching the planes and angles of it. "You're so much like her. Like my Heather come back to me again. You were all I ever wanted."

His words devastated her. Even pretending to be Heather wouldn't save her.

Another car drove by and he abruptly turned from her, shifted the car into gear and began down the twisting turns of Telegraph Hill.

She had to do something to stop him from going to that remote spot wherever it was. She had to stay where there were people to help her. In the city. Her city—and Paavo's.

She turned in a half-circle so that she sat on the hump on the floor board between the two front seats. She faced the back window. At her own back was the console between the front seats, the console where a hand brake was located.

She waited until he was past the twisting part of Telegraph Hill where he couldn't drive very fast. Suddenly, the car tilted downward, and she realized they were on one of the city's steepest hills. He stepped on the gas and all but flew down the first few yards.

This was her chance. She jutted out her bound hands

behind her, grabbed hold of the hand brake and pulled up on it as hard as she could. The back wheels locked, and the car went into a tail spin. Carter screamed with rage.

Paavo noticed that her answering machine showed "zero" messages. But he'd left one for her, so she must have played it. Maybe someone else had left a message, and that would explain where she'd gone?

He pressed the replay button.

"Angie. It's me."

He groaned at the thought of listening to his own awkward speech and looked for the fast-forward button. He found it just as his words were nearly obliterated by static. A mercy, he thought.

"... another murder...."

A what? He hadn't said that. He pulled back his hand. "Meet me..." Static erupted again at the words "Coit Tower."

Good Christ, he thought. He'd listened to his voice, except for those few, damnable words covered with static: another murder, and Coit Tower. Someone had tampered with his message, added words, someone who knew how to break into her answering machine, knew recordings, electronics ... Carville.

He called Central Station and ordered an immediate all-points bulletin for Angie and Wesley Carville, giving them the license number for a white Ferrari. They already had a bulletin out on a green Honda Civic. Fighting a sickening feeling at the pit of his stomach, he knew with an awful certainty that the Honda reported at Judge St. Clair's had been, in fact, Carville's.

He was standing, shouting into the phone at the dispatcher, who seemed too slow to act, too slow to comprehend, saying to start the search at Coit Tower and consider Wesley Carville armed and dangerous.

A lamp post stopped the Honda's mad spin. The car's front grill wrapped around it. The padded seats she had hurled herself between had protected Angie from being hurt, but crawling to her knees now, she saw the crack in the windshield where Carter's head had hit it. Blood streamed down his forehead and his eyes were shut. She wondered if he was dead.

And she thanked God that, for whatever reason, no airbag was deployed.

She worked herself over to the door. With her back to it, she groped until she felt the door handle. She lifted it, then had to lean against it to get the door to open. As it opened, she had no way to keep her balance and tumbled onto the street.

Bruised and aching, without being able to use her hands to help her, she had to use the car for support to get back up onto her feet. She went over to the driver's door and looked in the car. Carter certainly looked dead. His face was white and bloody. His knee must have hit the dash hard because his trousers were torn and the knee ripped open so deep it looked like some bone was showing. Her stomach flipped over at the sight, and the world went a little tipsy.

She was surprised no one was out here yet to help. She'd wait. Someone would surely come soon.

Then she saw one of Carter's fingers twitch. She jerked back, terrified, and began to run up the steep hill, her only thought being that going uphill would be harder for him in his condition.

By the top of the hill, she was gasping hard for breath. The gag made it nearly impossible to pull in the deep lungfuls of air she needed. She rubbed her face against her shoulder in a vain attempt to ease the gag downward toward her chin. Running the way she'd just done had been silly, she told herself. No need. Carter wasn't coming after her. He wasn't going to be able to move in the condition he was in.

Somewhere, soon, she'd find a house light on, see someone out walking or a car go by. She'd find help and everything would be all right.

But instead, through the fog, she saw the door on the driver's side of the Honda spring open.

39

"Is that her Ferrari, Inspector?"

Paavo, standing by Angie's car in the dark parking lot, had been asked that question at least three times already—by each patrol car that cruised by. "Yes. Now find her!" The car, with a slight dent by the headlight, had been found up against a bench with the engine running.

Another officer walked up to him. "I don't see any sign of her."

"Of course not. She's not hanging around the Tower. I can see that. She's got to be hiding somewhere on that hill. Look for her. Go through the bushes."

"What I'm saying, sir, is that she might not be anywhere around here. You said there was another car."

Paavo didn't want to think about that—about that bastard taking Angie to some place in his car. He wanted her hiding in the brush here, waiting for him to find her. He wanted her safe.

The policeman part of him, though, knew from bitter experience that if she was here, she was probably dead. He couldn't face finding her himself, but he couldn't bear to leave her out here in the cold, foggy night. He had nowhere else to search for her. No other leads to follow.

"Look a little longer, please," he whispered.

His cellphone rang. "Smith."

"Officer Manning, Central. We found the green Honda, Inspector."

His breath caught. "Yes?"

"It's been in a wreck. On Kearney, not far from Lombard."

His world tilted. "The occupants?" He could barely get out the words.

"The car's empty. But we found a billfold belonging to an Angelina Amalfi in the glove box, along with a cellphone and keys."

She saw a light in the upstairs window of a small house. Breathless, she stumbled toward the front door, but with her hands tied behind her, she could only kick it. Her arms, her wrists ached, her mouth burned where the tight gag pressed into her skin. She waited a moment, then kicked again, harder.

The light switched off. No! She wanted to cry out, but couldn't. Why was there no one to help her? From the corner of her eye she saw the black and white of an SFPD patrol car go by. She chased after it, but it had already disappeared into the fog.

She couldn't yell, couldn't wave her arms. Instead of coming to her aid, people seemed to shy away, to lock their doors instead of opening them. When had we come to this? Tears of frustration and fear filled her eyes. This was a big city, filled with people. But she felt completely alone.

A movement in the fog caught her attention. She stared at it, waiting, praying that it was someone who'd give her help. She took a step toward the person, then stopped, staring, not believing. He stumbled, his hand to his knee, but still he came forward, toward her, a figure in the mist. But she knew it was him. *Him.*

She turned and ran, praying that the fog had somehow shielded her. But since she saw him...

He could reach her easily. Grab her again. She ran. Looking at the street signs as she reached a corner, she knew where she was. Her church, Sts. Peter and Paul's, was nearby. Maybe there...

Running down the steep Filbert Street hill, without the aid of her arms to steady herself and help keep her balance, she was forced to slowed down, slipping and sliding, never actually falling, but coming perilously close. She expected Carter to catch up to her any moment.

Her lungs were ready to burst as she reached the ten-foot high doors of the church. Locked. She fell against them, her cheek pressed against the ancient oak as choking, gasping sobs broke from her.

She tried other doors, all were locked. Finally, she forced herself to stop, to listen for the sound of Carter's running footsteps reverberating through the empty night.

She listened.

"Where is she, dammit?" Paavo pounded his fist onto the roof of the green Honda, fear for her gnawing at him as he looked up at the rows and rows of flats and apartments surrounding them. Yoshiwara had shown up. Paavo wasn't sure from where, and now Yosh stood in the middle of the street directing the investigation. Yosh grabbed his arm. "Take it easy, partner," Yosh said. "We'll find her."

Paavo pushed himself away. He had to see the condition of the car. The front end was bashed in, and there was blood on the driver's side, including where it appeared the driver's head had hit the windshield. He didn't know what that meant about Angie—if she was there, or her condition. He could only pray it meant she hadn't been harmed.

He peered into the fog, up and down the empty, silent street. He didn't know which way to turn, where to begin. He'd never felt so helpless.

He couldn't help but think of the report he'd read out of Oakland—the police report of the way they'd found Heather.

"We've got to find her," he whispered. He alone heard his words.

The street was silent. Maybe it wasn't Carter that she'd seen in the fog after all? Or, maybe she'd lost him? Angie was back at the main entrance to the church. She kicked at the doors, but they were so large and solid they didn't even rattle. She forced herself away from them, to go on, back down the broad church steps to the sidewalk, onward, expecting Carter to appear before her any second.

At the corner, she felt a burst of hope and ran.

"Shhh! I t'ought I hoid somet'in'."

"I didn't hear nothin.'"

"I swear I did. Like a poundin'."

"You musta heard your brains poundin' in protest—from you tryin' to use'em."

"Shut up, you two! We ain't got all night."

"Maybe it's da cops. You want I should go check?"

"Forget it, I said. Or I'll give you a real poundin'. Who's first?"

"Not me. I hate being foist."

"You never been first for nothin' in your whole life."

"Go on."

"No, you go on."

"No, you."

Angie kicked at the door to Wings Of An Angel as loud as she could, but no one came to answer it. She was sure Earl, Butch and Vinnie were down in their basement apartment fast asleep. They'd help her, if she could just reach them.

The door was old, with a large, single panel of glass in a wood frame. Probably not safety glass—probably not even up to code. The only way to get in would be to break the glass, reach inside the door and unlock it. She tried kicking the glass, but she couldn't kick high enough to hit the sweet spot—the middle area which she knew was the weakest part.

She'd have to use her elbow and shoulder. Even through the leather jacket, it would hurt, but not nearly as much as Carter if he ever caught up to her.

She rammed her elbow into the window and fell back. Even her teeth vibrated at the blow. But nothing happened.

She tried again, smashing her elbow and shoulder into the glass with as much force as she could muster. The glass shattered. Not bad!

Using her elbow again, she knocked away the glass near the door knob, turned backwards and reached in with her bound hands, flicked the deadbolt latch, then grabbed the doorknob and turned.

She ran inside, slammed the door shut, looked through the shattered glass to the street—and nearly fainted.

Carter stood before her. Blood was smeared across his forehead and down his right cheek. The right lens of his glasses had a spider-web crack in it. His stare was deathly cold.

He reached through the broken window for the lock. She brought her elbow down hard on his hand, grinding it into the jagged glass. He shrieked and pulled it free, scraping it across the broken shards and sending rivulets of blood streaming down the door.

She ran to the kitchen. Behind her, she heard his curses and the sound of more glass breaking.

At the back of the kitchen she found some steep stairs, apparently leading to the basement. Her three friends were surely down there sleeping. Once with them, she'd be safe.

She started down, but on the third step her feet slipped out from under her, and she slid all the way to the bottom.

Slightly dazed, she looked around. To her surprise, she wasn't in an apartment at all, but in an unfinished, bare-walled basement furnished with three old army cots.

Scattered about on the ground were tools and a lit Coleman lantern. Above them, she saw a huge hole in the basement wall.

And sticking their heads through the hole, staring at her in stunned silence, were Earl, Butch and Vinnie.

"Miss Angie," Earl said when he found his voice. "What're you doin' here? What's dat t'ing over your mout'?"

She ran to them. Heavy footsteps and banging could now be heard overhead. Angie tried to tell them what had happened, but with the gag her words came out muffled and incoherent.

Her friends asked no more questions. Three pairs of hands reached for her and pulled her through the hole. She found herself in another basement, and looking at the merchandise all around her, she realized it was the basement of the jewelry store right next door to Wings of An Angel.

Earl removed the gag while Vinnie cut the ropes from her wrists.

"It's Carter," she panted. "He's insane. He wants to kill me. Call the police!"

"We don't have no cellphones, Miss Angie," Earl said looking scared and fearful.

"Good God!" Vinnie bellowed. "I'm too old for this stuff."

"Quick! Let's go up to the jewelry store," Butch said. "Maybe he won't know where to find us."

They ran across the basement and up the stairs to the ground floor. The door leading into the store was locked. Using a crowbar, Vinnie easily popped the lock, and they ran in.

The entire front of the store was windows. Outside street lights lit the interior for them.

"Let's get out of here," Angie cried. She ran to the front door of the jewelers, turned the lock and opened it, only to be stopped by a heavy metal gate that completely covered the entire front of the building—both windows and door. All four of them grabbed it and tried to force it open, but it wouldn't. It was padlocked.

Angie spun around. There was no back door, no back window.

They were trapped.

The streets were eerily empty. Through the fog, Paavo hadn't even spotted a *wrong* person to follow, hadn't even been allowed the faintest glimmer of false hope. He'd worked his way up and down Kearney and Grant. Now he was on Stockton. He turned off Stockton at Filbert to drive by Angie's church. Sts. Peter and Paul's.

The front of the church looked bare and empty. The doors, he was sure, were locked. God had closed up for the night, and only the godless remained out here on the streets.

Angie's restaurant "find" was somewhere near here, he

recalled. On Columbus. If she was near it—and able to—she might seek it out, a place where she'd been happy with people she'd liked. A sanctuary.

But at this time of night? Nobody would be there. Like the church, it'd be locked up tight. And besides that, he hadn't even bothered to ask her where it was. Why? Why hadn't he taken the time for her? What if—No! He couldn't, wouldn't, think that.

Gripping the steering wheel hard to rein in his rising panic, he gunned the engine and turned onto Columbus.

40

"Quick! Barricade the door," Angie shouted.

The three men began pushing anything they could find—a desk, a file cabinet, a chair—in front of the door that led to the basement.

She picked up the phone to call the police. It was dead. She dropped it and backed away. That explained why Carter was taking so long in the basement, why he hadn't run up the stairs immediately and tried to break in. But he was out there now, that was certain.

She ran to the back of the counter near the cash register and threw herself to the floor, searching for some kind of alarm. A loud thud hit the door, and the barricade moved back an inch or so.

The men threw their weight against the furniture, trying to keep the door from opening further. But Carter was stronger. Angie knew they were four against one—but her friends were small, older man. And Carter didn't seem human.

The door inched open. Carter's fingers reached into the room and gripped the door frame.

Earl, Butch and Vinnie backed away, their eyes wide and

fearful. Earl grabbed a heavy ashtray, holding it high. Butch clenched his fists like a boxer, and Vinnie found a fake pearl rope necklace that the jeweler hadn't bothered to lock up for the night. He wrapped it around his fingers like brass knuckles.

Angie was in tears, frantic to find the alarm. She found a button on the floor, near the counter's edge. She pushed it. Nothing. It didn't feel as if was connected to anything. Desperate, she pushed it again and again.

Carter must have cut those wires, too. He knew electronics, he'd said. Yes, he knew them.

He squeezed through the opening. A red blood-filled bruise the size of an orange lifted from the center of his forehead, small, jagged cuts radiating from it. Strips of flesh dangled from the bloodied mess that once was his hand. His eyes were wild and staring. He took in the three small men, and then Angie. "Hail, the gang's all here," he said.

Angie scrambled to her feet and backed away.

"You ran away from me, Heather." He moved toward her, his voice low and growling. "To other men. I don't like that."

"Get out of here, Carter," she cried. "The police are coming. They'll arrest you."

He pulled a long combat knife from his back pocket. "I don't think so," he said.

She cried out and bolted around the counter to her friends. Earl pushed her behind him.

Carter chuckled. "How noble."

He began to weave forward, making his way closer and closer toward them, keeping between them and the door to the basement.

Suddenly, he lunged at Earl with his knife. Earl tried to step aside, out of the way, and at the same time swung the ashtray at Carter's head. The heavy object struck, but too late. The knife went into Earl's side and came out bloody.

"Earl! No!" Angie cried, trying to catch her friend as he fell.

At the same time, Butch and Vinnie attacked Carter. They barely reached his shoulders. Butch grabbed the arm that held the knife and tried to pry it from Carter's fingers. Vinnie, reaching up, pummeled his face with the pearl knuckles.

Angie couldn't get close enough to do anything to Carter, but she saw that the path to the basement door was now clear. She broke for it.

"No!" Carter roared. He threw off Vinnie with ease. Vinnie's head hit the wall, and he dropped, unconscious. Carter whirled and smashed a fist into Butch's face. Angie heard the crack of his nose and saw his blood splatter over the room. The little man went down.

Carter lunged toward her. She skidded to a halt and spun away from the door just as he crashed against it.

A jeweler's stool had been pushed into a corner. She hurled herself at it and picked it up, holding the seat to her chest, its legs pointed outward.

"Keep away from me!" She screamed. "Keep back!"

"Heather, Heather, Heather." He shook his head, slowly brandishing the knife, first in one hand, then the other, as he stepped nearer. "Put the stool down, Heather."

She shook her head, perspiration dripping down her face, into her eyes, nearly blinding her.

He paced back and forth. "You're coming home with me. Again."

He reached for the stool and she swung it so that a leg hit his mangled hand.

"Bitch!" He grabbed the legs of the stool, tore it from her hands and tossed it aside.

———

Gun drawn, Paavo called for backup as he stepped through the shattered glass of what had once been a door. He saw the blood. The dining room was dark and empty. He ran through the swinging door to the equally empty kitchen.

In the back, stairs led down to the basement. Angie! His mind shouted. But what if his hunch about this restaurant was wrong? What if the broken glass was just some two-bit robbery —a coincidence—and Angie was still out on the street somewhere with Carville?

Still, every instinct told him this was the place he'd find her... and he prayed she was still alive.

He moved swiftly, silently, fearful that if she was here with Carville, the sound of someone approaching might cause him to kill her.

As he descended the steps, he saw a large hole in the basement wall. A hole to the jeweler's next door? Should he take time to pursue this? It all seemed so bizarre. But something, a vague feeling, told him to crawl through it.

That was when he heard a scuffling sound coming from the floor above, a voice.

"Bitch!"

His heart nearly stopped. Silently, he hurried up the stairs.

A scream! Angie!

He burst into the room—in time to see Wesley Carville toss a stool out of the way.

Paavo saw the knife, saw Angie backed into a corner, saw Carville slowly, menacingly step toward her.

"Drop it, Carville," he ordered.

Carville glanced his way, then smirked. "Forget it, Inspector. You can't stop me. No one can." He sprang at Angie.

She saw Paavo, and threw herself on the ground, giving him a clear shot. Mercifully, he took it.

The force of the bullet caught Carville in mid-leap and knocked him sideways against the wall. The knife clattered to his feet. He slowly sank to the floor.

The room fell silent.

Right behind Paavo in the doorway were two patrol officers, guns drawn. They had seen everything that had just taken place.

Angie crouched on the ground. Her eyes met Paavo's.

He reached her side in an instant and dropped to his knees, reaching for her. "Are you all right? Did he hurt you?"

She sat up, but her face crumbled as she looked at him. "I'm okay," she whispered, "but my friends..."

One of the patrolmen ran to Carville. He was still alive, but out cold. The other officer went to Vinnie who had just come to and waved him off. The officer then went to Earl. Butch was already there, trying to help Earl stop the bleeding where he'd been stabbed. They could hear the ambulance sirens already.

"Looks like they're being helped," Paavo whispered. "It's you I'm worried about. I was so scared ... so scared I'd lost you." He gathered her in his arms and held her tight against his chest, rocking her, comforting her, then buried his face in her hair and couldn't stop tears from filling his eyes.

41

In minutes, ambulances and what looked like the entire Central station officers were at the scene. As Carter was rushed to a hospital, other EMTs tended to the three older men who'd tried to help Angie. She refused any help.

Paavo wasn't allowed to work the crime scene since he had shot Carville. That meant there would be an inquest, and he'd be off duty until it was completed. That was fine with him, since he didn't want to leave Angie's side. She was wrapped in two blankets and sat on the end of the ambulance until it left to take Earl, Vinnie, and Butch to the hospital.

She'd been assured that some stitches and pain medicine would have Earl up and about in no time at all. The EMTs wanted Vinnie to be checked for a concussion, more because of his age than anything else. Vinnie didn't want to go, but Butch told him Earl needed company, so he agreed and joined him in the ambulance. Last of all, Butch also joined them. He wanted to see a doctor to give him some pain meds and also straighten out his broken nose, so when it healed, "he'd been pretty again," to quote him.

As soon as he could, Paavo called Serafina to let her know

he'd found Angie and not to worry about her. Angie listened in as he assured Serafina that Angie would call her soon, but at the moment, she was pretty tired.

"You're with her, Paavo?" Serafina had asked.

"I am," he said.

"*Bene.* Then I'll go to bed. It's late for an old lady!"

After telling Serafina goodnight, Paavo's last bit of duty was practical. "We need to go get your car," he said to Angie. "Are your keys on you?"

"In my pocket."

He asked a couple of patrol officers to follow him and Angie in his Mustang up to Coit Tower to retrieve Angie's car. They'd heard it was a Ferrari and were happy to oblige. But when they got there, he gave them the keys to the Mustang, and asked that they park it in Central's lot. He'd retrieve it soon.

Then he and Angie got into her Ferrari, Paavo in the driver's seat.

"I don't want to go home," she told him. "I don't want to be alone."

"Your parents' house?" he asked.

"No, not there either."

He met her gaze, and nodded.

At Paavo's home, the first thing Angie wanted to do was take a shower and wash away Carville's touch. Paavo told her what he'd learned about Carville and how he'd found her as they drove.

All he had to give her to wear were his flannel pajamas. After the shower and towel drying her hair as best she could, she put on the top. It reached half way down her thighs. Some of her dresses were shorter. Barefoot, she walked out to the living room to be with him.

He had built a fire, so the living room was warm and cozy. A bottle of white wine was on the coffee table. "I thought you could use something stronger than coffee or tea after your evening, and I know beer isn't your favorite," he said softly. "Would you like a glass? It's some kind of chardonnay."

"It sounds great," she said, and sat down on the carpet in front of the fireplace to let the heat take away the chill that had settled over her since Carter, or Carville, or whatever his name was, had pulled her out of her car.

He poured them each a glass and then sank down, cross-legged, facing her.

The light from the fire played against Paavo's features, surrounding him with a warm glow. Her eyes drank him in, the sight more heady than any wine. The gentleness of the man, his caring, filled her senses.

She cared too much, she knew that, and she had often feared he cared not nearly enough. But now, she remembered the tears of relief in his eyes when he found her alive. Now, she could see his feelings for her as clearly as if they were written across his brow. Tomorrow he would probably be Mr. Inspector again, but tonight, none of that mattered.

She reached for her wine, and he picked up his glass, then they leaned toward each other, clinging the glasses in a toast. As they raised the wine to their lips, they looked up and their eyes locked. Her entire body seemed to crackle with tension and she lowered her glass, her hand suddenly unsteady.

Paavo watched her every movement. She knew everything was written on her face, and knew there was no way she could hide the love or desire she felt for him. Nor did she want to. Without a word, he gently claimed her wine, placing it on the hearth beside his own. A charged stillness enveloped them. He got to his knees and took her arms, drawing her close as his lips met hers, leaving her breathless and wanting more.

She clutched his shoulders tightly as his hands enveloped

her waist, deepening their kiss. With tender care, he eased her onto the soft rug as if she were fine crystal. Stretching out beside her, he traced the contours of her body beneath his flannel pajama top as his gaze intensified. Responding in kind, she raised her hands to his neck, urging him closer for another passionate kiss.

Her fingertips traced the strength of his back as she mirrored the fervor of his kisses. His eyes captured hers as his hand traveled to her hips and lower, letting her feel the rapid pounding of his heartbeat, letting her know how much he wanted her. She began to unbutton his shirt.

"Are you sure?" he asked, seeking reassurance.

"I've been sure for a long time," she replied, sealing her words with a kiss that left no doubt.

Without his shirt, the scar on his chest where he'd been shot broke her heart. Tenderly, she traced her fingers over it, so thankful he'd been saved. His kisses paused, and he gazed down on her, as if questioning her thoughts. She ran her hands over his broad hard chest and flat stomach, watching his muscles ripple as she touched him.

She felt a tremor rush through him at her caress. Then, his kisses blazed, and he became her world. But even then, he was careful and cautious with her, as if he remembered that he was a big man, and she was a little woman. "It's all right," she whispered. He lifted his head and his eyes held a depth that touched her core, sending her soul soaring. She was lost in him. His love was all-encompassing, skilled and intimate, engulfing her on every level, physically, mentally—even spiritually, if such a bond were possible.

Eventually, they moved to the comfort of his bed. He was everything to her that night. She didn't sleep, but lay in his arms, unwilling to move, listening to the strong steady rhythm of his heartbeat. "Hungry?" he asked once, deep into the night.

She ran her fingertips over his cheekbone. "Only for you."

His look was open and warm. "Angel," he whispered as he kissed her, pulling her close to him again.

After a while, he slept, but sleep still wouldn't come to her. She held him close. Earlier that night, she'd witnessed, felt, the ugliness of his world. She'd watched him almost killed a man —word had come from the hospital that Carter would survive. Still, she expected Paavo would have a storm of emotions to that shooting in the days ahead as an investigation and inquest unfolded. She knew he'd been right in what he had to do, but she knew it would weigh on him, and at times, the press and public could be hard on an officer involved in a shooting. Somehow, she would help him get through the dark days she expected would come.

Her thoughts swirled. Why, of all the men in the world, did she fall in love with this man? Why this man, whose life was so different from hers, and far too frightening?

But despite all the warnings from family and friends, despite all their ups and downs, she couldn't help it. She loved him.

42

Two weeks later, Vinnie, standing tall in a black suit, greeted Angie and Paavo at the entrance to Wings Of An Angel. The restaurant was filled to capacity for its Grand Opening. Three more tables had been added, and two couples sat by the entry waiting for the next available place.

"We saved a table for you an' the Inspector, Miss Angie," Vinnie said. He seated them, then hurried back to his station at the front door and the cash register. The red checkered tablecloths had been changed for tonight's event to white ones, with white napkins. The restaurant actually gleamed.

"I can't believe this," Angie said, marveling at the decor and the crowd. She'd dressed in a cream-colored chiffon dress that dipped to a V in front and diamond earrings that sparkled with every turn of her head. And she'd convinced Paavo to wear a suit for the occasion.

Earl walked up. "'Ey, Inspector, you made it. Awright!" He handed them each a menu. "Dey jus' came in today, Miss Angie."

On heavy, slick white paper, in gold foil lettering were the words: THE WINGS OF AN ANGEL. Below, Butch's specialties.

Angie jumped from her chair and kissed him on the cheek. "It's beautiful, Earl. Congratulations to all of you."

A blush started at the neck of Earl's white shirt and quickly traveled up his face to his shellacked hair. "T'anks, Miss Angie. You helped a lot, too."

She laughed as she sat down again. "How's the spaghetti and meatballs today?"

"Same as ever."

"All these people obviously think they're terrific," she said. "Of course, my article in *Haute Cuisine* praised this restaurant to the hilt, and—I know it's not very modest of me—but I'd say the recommendation of Angelina Amalfi carries some weight in this town." Facing Paavo, she beamed. "This is such a *find* for me."

"It certainly is," he said with a smile and a nod.

"An' da food's okay, too," Earl said. "A lotta dese people say da place smells really good when dey pass by, so dey come in." He turned to Paavo. "Inspector, me and da boys wanna say t'anks for explainin' how dat hole in da wall was just 'cause we was tryin' to fix a leak in a water pipe. We didn't mean to go all da way t'rough to da jeweler's store. Honest."

Paavo fixed a steady gaze on Earl. "The guys at the Hall of Justice understood perfectly. I told them you three promised the next time you had a leak, you'd call a plumber. Right?"

"Sure t'ing, Inspector."

"And I'm glad to see you're back on your feet."

"Yeah. It was just a nick. An' da swellin' on Butch's nose an' his black eyes is almost back to normal, too. I'll get your dinner."

Angie reached for Paavo's hand. He took hers and gave it a light squeeze. She'd stayed with him these past two weeks, seeing him through the inquest, and the times when he would feel bad about having nearly taken a man's life. And he'd been there for her during the times she'd have a flashback to how frightened she'd been, or when she'd cry out in terror from one of the nightmares that had awakened her every night for a week after the horror happened.

Each time it happened, he'd held her until she fell asleep again. And then one night he confessed she wasn't the only one who had nightmares. One plagued him over and over; the one in which he was unable to find her no matter what he did, no matter where he looked. The one in which Wesley Carville won.

They both were doing much better now, and Paavo was cleared to go back to his job on Monday. "I was thinking, Paavo, that after Easter dinner tomorrow at my mother's—oh, I did tell you all my sisters and their families were going to be there, didn't I?"

He grimaced. "You hadn't given me that good news yet."

"Well, anyway, I thought after that it'd be time for me to go back to my apartment. It's probably time we both go back to our normal lives."

"I can see that," he murmured. "You have a beautiful apartment, a great view, while my place is just a simple, very old cottage."

"On the other hand, I do like staying there with you."

"You know, there's no need for you to rush off on my account," he replied.

Joy filled her. "There isn't?"

"No. I'm not sure that you're fully recovered yet. We should be sure there are no more nightmares."

"We should?" she asked.

"That could take a while, Miss Amalfi," he said.

"You may be right, Inspector."

"Good." He leaned back and lifted an eyebrow. "Because I do love... having you stay with me."

"That's good." She leaned back, her eyes dancing. "Because I do love... staying there."

They looked into each other's eyes.

"Here you go," Earl announced. He carried a tray with their meal and put their plates before them. "Enjoy."

"This is it, Paavo," Angie said excitedly. He picked up his fork. "These are the special meatballs and the wonderful spaghetti sauce I was telling you about. Butch still won't tell me what the secret ingredient is. Whatever it is, though, he should package it. He'd make a fortune."

She watched expectantly as Paavo took a bite of the spaghetti.

"Secret ingredient, you said?"

"That's right."

She watched as he cut into the meatball and tasted it, then eyed the meat, then Angie, then the meat again. And then he grinned.

"What's going on?" she asked, worried by his reaction. "Don't you like it?"

"I do like it, but there's no secret here. Not to me, anyway. Although I can see why it is to you." Then, he lightly chuckled. "Yes, I can well imagine someone with a gourmet background, and even from an Italian household, would very likely be puzzled by it."

"Paavo?" She didn't understand what he was trying to tell her.

He put down his fork and touched the napkin to his lips.

She gripped the tablecloth. "What's wrong? What aren't you telling me?"

He looked at the plate of food. "It's institutional memory, I'm afraid."

"Institutional what?" She clasped her hands. "I don't understand."

"You see, Angie, it's all of a piece."

She twisted her napkin. "You're talking in riddles," she cried. She hated it when he talked in riddles.

"In Homicide the other day, me and the guys were discussing Earl, Vinnie and Butch," he began. "And Yosh, who knows a lot of old songs, remembered one from back in the 1930s or so, with words something like 'If I had the wings of an angel, over these prison walls I would fly.'"

She felt her throat tighten. "Prison walls?"

He nodded. "Army vets, like me, and ex-cons have one thing in common. Unforgettable memories of institutional food. I remember. Butch *really* remembers."

She didn't want to hear anymore. Visions of another assignment for *Haute Cuisine* flew away, just like those wings over prison walls. But she couldn't stop herself from saying, "Tell me, Paavo. What's the secret ingredient?"

"You really want to know?" he asked.

"I really want to know," she answered.

"Butch didn't use a lot of it," he said, as if that was some sort of consolation. "It's basically just to stretch the meat."

She groaned aloud. Gourmet restaurants did not *stretch* the meat. Barely able to speak, she whispered, "Out with it, Inspector."

"Don't say I didn't warn you," he said. And then, although he spoke in the lowest possible voice, his words seemed to reverberate throughout the entire restaurant. "The secret ingredient, Angie... is Spam."

***

I hope you enjoyed The Marinara Murders, *and will continue with the next Cook and Inspector Mystery,* **Close Encounters of the Deadly Kind.**

ABOUT THE AUTHOR

Joanne Pence was born and raised in northern California and now lives in Idaho. She has been an award-winning, *USA Today* best-selling author of mysteries for many years, but she has also written historical fiction, contemporary romance, romantic suspense, a fantasy, and supernatural suspense. All of her books are now available as ebooks and in print, and most are also offered in special large print editions. Joanne hopes you'll enjoy her books, which present a variety of times, places, and reading experiences, from mysterious to thrilling, emotional to lightly humorous, as well as powerful tales of times long past.

Visit her at www.joannepence.com and be sure to sign up for Joanne's mailing list to hear about new books.